ORACA DISCOVERY

STAR REACHER SERIES BOOK ONE

J PULK

SPARKSTONE PUBLISHING LLC

"I will not deny myself the prize, should it find its way into my collection. But as a fallible being, I must also consider whether I could be trusted to keep it."

— FROM THE JOURNAL OF FERNIUS POH

PROLOGUE

"Activate the secondary weapon systems."

The order came from a slender being with shimmering green skin and short white hair as she surveyed the assortment of ships in nearby holding positions. On the nightside of the system's largest planet, the glowing orange and white backdrop of its upper atmosphere cast the other vessels in dim silhouette.

A small holographic image of an emerging wireframe pattern formed at one of the human crew stations. "Compression threshold detected."

"Reorient the ship toward the arrival coordinates."

The short fur-covered species that crewed most of the bridge tapped at their interface consoles, and the attack cruiser *Emu Ja'* slowly pivoted.

"Compression field is collapsing."

Nearby space distorted as an interstellar exit point twisted the laws of physics, then collapsed into a dusky olive haze as it submitted to the conventional cosmic order. A forty-meter freight transport emerged from the mist, its quad engines swiveling to counter the ship's residual momentum until it came to a relative stop directly in front of the *Emu Ja'*. A black scar ran across the entire top side of the comparatively small vessel, likely the result of an encounter with at least a class four energy weapon.

"Freighter *Rusty Bucket* has arrived at the designated rendezvous coordinates."

The green being's silver eyes narrowed. "Broadcast on general communication channel."

A chirp sounded from a workstation. "Transmitting."

"Captain Ketsa, this is Exalted Daihn of the Chekt Imperium. You have exceeded the delivery date specified by our contract and are in default."

An image of the freighter captain appeared in the bottom corner of the forward window, but Daihn didn't bother to look at it as the captain replied. "I know I'm behind schedule, but I'm sure I'll find your merchandise soon. I want to negotiate a new delivery date."

Daihn studied the other ships that hovered in space, a few of the larger ones slowly turning as if to get a better view of the event. Her tiny prehensile earlobes swayed as she answered in a tone that became more relaxed with each word. "I am entitled to alternate compensation in accordance with our agreement."

"No, please. I made a mistake, but our contract—"

"Close communication," Daihn said, and Captain Ketsa was cut off mid-sentence.

The freighter's swiveling bow thrusters spat out blue jets to push its nose toward the planet as its main engines ignited, but the attempt at escape was pointless.

"Commence salvage operation."

The crew took coordinated action, and the room's crimson accent lights dimmed as workstations growled computer tones.

The *Emu Ja'* rocked as a dozen projectiles launched from missile and weapon ports, each displaying its own unique trail of light and color.

At nearly point-blank range, the firepower tore away at the freighter, sending pieces of its hull plunging into the planet's atmosphere, and for a moment the ship was swallowed by aqua and emerald fireballs.

The assault ended abruptly, and the sound of small pieces of wreckage bouncing harmlessly off the hull replaced the din of weapon annunciators on the bridge. Her ship's primary energy weapons would have done the job faster, but the attack wasn't designed to be efficient. It was intended to impress.

Daihn stepped from her elevated platform and walked to the viewing window, trailing a long white robe that was a symbol of her status in chekt society. Debris drifted from a huge tear in the target's cargo hold. "Deploy salvage craft."

Automated drones launched to collect any undamaged cargo the wrecked freighter still contained while Daihn kept her attention on the ships that had been observing the event. She was more interested in who might be watching than in any value the wreckage held. But the other ships simply hung in space, giving no indication of their opinion on the matter.

1

A pre-dawn breeze followed Tom Sparker as he rushed into the pilot station and grabbed his uniform hat from the rack. The shift supervisor looked up from the status monitor in his adjacent office. "You're fifteen minutes late this time, Sparker. I'm docking you."

Tom grabbed his flight notes and uniform jacket, barely slowing his pace as he headed for the hangar door. "Don't worry, I'll make the flight on time."

"We don't rush preflight here. I've already delayed the tour thirty minutes." The supervisor pointed an accusing finger at him. "And you'll be docked for the full half hour."

Tom shoved the heavy door to the flight hangar open and tramped up the nearest ramp to the elevated walkway as he pulled on his tour guide cap, which mostly tamed his wild hair. There were too many rules in Copania's tourist industry for his taste, but there were also few options for a Trades Academy dropout to earn a living. No shipyard or repair shop would hire him for even low-level maintenance work, and although he could have earned slightly more as a construction laborer or restaurant server, it was better to have his hands on flight controls instead of a broom handle or a waiter's notepad.

The lead deck mechanic looked up from the service floor as he wiped a greasy component with a rag. "Hey! Look everyone, the late shift is here."

The other workers smirked but continued their duties. Tom's foot caught on the edge of the ship's ramp, and he stumbled, then glanced back as if someone had put it there since he last walked the path. "At least I'm up here . . . where it's not dirty." His own awkward comeback made him feel more uncomfortable than the teasing did, as if it somehow confirmed the mechanic's sharper wit.

The team lead didn't miss a beat. "Flyers get sunny—" He bumped fists with another worker as they finished the adage in unison. "But wrenchers make money!"

A third technician looked up from her work and pushed a lock of bright red hair from her face with an oil-covered hand. "We're on triple-time mechanics' pay!"

Tom pretended to ignore their comments and ducked into the shuttle hatchway as he signaled to a deck hand that he was starting the preflight checks. He sank into the pilot seat—the only place he ever felt at ease. The soft hum of the warming engines welcomed him back, and as he flipped switches, the tiny echoes off the cockpit walls relaxed him.

It took him only moments to ready the ship, but the deck crew shuffled around at a pace that would make a sharta slug look like a galloping hunge. When the lead technician finally gave the signal for takeoff, Tom moved the flight controls by instinct. The ship leaped into flight and sped toward the passenger boarding dock, making two of the deck crew duck to avoid getting knocked over by thruster exhaust.

Thirty passengers filled the nearby terminal. A few eagerly

eyed the shuttle as Tom approached, but most read the tour company brochure or wrangled their young while they waited in the early light at the outdoor boarding queue. The ship gently bumped against the platform as it hovered, and the passenger door popped open.

The impatient tourists flooded in, and a cacophony of excited conversations mixed with children's laughter instantly filled the passenger compartment.

"Good morning, everyone, and welcome aboard," Tom said over the intercom. "My name is Tom, and I'll be your pilot and guide today. We'll be taking off as soon as we're all seated."

The fully booked shuttle was filled mostly by members of an alien species on a chartered trip from Oorano—a boggy, forested planet in a nearby star system. The rest were local humans and their children, taking the morning tour together as a family outing.

"Translation devices are available on the seat pockets in front of you if you need them. Please remain seated once we're in flight, but feel free to take plenty of images during our trip."

The boarding hatch was secured with a clunk, and Tom pulled away from the dock, accelerating as he followed a kilometer-long row of flight markers on the ground. "Hold on to your belongings as we get ready to rise to cruising altitude."

Features of the neatly maintained park beneath them quickly turned into a blur as they accelerated, and Tom gave a pull at the controls to make a hard turn skyward. The maneuver drew excited yelps from the children and a few grunts from the adults as they steadied themselves against sudden queasiness. The thrill ride was a traditional and expected part of the tour, but it lasted only seconds.

"We'll be visiting several of Copania's most spectacular

features today, but it will take us a minute to reach our first destination, so sit back and enjoy the ride."

As the oldest settlement of the five human colonies, Copania was the most thoroughly explored, and because of its clean environment and natural beauty, it was the most popular tourist planet among the seventeen core systems. Since each tour visited the same locations in the same order regardless of the time of day or weather conditions, Tom recited the same tour script during every flight.

"In a moment, we'll be passing near one of the jewels of Copania's northern hemisphere. If you look to your right, you'll be able to see Missom Spires, a series of four massive pillars—each of which is nearly four hundred meters tall and a hundred meters wide at ground level. Scientists have recently uncovered the remains of an ancient city at the base of the spires, and an archaeological excavation is ongoing. We'll be passing by them quickly so look now or you might *miss 'em.*"

Even after three years of faithfully reciting the corny joke, Tom still cringed at the required attempt at humor. A few of the human passengers laughed, but puns like that rarely translated to other languages.

"Past the spires, we'll head out over the Alic, which is Copania's only ocean. It gets its bright green color from the algae that grows on its shallow seabed, and while it covers almost half the surface, the deepest part is less than twenty meters. If you notice a moving dark patch under the surface, it's most likely a school of grazing olfs migrating to their daytime feeding grounds."

The tourists captured images of the endless green ocean as sunlight broke over the water, and Tom's smooth turning dive toward their next destination provided a moving panorama of the glimmering horizon. The sight was awe-inspiring—at least to anyone who hadn't grown up on Copania. A typical native would see the glint of violet that accompanied each sunrise as mere daylight and a signal to prepare for school classes or a mundane job.

"We're coming up on the root caverns of the Salamander Swamps. They're formed by thousand-year-old trees that grow in clusters above the shallow salt water. There's more wildlife here than anywhere else on Copania, so you might see some of our indigenous friends. But look closely, because most of the animals here only grow to be about as big as your hand."

Tom leaned the shuttle to port and swooped down into one of the cavern formations as he slowed the ship. External spotlights blinked on to illuminate the moss- and leaf-covered walls. An ooranoan passenger stood, and one of the translators squawked. *"This is not swamp. It is swimming pool for children."*

The other aliens sputtered a sound that must have been laughter at the veiled insult about Tom's home world. He'd already endured enough taunting for the day and gave a quick jerk to the control yoke, making the alien fall back into his seat.

"We've hit a little turbulence. For your safety, please remain seated while we're underway."

The shuttle slowed more and drifted forward through the dim growth as Tom continued. "Nearly all of the animals that live here spend their entire lives inside just one of these tree clusters and rely on the small ecosystems within for their survival. They'll only leave if their original habitat is threatened, then they'll move to the next available cluster. When that happens, many creatures don't survive, since the clusters can only support a certain amount of animal life as they reach a natural equilibrium."

The tourists chattered among themselves as they leaned

toward the windows like every tour group before them. For some, it was a once-in-a-lifetime visit to Copania. But years of tour piloting left little mystery for Tom.

"The lichen covering the upper canopy actually communicate with each other by sending chemical signals through connecting hyphae. We don't know what purpose it serves, but it could be an indication of a kind of developing sentience."

They floated past the mossy green-brown walls of the cavern and all of the life that clung to them. Talka birds flew back and forth from sod nests built near the waterline, and long hanging vines brushed the shuttle as it passed. His guests' attention remained fixed on the attractions as they approached the exit, but Tom stared flatly ahead where a talka chick nudged a sibling out of their nest. The fluffy bird plopped into the water and bobbed on the surface for a second before its mother plucked the chick up and tucked it back into the safety of the tightly woven cup of twigs.

As the shuttle emerged from the shadowy canopy, most of the passengers resettled into their seats, but the heckler made another stab. *Maybe now we see some real animals, not tiny pets.* More sputtered chortling.

Tom let out a resigned sigh. He'd have to endure another two years of tours to save enough credits for a decent ship of his own. Hardly anyone who worked in the tourism industry would risk losing a steady paycheck, but the thought of one day escaping his life of schedules, scoldings, and bullies was the only thing that kept him coming to work each day.

Sunlight streamed into the shuttle windows as he pulled at the control yoke. "Next we'll visit the Shadow Cloud, a thick vapor mass high above Copania that never dissipates. It will take a while to get there, so if you're thinking about purchasing a souvenir, now would be a great opportunity to browse our gift catalog."

-------◆◇◆-------

As Tom entered the pilot station, the shift supervisor looked up from a nearby display. "Tom, I need to talk to you in my office."

Everyone else in the room stopped their work and watched as Tom hung up his flight jacket and followed the supervisor. He hadn't been in the office since he was hired, and it felt smaller than he remembered.

"Tom, I just had a conversation with the regional manager, and he isn't happy with the number of flight delays we've had in the past few months."

Aware that a dozen people would be trying to eavesdrop, Tom kept his voice quiet and calm. "I promise I'll get to work on time from now on. It's just that I've—"

The supervisor held his hand up. "We're also getting complaints from guests. I've been instructed to replace you immediately."

Tom lost his relaxed tone as he searched for words. "You're . . . firing me?"

"You're one of my best pilots, Tom. But competition is tough, and corporate won't tolerate less than perfection."

"I've only been late . . ." He began counting on one hand then had to switch to the other before realizing he wasn't helping his case. "Listen, I'm great with tourists. Where else are you going to find someone who's willing to—"

A young ooranoan walked into the office and sat in a corner chair. Tom glanced at the newcomer and jerked a thumb at him. "Who's this guy?"

"He's your replacement. I like you, Tom, but I need your
ID badge."

2

Daihn strolled through the corridor that led to her ship's private lounge. She paused at a viewing window that overlooked the bow of her ship to gaze at the elegant finish and clean curves of the hull. As a symbol of wealth and status among her people, the *Emu Ja'* represented most of her fortune, and it was among the finest craft in all of chekt society. A smile pulled at the corner of her mouth as she continued across the pigmented glass floor to check the progress of her current venture.

Select members of her loyal saazu crew worked at small workstations along the walls of her private lounge, their white stripes of fur taking on hues of amber and blue from indicator lights on their station panels in the otherwise dimly lit room. All chekt vessels had a complement of the hardworking species who were bound to the chekt both by honor and a symbiotic relationship that had endured for centuries. Humans were better skilled in many fields, but the saazu's history of loyalty had made them the only alien species to ever earn permanent status in chekt society. The Imperium rewarded their loyalty and diligence with fervent protection and unquestioned trust, making them the preferred choice for the most sensitive tasks.

Near the center of the room, a human wearing a thin cloth overcoat pushed his magnifying spectacles to within a centimeter of a stone tablet. The weathered artifact sat on a blocky pedestal that was out of place among the room's swooping architecture.

Daihn stopped at the display and folded her arms. "What have you found?"

The historical specialist, Uolo Sou, looked up from his work and stared at her through the bizarre goggles that distorted his face. "Oh, I wasn't expecting you so soon."

Daihn stared at the man as she awaited his reply to her question. She had observed that eccentric scientists like Uolo sometimes needed extra time to properly focus on a conversation, though it always tested her patience.

"I think I've matched a few of the carved symbols," he said. "Did you get the second tablet?"

"The freighter captain failed to retrieve it." She turned to the artifact on the table. "What do the markings represent?"

"They aren't included in any common reference databases." His spectacles blurred his vision beyond a few centimeters, and he pulled them off to properly address his employer. "But a few do seem to correlate with one of the older texts I brought. I'm still working on syntax though. Until I have some basis for grammatical placement, I won't be able to reliably translate any of it."

"Remember that your primary objective is to verify the artifact's authenticity. A translation is useless to me unless the information it contains is genuine."

Uolo made an enthusiastic pitch for his approach. "But deciphering it would help me verify that. If the translation correlates with your dating analysis of the stone itself, it would be reasonable to think that the postulated seven-thousand-year age is accurate."

"And what of the grooved slotting on the edge?"

"As for that, I think you were correct in thinking that it's an attachment point." He ran his fingers along the lightly rabbeted channel. "It's too bad you didn't get the other tablet."

Uolo's pondering eyes drifted up from the artifact to meet Daihn's piercing stare, which jolted him back into the moment. "Since the symbols are close to the edge on that side of the tablet, it's possible that another one would mate with the edge to add to the inscription, but unless I can find a language pattern, I won't be able to tell if another piece would contain a continuation of text."

Daihn offered a nod. "So you believe the carvings represent a language."

"Maybe." Uolo shifted his head as he worked to narrow his reply. "Probably. Or it might be a system of pictograms or glyphs. Like I said, I have more work to do before I can give an informed opinion."

Daihn's eyes narrowed as she considered the object of his study. "How long will it take to complete your work?"

"It's hard to say. I have several more reference sources to check, including the library at Dacruul."

Daihn gave a slow nod as she turned toward the doorway. "I await your final report." She held up a cautionary finger. "And I expect a conclusive interpretation."

3

Tom stared at the data pad as he hunched over the secondhand eating table in his one-room apartment. The windows that faced the street let in plenty of daylight, but were oversized for the tiny room and made the space feel even smaller than it was. A deep gouge in the wall over his bed had been painted over before he'd moved in a year earlier, and a kitchenette at the far interior end had built-in appliances that he hardly ever used. A tray of half-eaten dough covered in sauce sat in a restaurant container from the night before. His favorite dish had done little to console him after being fired, and he hadn't been able to muster the appetite to finish it.

His forehead wrinkled from the stress of the past day as he scrolled through lists of used spacecraft. The lingering scent from the partially dehydrated remains made his stomach rumble, but it wasn't enough to distract him from pining over ships that he couldn't afford—any of which would be a joy to fly as a freelance planetary courier or as the captain of his own private tour ship for upscale visitors. But the prices were more than triple what he had in savings, and he wouldn't qualify for a loan after such a recent job termination. His eyes burned from staring at the pad, and he set it down to blink away some of the heat.

The sunlit windows dimmed, and the planet bellowed a rumble of distant thunder. Tom looked up, and as the darkness of the approaching storm made the room lights automatically activate, he caught the shifting silver glimmer from the collection of dented piloting trophies saved from his youth. The mementos sat on the table, pushed against the wall, as the only decorative items in his sparsely furnished home.

He pulled the tallest of the trophies close enough to read his name on the champion inscription. The ornament mounted at its top was a replica of the single-pilot racer he'd flown to win the contest—a ship with sensitive controls that required not only dexterity to pilot but also the ability to anticipate how the ship would react while swooping through the shifting artificial gravity fields that dotted the course. It was much more advanced than his dad's bulky delivery transport that he'd learned to fly in, but to his eleven-year-old self, that ship had been more exciting than the fastest racer. After his father had let him take the controls during a routine delivery, he'd begged to go with him at every opportunity, and with practice he'd learned the basics of flight a little at a time.

The award was a testament to his skill, but also to his father's instruction. When he'd told his dad that he wanted to be as good a pilot as his father was someday, the quiet man had smiled and told him that he shouldn't try to be *as good*, but he should instead work to be *better*. Tom's face softened. It was a great memory—and one of too few, since a military battle with aliens in a far away solar system had made sure his dad would never return to finish his lessons.

Still, the encouragement had nurtured his enthusiasm, and by the age of sixteen, Tom had already set records in the Copanian Junior League flying competitions. He'd even impressed the instructor of an aerobatics workshop with his ability to focus under pressure, but while his talents had eventually led him to a career as a pilot, that kind of discipline had never translated into any other part of his life.

He set the trophy back in its place and dragged a half-empty cup from his stale meal across the table. Rehashing old memories wasn't going to help him find a ship—or a flying job, for that matter. Without a reference from his previous employer, he wasn't going to find *any* piloting work in the highly competitive field, and after years of doing something he loved, the thought of working another kind of job felt like punishment.

His eyes drifted back to the trophy. It had been packed and unpacked many times over the years as he'd moved from rented rooms to employee living quarters to his current apartment. The old award had endured its share of drops and scrapes, and half of the silver finish from the tiny model's plastic core had fallen away. He ran a finger over the miniature ship, and another small fleck fluttered to the tabletop. But it wouldn't matter if every bit of finish dropped away. The award was a reminder of the pride he'd felt on the day he'd won it, and even though it was worn and gouged, he could still tell it was a ship. He gazed at the tiny model as the thought recycled. *It was still a ship.* Maybe he needed to change his approach.

Tom sat straighter and reached for the data pad. For years, he'd flown progressively newer and more elegant craft with the most convenient features and modern controls, and he'd built his career dreams around imagining himself in one of the fancy light freighters or ferries he'd seen at spacecraft shows. But if there was a ship available that he *could* buy and still have enough credits left to pay for some light maintenance, he could trade up for the ship of his dreams once he got his business running. The options wouldn't be fancy, but it would be better than accepting failure and working a job he'd loathe.

New search parameters for anything within his budget returned only a single result. The listing was vague, with no image of the ship, and the description read only "HF industrial shuttle."

Tom drafted a message on the pad to the listing dealer inquiring about the ship, then he paused. Industrial ships weren't sold until they were near the end of their useful service life, which meant it would probably need repairs of some kind. He wasn't much of a mechanic or even a decent technician, but he wouldn't be able to afford to pay anyone to make repairs, so any needed work would be up to him. He looked out the window and watched a distant spacecraft approach a nearby port as he considered sending the message. Raindrops began tapping on the glass, and reflections from approaching lightning bounced into the room. He did have *basic* maintenance training. If he could change a tire on a land vehicle or swap out a relay in a hovergrav pad, why couldn't he manage basic repairs on an old industrial ship?

He sent the message and received a quick reply. The dealer confirmed that the ship was still available, but they didn't expect it to be on the market long, and that Tom could see the mining ship that evening. He tapped in a reply that he'd get there as soon as possible but might not make it until after hours. The dealer responded that would be fine, since she'd be working late, and he should ask for Margo.

The flash from a bolt of lightning lit the room, and another rumble of thunder shook the building. He reached toward a row of hooks on the wall, and his shoulders drooped at the sight of the empty space where his raincoat should be. The embarrassing firing had rattled him, and he'd forgotten to take his belongings from his locker before he left the tour center. It would be humiliating to make another appearance there, but he also couldn't afford to lose any of his personal items—especially without a source of income.

Waves of rain crashed into the windows, and the howling wind made the panes vibrate. He'd get to his locker later. Right now, he had to stay on task—find some way of making a living that he could tolerate. He had to find a way to fly again.

4

The driving rain made it hard to see through the locked glass doors of Zenk's Preowned Spacecraft. Tom shielded his face from a gust of wind and knocked to get the attention of the worker walking across the showroom floor. He shouted through a pane as if it were a giant microphone. "My name is Tom!"

The dirty-faced employee glanced at him but continued walking.

"I've come to see a ship. I'm supposed to ask for Margo."

It was already after closing time, and the worker scowled as he came to the door. The glass muffled his voice. "What do you want?"

"I'm here to see Margo. I got here as soon as—"

The employee held up a hand and turned back into the showroom. "Hold on."

Tom's messy hair and tattered olf-skin jacket flapped as waves of drumming rain echoed off the windows. Copanian rainstorms could be severe, and this one had already knocked him off his feet twice. His holocom band chimed, and he tapped it to answer the incoming call. "I can't talk now, Marcus."

Blowing raindrops and mist distorted the tiny holographic image of his brother that hovered over his wrist. "Hey, you in the shower?"

"I'm going to look at a ship."

"Stop wasting time with that and come over. We need another player for a game of three-handed Yobi tonight."

"Maybe. I'll call you later."

"Bring money."

The image disappeared as Tom scowled, yanking up the collar of his jacket in the howling wind. Working on his career was hardly a waste of time. And even if it was, it was a better use of it than gambling away his credits to his overachieving sibling. Unlike Tom, Marcus had not only graduated from the Trades Academy, but he'd done so at the top of his class, earning him a high-paying job at a local engineering firm. Marcus had disposable income to risk in games of chance, but Tom had different plans for his modest savings.

The growing whine of a hoverpod speeding along the empty street made Tom turn. The pod didn't slow as it passed, and a wake of water jumped from the gutter hard enough to force a spout up his nostrils. The vehicle made a quick stop, and the driver popped open a window. "Sorry about that . . . Hey! Look everyone," the lead mechanic from the tour shop floor called into his vehicle. "It's the *late again* shift. It's after hours, Sparker. You should buy a watch." Subdued chuckles drifted from the window.

Tom looked at the mechanic through his hands as he wiped small bits of debris from his face, but he couldn't find any words to counter the wave of embarrassment that hit him harder than the splash from the street. The female mechanic leaned out into the rain on the passenger side, her red locks tossed by the wind. "You okay?"

Tom raised a hand and forced a nod, and another voice inside the pod urged the driver to leave. The mechanic gave a quick shake of his head and closed the windows, forcing the woman on the other side to duck back in before the vehicle sped away.

The whoosh of the dealership doors brought Tom's focus back to his reason for being there. He spun and entered the main showroom, which looked less inviting than it did from the street. "Thanks. I know I'm a bit late."

The waiting employee tapped at the door panel to relock it, and the doorway slid shut, silencing most of the storm. "Wait here."

The worker left, and Tom wandered across the mostly empty showroom. Tall windows bordered with cheap blue accent lighting reached five meters to touch the second-floor sales offices, and the two-story-high ceiling decorations hinted at the century-old building's original design—though dated renovations covered most of the interior.

The water in his shoes squished with each step he took across the otherwise quiet area, and his wet clothes clung to him as if they were pasted on. After only a few moments, his saleswoman appeared from the top of the open staircase to greet him. A spicy odor preceded her as she made her way down the stairs with a forced smile. "I'm Margo. You must be Tom."

"Yes ma'am."

"C'mon." She motioned with her hand for him to follow her. "It's in the back hangar."

She grabbed some papers from a nearby desk and headed

across the showroom floor. "You're going to love this little ship."

Tom stumbled over a wrinkle in the old carpet, but Margo didn't miss a step as she entered a narrow hallway with greasy handprints on the walls. "Careful, the floor's slippery."

"Did you say it was a mining ship?"

"It came in this morning. I've already had a few calls about it, but you're the first to take a look."

It was easy to believe there was interest in the only listed ship in its price range, and getting the first look was a lucky break.

The hallway opened into a large service hangar containing late-model space cruisers, haulers, and transports.

"I used to sell a lot of them, but this is the first one I've seen since last season."

On the other side of the room, another doorway led to a much dirtier space filled with dozens of aging utility transports, personnel shuttles, and automated maintenance vehicles in various states of disrepair. The concrete floor was dotted with fresh puddles from roof leaks, and the place smelled like stale thruster exhaust. In another few meters, they stopped in front of a plain-looking craft.

"Here it is." She beamed. "Only twelve thousand hours on the air regenerator. HF-T550."

Tom's lowered expectations were entirely fulfilled by what sat before him. It was an old magma-mining ship that was specially designed to retrieve precious raw materials from deep within a planet's molten core, and its dull gray hull had been scraped and battered from decades of heavy use. He'd never flown a ship that was designed for heavy industrial service, much less one that was intended to operate inside a planet, and he couldn't have found a ship that looked less like what he'd dreamed of.

"It was decommissioned by the Sardian Four Mining Consortium just before they went out of business—upgraded thrusters and standard ion drive."

Tom eyed the ship carefully as he slowly walked the perimeter, looking for reasons to like the old shuttle. The sleek, upswept nose and smoothed-out rear made it look more elegant than a typical utility vehicle, but the purpose of the design was to improve the fluid dynamics of the hull, making it easier for the craft to move through viscous magma. One of the ship's magnetic propulsion drives was mounted between two built-in ore-collection pods at the bottom of the craft, and its companion drive housing was molded into the top rear section of the hull. Those devices were used during mining operations in thick liquids and were standard equipment, but Tom didn't intend to use the ship underground, so he didn't waste any time checking them.

The fill and discharge gates on the ore pods had all been left in their open positions, and the interior chambers were covered with a layer of lumpy magma slag. With some cleaning, they might be usable for small cargo or as storage compartments.

Margo hovered at a distance. "I've got a recent hull survey for it, but no mechanical checks."

"Any problems with the survey?"

"Nah, but I could have told you that without seeing the report." She pounded a fist on the thick hull, and it thudded like a wall of stone. "These ships are practically indestructible. They only started decommissioning them because of the new automated drones."

A sound hull was a good start, but without a systems survey, there was no way to be sure that the ship could be made spaceworthy again. And given his limited mechanical expertise, Tom would have to rely on a visual inspection or risk losing the deal to other potential buyers. He ran his hand over the front of the ship as he rounded the windowless cockpit. Viewing windows weren't practical for subsurface craft that worked in extreme environments, so the ship was equipped with recessed and magnetically protected cameras and sensors that projected external images onto viewscreens in the cockpit.

Below the ship's nose and between its twin forward maneuvering thrusters, Tom yanked at the barrel of the original breaker gun like he was kicking the tires on an old land vehicle. The high-speed railgun was used to break up hard pockets of magma, generate flow through still chambers, or create openings between otherwise unconnected pockets of molten rock. "Does this still work?"

Margo shrugged as she checked a message on a data pad that was strapped to her forearm. "You could always scrap it and replace it with a storage pod."

He moved to an engine exhaust port on the side of the shuttle. The opening was caked with coppery soot, and the pungent odor reached out to him. "How about the engines? Are they original?"

"The ion drive was replaced a year ago, but there's no warranty on anything. They did their own maintenance and didn't keep records."

Aside from a small emergency hatch on top of the ship, the small craft had only a single entryway with its ramp already lowered, and Tom stepped inside. The main cabin was cluttered with parts and debris, but it was large enough for three or four workers to maneuver. Several access panels had been pulled from the walls and stacked against an open box of standard impact breaker gun charges, and one of the gravity deck plates had been removed to reveal the railgun's magazine beneath the floor.

To his left, the aft section of the ship had a head complete with a small wash sink, but most of the space was open, and drag marks on the floor were an obvious sign that it had been used for transporting cargo at some point. After some cleanup, it had possibilities, and he could imagine making the largest of the rooms into a living space. A twinge of excitement returned at the idea of living in his own onboard home—without having to pay rent to a landlord. His voice echoed off the bare metal walls as he pointed at the clutter. "Are these all parts of the ship?"

"Some might be, but I think they were using it as a salvage transport for a while. It's all included with the deal, so you can sort it out later."

Tom twisted his lips as he scanned the interior and began an internal debate. The shuttle was beaten up, but it was an industrial craft, after all. And how it looked wasn't as important as how well it would function. A bulkhead separated the pilot station from the main cabin, and he pulled the door open with a metal-on-metal creak. He ducked slightly to step through the oblong hatch into a space just large enough for two pilots to sit. Here, the ship had obvious problems. Circuit panels and wires hung out of every access opening in both the forward and ceiling consoles, and a tangled mess of cables had been stacked in front of the copilot station. It was a good bet that an overhaul would be a huge job—maybe too much for him to tackle.

He maneuvered around a box of parts that partially blocked the tiny aisle and slid into the dusty pilot seat. The flight yoke was perfectly positioned, and the old foam upholstery cradled him as if he'd worn it in himself. He relaxed his shoulders into the backrest and ran his hands over each of the throttle levers and control panels as Margo leaned in behind him to continue her sales pitch.

"It shouldn't take much to get it flying again. They made so many of these that parts are easy to find. With a few hours work, it'll be good as new."

He leaned over and heaved open the hinged copilot seat to find more parts stacked in the storage compartment underneath.

"I'm firm on the price, and I'll throw in a spare set of used thruster ignitors. But you've got to have it towed out of here by tomorrow. I have more stock arriving and this is in the way."

Tom let the seat drop and choked on a blast of dust. He sat back and ran his hands over the flight controls. While far from what he'd imagined buying someday, the shuttle was a perfect size for starting his own courier business or light hauling service. He let his gaze drift across the cockpit. This was his chance. He'd have to either find work that would keep him planet-bound or jump into an uncertain business plan that could bankrupt him. "I'll take it."

"Great! Let's go do the paperwork. You're going to love this little ship."

The awareness that he was about to spend most of his life savings sank in as they walked back to Margo's desk to start the hour and a half session of document signing, money transfers, and a review of the ship's latest survey report. If he couldn't get the ship flying, he'd be not only unemployed but also nearly flat broke.

Margo tapped at the last page of the registration data pad. "Okay, what ship name should I enter?"

Tom blinked. He'd spent countless hours thinking of the perfect name for his first ship, which he'd always dreamed would be a modern swift-skip or at least a reconditioned Ravarian ferry. But *Sparker's Speeder* or *Excelsior* would be ridiculous choices for an old mining shuttle.

Margo drummed on the edge of the pad as she stared at him. "I don't want to rush you, but it's late, and I need to be back here early in the morning."

A ripple of panic washed over him as he searched for a last-minute choice.

Margo seemed to spend her last bit of patience in a forced half smile. "How about we just use the registry number for now, and you can add a name when you decide on something. It won't cost much to update it later."

The suggestion felt like someone offering him a hand after taking a fall. "That's fine."

She quickly entered the registration code. "Okay then, HF-T550-1451 is all yours."

Tom accepted the data pad from Margo and stood to follow her to the exit. "I'll get a tow set up for tomorrow morning."

Margo scratched her nose with the back of her hand. "We open at seven sharp."

She tapped the door control and Tom gave a nod as he stepped into the rain. Most of his savings were now spent, and there was no turning back. His next challenge would be to turn his broken-down shuttle into a new career.

5

Tom gave a gentle knock, and the pilot station door opened almost instantly. The female mechanic smiled at him from beneath a bright red lock that hung across her face. "The supervisor saw you coming. You need to get your things?"

Tom nodded. "Yeah. It'll only take a minute."

"He said you need an escort." She wrinkled a nostril. "Company policy for nonemployees. I told him I'd take you back."

He winced at the reminder of his disgrace. "Thanks." Under other circumstances, it would have made him turn and walk away, abandoning his belongings to avoid the certain stares that waited for him inside. But given that he was now the owner of his own ship—derelict that it was—he privately nurtured a tiny flame of pride to shield him from the upcoming parade of shame.

Tom stepped inside and followed along the route he'd walked a thousand times before, doing his best to focus on his task instead of the other workers. His escort shoved the hangar door open and turned toward the catwalk stairway leading up to the employee lockers. "I'm glad I was here when you got here so I could apologize for the other night on the street."

"There wasn't any harm done."

"No, but Denik was rude." She shrugged. "I just felt bad. You know, he's not so bad when you get to know him."

Tom attempted a smile. "I'll take your word for it."

They arrived at a long row of narrow vertical doors. He touched the bio-lock mechanism of his old locker, and the door popped open. At least they hadn't deleted his access yet. Another trip through the pilot station to the supervisor's office for a temporary access code would have added insult to the experience.

"I'm Tau, by the way." She extended her hand. "I only started on the pit crew a few days before . . ."—she winced—"you left."

He shook her hand. "I appreciated you asking if I was okay the other night."

"I don't think he splashed you on purpose."

Tom grabbed his raincoat from his locker. "Too bad I didn't have this with me." He pulled out a short-brimmed cap he'd forgotten about and put it on.

"Were you at the dealer to buy a ship?"

Tom hesitated and glanced behind him to make sure there was nobody else within earshot. Tau seemed friendly enough, but he didn't want to risk anyone mocking his dream. "I'm hoping to go into business for myself. Maybe fly private tours or something."

A kind smile showed from beneath the hair that she couldn't keep from draping across her face. "That's exciting." She took a quick glance of her own to make sure she wouldn't be overheard. "Everyone knows about your flying awards. You should know that some of the guys pick at you because they're jealous."

He lifted an old pair of boots from the locker floor. "Oh come on."

"Really." She looked at him with wide eyes. "I mean, they'd never give up their mechanic pay to become pilots, and they'd never admit it, but they all know you're top-notch at what you do."

"Well, you know what they say about being a pilot in the industry. It's like digging ditches." He pulled a mostly empty duffel bag out and swung the locker door shut.

Tau finished the saying. "No matter how good you are, there's only so much an employer is willing to pay for a top quality ditch."

Tom gave a nod.

"Well," Tau said as her face blossomed into a bright smile, "I'm sure you're going to do great, no matter what you do."

They stepped to a nearby exit door at the corner of the hangar, and Tom leaned on the unlocking mechanism. "Thanks, Tau. I hope you're right." The door swung open.

"It was nice to see you, Tom."

Tom gave another nod as he turned away, stuffing the boots into the duffel bag as he walked. The visit hadn't been what he'd anticipated. The expected taunting and smirks from other workers never came. In fact, the experience left him with an unexpected boost of optimism, and he picked up his pace.

6

"Ow!"

For the fifth time that day, Tom hit his head on the underside of the flight console while squirming out to get a tool. He rubbed a greasy sleeve on his newest bruise and fought the temptation to pound the panel in frustration. It was time for a break.

The "few hours" of repair work that the saleswoman promised had already turned into more than eight days. The navigation system was a mess, and a more thorough inspection revealed that most of the other systems had been field-patched over the years. In the short term, only life support, navigation, and propulsion were critical. But considering the tangle of wires hanging from the fuel control panel, even getting the engines to fire would be a major accomplishment.

Tom grabbed the last half of a sandwich and sat on a damaged cargo box between his ship and a rolling cart stacked with a jumble of tools and repair manuals. He'd moved from his small apartment into a utility garage to avoid paying maintenance bay fees at a shipyard, but his savings would only cover two months' worth of rent. He'd have to either get his ship flying by then or scrap the whole project.

As he took a bite, Tom rubbed dust from the HF-T550 model designation cast into the hull by the manufacturer's mold. Nearly everyone registered a custom name, but naming a ship that might never get off the ground again made about as much sense as trying to make it look good, which was also pointless, since the tough pecrite hull would resist any molecular bond, making an attempt to paint or refinish it a waste of time.

He stuffed the rest of the sandwich into his mouth and dragged the cargo box to the front of his ship to use as a target. The breaker gun wouldn't be of any use on a courier ship, but a quick test would give him an idea of its resale value.

Tom dropped into the pilot seat and switched the firing control into single-shot mode. The device only had a twenty-degree range of movement, but it was enough to center the sight on his target. A gentle squeeze of the trigger made the ship jolt, and the sound of the breaker gun made him flinch. The high-velocity impact obliterated the cargo box, and tiny flakes of the crate's composite material floated to the ground like Hydrenian sand snow. The force produced by the old device was more than he'd anticipated, and he cringed at the divot that was left in the concrete wall behind the crate. With finances as tight as they were, he'd need his security deposit back.

The next test would be the most important one so far. If his ship couldn't fly, there wouldn't be any sense in continuing his efforts. A few flips of the planetary engine power switches brought a hum of energy from the drive coils as they charged.

The ignition indicator lit, and the ship growled as the engines rumbled to life, sending the smell of fresh exhaust into the cockpit. The milestone put a grin on Tom's face, and he tapped the control to raise the loading ramp. It moved slowly, but once sealed, the sound of the engines diminished to blend with the thrumming of the ship's other systems. He scanned the panel indicators with unblinking anticipation as he gently increased power to the engines. The craft lifted itself from the decking, which groaned with relief. He allowed it to hover for a moment, then he eased the throttle output back until the ship was again safely resting on the bay floor.

Tom threw his fists into the air in triumph and accidentally punched the low overhead panels. "Ow."

The success was a great morale boost. His hard work had paid off, and the prospect of actually working for himself felt within reach. If the computer's analysis of the engine test data checked out, he could perform an orbital test flight soon.

⸻◇⸻

THE CIRCULAR SKY door of the garage twisted open like an ancient camera aperture as Tom keyed in his liftoff request to Copania's Flight Control center. Already strapped into the pilot seat, he ignited the main engines. As if to punctuate the startup roar, an automated message crackled through the comm system. *"Craft HF-T550-1451, your submitted flight plan and takeoff are approved for zero eight four eight local time."*

He eased his ship into the sky. The cabin pressure was stable, the engines hummed in perfect synchronicity, and the only fault indicators on the cockpit consoles were for the open doors on the ore pods that he wasn't using anyway. Rising above the nearby buildings, he pushed the twin throttles forward and eased the flight yoke skyward.

Monitoring his new ship's unfamiliar controls made the trip into space seem quicker than it was. The ship was buffeted as it gained speed, but the ride evened out as he approached the edge of Copania's atmosphere. Several dozen ships were visible on the daylight side of his home world, some by contrasting marker lights against the blackness of space, and others passively lit by the bright algae green of the planet's pastoral ocean. A handful of specialized shuttles and satellites moved in synchronous orbit, above either scientifically significant areas or military facilities, but all were carefully orchestrated by Copanian Flight Control.

Tom had logged hundreds of orbital flights around his home planet in tour shuttles wrapped with large viewing windows, outfitted with expensive flight stabilizers, and equipped with the latest soundproofing technology. By contrast, his ship's smaller viewscreens offered a more limited view, the whole craft vibrated during flight, and the sound of the engines rumbled through every compartment. The interior also smelled like used industrial lubricant. But it was *his* ship, and it was flying. More importantly, *he* was flying again, and he relaxed into the worn seat.

Thrusters and flight controls functioned. Life support and navigation systems both worked fine. The ion drive was designed for unmanned trips on autopilot and would be too slow for his needs, but he test-fired it to verify that it gave the expected amount of thrust. Even the commercial-grade gravity decking in the cockpit seemed to work. It was a luxury on basic transports and ships designed for private use, but it was a solid investment in worker safety and productivity for industrial crafts in hazardous service.

Even though he was looking at his home planet on viewscreens instead of through actual windows, it had never looked better than it did from the cockpit of the ship that he'd made fly. Tom pulled at the controls and made a slow barrel roll to begin his deceleration into the atmosphere along his planned flight path. The black horizon drifted from his screens as the ocean filled them. Even without a Trades Academy diploma, he'd proven that he had enough skill to perform a basic overhaul—with a little help from the repair manuals. It was something to be proud of.

But a moment after his ship began to fight the friction from the increasing air density, the port engine abruptly failed, and the sudden imbalance sent the ship into a dizzying counterclockwise flat rotation. Tom gripped the flight yoke as an ear-piercing alarm wailed. He worked the flight controls in a vain effort to counteract the wild thrust of the single working engine, but the ship spun faster with each passing moment.

A few seconds after the engine failed, the shuttle's emergency system sensed the imbalance and tried to reduce power to the starboard engine to minimum. But instead of the engine shutting down, it began to pulse, which only made the spin more erratic. The flight control backup programming made the maneuvering thrusters scream at full power to compensate, but they couldn't counter the more powerful thrust of the large engine. The ship was out of control.

The wildly varying centrifugal force made it difficult to even see the flight console, but the dire situation drew Tom's concentration to a razor edge, and time seemed to slow down as he focused. Cutting power to the engine was the only way to stop the wild ride, but the disconnect was located to the right of the copilot station—too far to reach from his seat. There was no protocol for an engine failure plus an emergency system malfunction without a copilot to assist, so he timed the lull in the engine pulsation and did what every flight instructor and rule book told him to never do. He slammed the release on his safety harness.

With an upward shove and midair twist, he planted a foot on the wall of the cockpit as his body was thrown to starboard, right next to the engine power breakers. In a split second, he yanked the conductor handle, and the inertia that pushed him against the wall subsided. The thrusters slowed the spin, and Tom landed an awkward fall onto the copilot seat. His legs tangled between the seat and the wall, while his shoulder fell farther to hit the gravity decking under the forward control console.

With no counteracting force to work against, the safety system stopped the spin and slowly pushed him into an ascent course back out of the atmosphere. Tom twisted to free his legs as he dragged himself into the pilot seat, then strained to get his eyes refocused enough to find the alarm silence switch and tap the communication panel. "Control, this is HF-T550-1451 in distress. I have an engine failure and require assistance."

The response from Control came immediately. "Craft 1451, do you have orbital and maneuvering capability?"

"My backup system is re-establishing orbit, but I'll need a transport tow to the surface."

"Copy, 1451. Maintain your current course, and we'll clear traffic for you. A maintenance ship will rendezvous with you in four minutes. Keep this comm channel active until you're docked and secure."

"Copy. Maintaining current speed and heading."

Tom shook inside as he fought off a bout of nausea from

his fading adrenaline rush. Flashing lights on the cockpit panels showed a complete power loss to the port engine, but there was no indication of what had caused the failure. His side ached, and he wrapped a rag around a cut on his hand.

The emergency system decreased thruster power just as the service ship arrived with its docking bay door already open. "Craft 1451, this is Maintenance 083. Shut down all thrust power systems for docking."

Tom reached across the cockpit and flipped the disconnect switch for the flight system. "Copy, 083. Thrust system power is off."

"Craft 1451, we're commencing with docking. Stand by."

Floodlights bathed his ship as the rescue craft backed over it. Its bay door swallowed the shuttle with a huge hinged jaw and sealed him inside as an automated strapping system clunked into place for the trip to the surface.

"Craft 1451, we have you secure and pressurized. Please shut down all systems for the ride down."

"I'm powering down now."

He pulled the overhead main power breaker, and his ship went dark and silent except for the hum from the rescue ship's engines. A gentle sway told him the tow vessel had started its descent, and he took a deep breath. What had first seemed like a career triumph had become a narrow escape from disaster. His piloting skill had saved him this time, but it was clear that he'd missed something during the overhaul. The whole project started to feel like a bad idea.

THE SUN WAS SETTING by the time Tom got unloaded at the emergency terminal and paid for his ship to be transported back to his garage, which cost his next month's rent. Now he was over budget and short on time to get the ship ready—if it could ever be. With luck, the problem would turn out to be something easy to correct, so he rolled up his sleeves and pulled off the starboard engine service cover.

The access opening was small and didn't allow him to see much, so he snaked his arm into the compartment to feel around for anything that felt out of place. Sharp edges bit into his arm as he blindly explored, and his cheek pressed against the housing as he stretched to reach under the engine. There, his fingertips bumped into a thick, freely swinging cable that could only be the main power line. He slid his hand along the short length until it reached the connector at the end, which crumbled in his fingers. Most of the bits fell away, but he maneuvered his arm out of the tight space and stared at the dry-rotted pieces that he'd managed to grip. His gut went hollow, and he slid back to sit on the floor. Part of his ship had literally fallen apart during flight.

The bits of plastic disintegrated as he turned them over to examine them. Given the age and condition of his ship, there was a good chance more parts were in a similar condition, and with his limited expertise and equipment, there was no way to test every component. There would always be a danger of another failure.

He could ask Marcus to help him check the systems, but that wasn't his first choice. Marcus always had good intentions, but he wasn't very good at expressing them, and his input often felt like biting criticism rather than helpful advice. Plus, going into business should mean relying less on others, not more—and asking for help would make him feel even less capable than he already did.

Once he replaced the cable and got a commercial flight

permit, he'd look for suborbital jobs that would be easier on his ship. Then, with the profits, he could afford a proper overhaul and safety check. That was a better plan than opening himself up to criticism of his impulsive enterprise, but the idea that something else on the aging ship could break without warning still gnawed at him.

7

The miners' voices echoed off the cheap but functional corrugated walls of the meeting room, where at least one representative from each of the remaining families of the second Kala asteroid mining venture attended the informal discussion. Winnet Aramine, the appointed financial organizer, stepped to the front of the group. "Since it's the main reason we're here, I'll start things off with a report of our financial situation."

Private conversations among the miners turned to whispers as she spoke. "As you know, shaft seven isn't producing as expected. After paying for our latest shipment of air recycling media, drill heads, and noble gases, we're nearly out of funds."

A miner at the front of the room sat with his arms folded. "I thought the core samples from shaft seven showed it would produce grade five ore."

Grade five was premium quality pecrite ore, and it could be used almost without refinement for reactor catalyst grids and interstellar drive generator housings. The still-valuable but lower-purity ore that was used for plasma smelters and ship hulls could turn enough profit to keep a mine running, but wildcatters weren't interested in toiling for seventy hours a week just to make ends meet.

Administrator Shek Windham, a broad-shouldered man whose voice made the walls vibrate with baritone harmonics, spoke as the only elected official in the colony. "It did, but the readings have shifted again. Tests say we need to go deeper."

Murmurs swept the room and heads shook. Decisions regarding the day-to-day operations were left to the administrator and his staff, but after the failure of the first Kala mining operation, the remaining fourteen families had decided that any major financial decisions would be resolved by the group.

Shek's eyes swept the room. "We have enough equipment and resources to complete shaft seven to our original target depth, but the samples all point to the higher grade ore thirty percent deeper than the original projection."

Winnet took a half step closer to the group. "We can take out a speculation loan to cover the cost."

The man with folded arms stood and looked at the others in the room with conviction. "I'm not willing to spend more than we have. I'd rather stop than go into debt."

Another miner nodded in agreement. "We can go back to working for Froster or one of the big outfits on Qinter and come back here when we've saved enough to drill more."

Winnet's mouth hung open at the suggestion. "And leave with nothing more than low-grade ore to cover our trip home? If we abandon the settlement, anyone will be able to claim it. Do you really want to let anyone who comes along just take what's ours?"

The man unfolded his arms and anchored his palms to his waist. "That's the same argument you made before we drilled shaft six, and now we're broke. I don't know about everyone else, but I'd rather call it a bust and move on. We can try again later, but borrowing money on a speculation mine has a way of spiraling out of control."

Most of the attendees exchanged silent nods with one another.

"If that's the consensus," Shek said, "then it's settled. We'll finish shaft seven to our original target depth and pull out if it doesn't produce the good stuff."

The group sat in silence, and the lack of any further argument signaled their agreement. This would be the end of K2. The decision made the other scheduled meeting topics irrelevant, and Winnet watched in silence as the miners filed out. Only she and a wiry man leaning against the wall at the back of the room remained. His eyes shifted from her to the doorway as he fiddled with a decorative metal strip on the front of his jacket—a nervous habit that Winnet ignored as she paced slowly toward him. "Why didn't you speak up, Firkis? I know you want to stay."

"You also know that I like to keep a low profile. Besides, there's barely enough of us to keep this operation going. If even a handful left we'd have to quit."

Winnet lowered her voice. "I'm not giving up my investment. We have to find a way to finance shaft seven to the new target."

He began rubbing harder at the metal trim. "I can only think of one way to do that, short of hijacking a credit barge."

"Are you suggesting we make a deal with another mining outfit?"

Firkis raised an eyebrow. "Who would want to team with a failing mine?"

"But if there's a way we can get the funds . . ."

"You just announced that we're out of cash. The decision's been made. We're leaving."

She stepped close to him. "If we can get the money, I'll tell everyone that it was an accounting error or something."

"Do you know what they'd do to you if they found out?"

Winnet's nose lifted a bit. "They'd thank me for making sure we succeeded." She leaned against the wall next to him and reduced her voice to a loud whisper. "I can't stand the thought of losing my investment when we're so close." She turned her head toward him. "What's your idea?"

Firkis squinted and glanced at the open door.

"It's risky. I'd rather not talk about it here."

8

The Office of Commercial Vehicles buzzed with the typical noises of everyday business as the government employee spoke in a clear and businesslike tone. "You can apply for a recreational or hobby permit, but use of a ship that's more than forty years old for commercial purposes requires recertification by a licensed mechanic."

Tom stared across the counter like a child being denied dessert after finishing his meal. A pile of somewhat wrinkled registration documents, pilot license endorsements, and completed applications were spread out on the counter between them. "But recertification for my ship would cost almost as much as I paid for it."

"I'm sorry, sir. There's nothing I can do."

Tom scraped the documents from the counter and stormed out of the building into the normal pedestrian traffic of the weekday lunch hour. His entire business plan had just been stopped by a single unexpected rule, and the denial of a business permit meant he only had one option left. His index fingerprint was coded to quick-dial Marcus, and he tapped his holocom band. A single chime later, an image of his older sibling sitting in a Copanian mineral bath popped up.

"Have you got some time?" Tom asked.

"Come on over, the water's great."

As he turned to head for Marcus's place, he nearly tripped over a street-cleaning bot that maneuvered out of his way at the last moment to avoid bumping into his shin. The tiny autonomous devices that kept downtown Copania neat were a nuisance, causing a perpetual tripping hazard throughout the most densely populated part of the city. Tom shook his head as it burbled an apologetic tone and continued its programmed task.

The bots polished the epoxied terrazzo walkways to a high gloss. Inset strips of light showed color-coded pedestrian routes that ran throughout the core of the city—a tourism gimmick designed to draw visitors to the downtown businesses. The movement of light made the streets look almost alive, even when no people were using them. Of course, inset electronic screens also presented paid advertisements for the tourist industry.

Marcus lived on the thirtieth level of one of the nicest places in the downtown district, and even from twelve blocks away, it was hard to miss the clean glass building that rose forty stories. Marcus didn't share Tom's childhood passion for flight, but had instead fallen in love with the mechanics of things, which turned out to be a much more lucrative interest than piloting—at least on Copania.

The foot traffic became lighter as he made his way farther from the center of the city. Jingles from advertising recordings drifted out of open shop doors. Hoverpods and wheeled land vehicles sped around corners as they dashed to meetings or transported luxuries to the many expensive residences in the district. High above, thin streams of slow-moving air traffic silently worked their way across the sky. The procession seemed to taunt him as unseen forces conspired to deny him access to their aerial parade.

The municipal buildings in the core district were all coated in a heavy commercial finish, but each one he passed on his way to Marcus's apartment was slightly more polished than the previous, and the urban terrain shifted from concrete to plasteel to prism-ceramic construction. Even the ambient sound changed from the whine of vehicles to soft echoes, as the arrangement of buildings in the more modern part of the district were designed to dampen the sounds of engines and repulsors into smooth white noise.

The skyscraper with its ground floor walls made of permaglass blended with dozens of others that had been built from the same plans. Its lobby walls were lined with cylindrical elevator cars, and Tom stepped into one. The wall of the plain but impeccably clean car swiveled to encapsulate him and began its ascent toward the prime level. The sweet scent of roasted faery flower pods accompanied a flowing melody that was piped into the lift, and in a moment the door swiveled open. After only a few steps onto the floor, he reached the chime panel on Marcus's door and tapped it. His brother yelled from somewhere inside, "It's unlocked!"

The clean suite was brightly lit, and while only a little more than twice the size of Tom's apartment, it was decorated with modern cushioned chairs and furniture in contrasting hues of almond and mocha. The kitchenette featured a serving lift to deliver made-to-order food from a central gourmet kitchen, and the floors shone in a way that only a professional cleaning service could produce. Near the open balcony doorway, Marcus sat in a steaming lounge tub as he watched a mechanized combat program on a holographic display. Thin streams of effervescent ocean minerals rose to the surface of the cloudy water and created a mist that hung in the surrounding air.

"Grab a seat. This is day two of heavyweight eliminations. It's a repair period now, but the best round is coming up."

Tom sat on one of the plush outdoor chairs. "I heard Gombra was fighting today."

Marcus kept his eyes fixed on the contest. "Yeah, I bet a day's pay on him. Help yourself to a drink."

Tom might have enjoyed some time in the opulent surroundings if the pressure of finding an income wasn't weighing on him.

"Thanks. Hey, um . . . I bought a mining shuttle. Do you know how I can get a cheap commercial certification for freight hauling? They told me I need one since it's over forty years old."

The station switched to a commercial break, and Marcus reached for his bottle of ale. "Bought what? I thought you were a couple years away from buying one of those decommissioned Ravarian ferries."

"That was my original plan, but I lost my job, so I needed something quick."

"You bought a ship before making sure you could get a cert?"

In fact, he hadn't thought about certification at all until the clerk at the Office of Commercial Vehicles told him he needed it, but getting a lecture about it from his overachieving brother wasn't going to help. "I just didn't know about the forty years rule, that's all."

"Did you say a mining shuttle?" Marcus shook his head. "That's an industrial ship. I'm not licensed for anything that extensive. I know guys who can do it, but it's not cheap."

Another dead end. Tom's shoulders slumped, but he did his best to hide a sigh. Marcus took a drink, then abruptly pulled the bottle from his mouth. "Wait, you lost your job?" His cheeks puffed out as he whistled a quiet exhale. "Are they laying off at the tour place?"

Tom tried to sound nonchalant. "Well, I've wanted my own ship for a long time. This just pushed my schedule up. But they won't give me a business license without a current cert."

Marcus turned back to the match that was preparing to continue. "I'd sell the ship and just get another piloting job."

It wasn't helpful advice, and Tom shifted in his seat. "Considering I got fired, that might take a while."

That grabbed Marcus's attention. "Fired? How could you get fired? You know you'll never get another flying job without a recommendation."

Here was the lecture that he'd known was coming, and he wanted to move past it. "I know, but that's my situation, so I need to get something else going."

Marcus nodded. "You're right. I didn't mean to criticize. I'm just surprised is all. You could probably get a laborer position doing waste collection, or maybe even landscaping work. Wait tables for a while and try again in a few years."

His brother's softened tone was a relief. "I thought about that, but I want to keep flying if I can."

Marcus motioned to his old military unit insignia that he had framed on the wall. "Then why not sign up for military service? I'd have made a career out of it." Before trade school, Marcus had served for two years in the Copanian Guard, where he'd been decorated before an injury forced him to take an honorable discharge. "Plus, you might learn some self-discipline while you're there."

Tom tensed at the renewed lecture.

"I know you were the first to barrel roll the Zymezia course in under four minutes, but you need more than a bunch of flying awards before a company is going to want to keep you."

Tom had never told Marcus that he'd taken the defense enlistment test three times with the hope of becoming a military pilot and failed with a slightly worse score at each attempt. "I doubt I'm cut out for a military job." Tom bit his lip. "Maybe you could get me a temporary position at your company, just until I find someone to do the cert at a good price."

Marcus gave a solemn shake of his head, and Tom leaned forward. "Even as an assistant in the garage?"

"Nah, there's a hiring freeze in most of the industry. Hand me another, would you?"

The lid of the cooler automatically slid open as Tom reached for a fresh bottle and handed it to his brother. "What I really need is to get out of this rut of being an employee and fly for myself. I'm sure I could run a successful business of my own."

Marcus twisted the top from the bottle. "How about going out-system? Someplace where the rules are more flexible."

It was an idea that had never occurred to Tom. They'd grown up on Copania, and the farthest he had ever traveled was an overnight asteroid study trip with school.

"You mean for freight hauling?"

"For anything." Marcus shrugged. "Cargo, passenger, courier service, whatever."

"They'd let me fly without certifications?"

"I don't know about the big systems, but for sure in industrial ones like Doulier or Feth. They're focused on profit, not safety."

The thought of exploring the fringe systems was thrilling,

but his experience during the test flight kept his rush of excitement in check. Leaving Copanian space would mean he'd be on his own if he had another emergency. He pulled a drink from the cooler and twisted the cap. "I hadn't thought of leaving Copania."

Marcus focused on the mech battle that had resumed. "I'm not saying you should, either. It was just an idea."

Tom stared into his bottle. His ship had large engines for maneuvering and a staged ion drive that would normally be used with an autopilot system to make slow, unmanned deliveries, but neither was practical for traveling to another star system. "I'd need a tagalong drive."

"Yeah, a transport tow would be expensive."

"Plus, I'd need it in case I found work between systems. Do you know where I can get one on a budget?"

Marcus winced at the mech battle as a small explosion damaged one of the combatants, showering sparks that terminated at the edges of the holoimager projection matrix. As the station went to a commercial, he threw his hands up, sloshing ale outside of the tub. "Gombra's finished in the next round. I can't believe that homemade piece of junk is beating the division champ."

Tom's forehead wrinkled in thought. "Maybe I could salvage an old drive and get it working."

Marcus pulled his attention from the display and pointed the neck of his bottle at Tom. "Never use salvage drives. They're in the scrap pile for a reason, and you don't want to get stuck someplace without a way to fix it." He squinted as he searched his memory. "We used to have an old kit drive kicking around our shop. It was a low-end model, but it was never actually used."

"And it works?"

"Someone got it half installed in their ship before they gave up. They wanted us to finish the job, but when they found out how much labor would cost, they ended up just buying a new drive that included installation. I could probably get you a deal on it, but you'd only get a ten-day warranty since it was a trade-in."

"I'd be able to test it in ten days . . ." Tom took a breath. "If I had some help."

"Let me guess. I'll be helping you install it?"

"It's either that or I lose my ship."

Marcus took the last drink from his bottle. "Come by work tomorrow and I'll find out if we still have it. There's no credit for secondhand parts either, so bring cash."

"I'll bring everything I have."

Marcus cocked his head. "And you're going to owe me for this."

Tom hopped up and set his drink down. "You're right. I'll owe you big. Thanks, Marcus."

Marcus raised his empty bottle in a salute as Tom hurried out of the apartment and down to street level.

Staking his business claim in the fringe systems was Tom's only chance to breathe life back into his plans, but his ship would need several upgrades before he could leave Copania, and there was one that was vital. Since his mining ship was designed primarily for atmospheric and orbital use, traveling between star systems—at least within a practical amount of time—required an interstellar drive. Full-scale drives required large generators and charge cells to form interstellar compression fields, and typically only governments, corporations, or the very wealthy could afford them.

However, there was a common way to use an interstellar drive without owning a full-scale unit. A tagalong drive was technically an interstellar drive, but it didn't need its own generator or charge cells. It was much smaller and less expensive, and it was designed to use waste energy that was thrown off in the wake of a larger ship's fully equipped system. Using that energy, it could propel a small craft to an interstellar speed for a limited duration. If a destination was within range, only a single tag might be needed, but long distances required careful planning between ports to ensure that enough waste energy from other ships would be available to complete a trip using multiple tags. Most tagalong drives were professionally installed, but a skilled mechanic could install an aftermarket unit. Tom didn't fit that description, but fortunately Marcus was a drive expert.

9

Tom crouched next to the tagalong drive and upgraded navigation antenna array that represented nearly the rest of his savings. Marcus had subtracted his employee discount and had even gotten his company to include a drive mount and small energy shield at no charge. Tom's ship's cast-pecrite hull was a perfect heat resistant material for traveling at speed through planetary atmospheres, but without the shield, any add-on devices would be burned up seconds after being exposed.

The Litadyne Tagalong 111A was originally marketed as a hobbyist kit, but installation had proven far too complex a task for the average handyman, so it was only sold for about a year before the company went out of business. Replacement parts would be difficult to find, but he was glad to have it.

He pulled one of the mounting brackets from its tattered packaging and climbed the ladder next to his ship. Placement of a tagalong drive on a ship wasn't critical, since the compression field could be adjusted to encompass any hull shape. He wasn't using the magma drive, so the logical place to install the new devices was on top of the upper magma drive housing where the drive ports would make ideal attachment points, and the three exhaust-energy collector panels could be installed to wrap over the top of them. It would take an hour to get the brackets attached, but that should be quick enough to get it done before Marcus was ready to test the configuration.

It was the third day of the project, and Marcus was working on calibrating the flight computer. Tom climbed down to where his brother was cross-referencing between four volumes of the drive manual.

"I know it's going to look clumsy," Tom said. "But it shouldn't interfere with planetary flight much."

"Just make sure that shield works." Marcus said without looking up. "Otherwise, you'll only get to use your new toy once."

Tom had to admit that Marcus really knew his stuff, and without his help, he wouldn't have had a chance of getting the drive working. He'd filled his brother in on the details of his test flight, and Marcus had agreed to help reload the emergency flight programming and apply his skills to an inspection of all critical systems before they started the new installation. "I'm still surprised you didn't find anything else that was falling apart. I was sure there would be some other component or cable that was worn out or crumbling."

Marcus looked from one of the manuals to another, then back again as he triple-checked the calibration procedure. "Yeah, you're lucky to have survived that engine failure. I doubt anyone else would have."

The memory of the dizzying spin was still fresh. "You'd be surprised at how a death spiral at the threshold of planetary burn-in can motivate you."

Marcus didn't miss a beat. "Modesty is olf splatter. Take some credit. What you did was pretty amazing."

"What I did was almost crash my ship."

Marcus looked up. "That's what makes it so impressive. You might do better in the military than you think."

Too bad the military didn't agree, but his brother's sincere compliment was more credible than any standardized government exam. Marcus's confidence often sounded like arrogance, but his no-nonsense nature had been learned during his successful military career where communication was key and empty platitudes could get people killed. When he gave a compliment, he meant it.

"That's high praise from a war hero."

"It's just true, that's all. I'm glad to see you finally capitalizing on something you're good at, even if it is with a hunk of junk like this."

"My plan is to trade up as soon as I can."

Marcus nodded in approval as he looked back at the manuals. "Something easier to maintain would be a good start."

"I'm hoping to get something that doesn't need any work at all, but that'll depend on what kind of work I find."

Marcus looked up from his studying. "You mean you don't have any work lined up yet?"

"Well, no. I mean, I'm sure there are lots of jobs I could get, but I've been busy working on my ship."

Marcus raised an eyebrow. "You know, business can be pretty cutthroat, even in the more civilized parts of space, and you're heading to the fringe."

Tom had been so excited about his plan, and so busy getting ready to leave, that he hadn't even considered the possibility that he wouldn't find work, but he did his best to project confidence. "If there's any work out there, I'll find it."

"Sounds like a risky bet."

"Well, I'm not going to find any piloting jobs here, so I'll take my chances." Tom gestured to the manuals. "Any luck with those?"

Marcus turned back to the schematics and data tables. "I think I've got it figured out. The drive doesn't have any auto-calibration, so we'll have to do everything manually."

"How will that affect the operation?"

"It shouldn't, once it's set up, but if it ever loses calibration, you'll have to redo it from scratch, so I'd take notes if I were you."

"I passed the basic ship systems classes, you know."

"Suit yourself," Marcus said. He pointed to a data port with one hand and a page of one of the manuals with the other. "Since the drive kit for the tagalong uses its own flight computer, we won't have to merge flight systems. Plus, if the tagalong has a problem, it shouldn't affect the other engines."

Tom nodded. "So if I lose one system, the others will still work."

"Exactly. Also, there are thirteen quad sequencers split into binary pairs that all feed data into the program."

Tom picked up a data pad and quietly tapped out notes as Marcus began his explanation. He still barely had a grasp on even the basic principles of interstellar travel, but after several hours of tutoring and testing, the tagalong's self-diagnostic confirmed a properly configured installation, and it was ready for use by the end of the day.

While Tom reattached the control system service cover, Marcus stuffed some calibrating instruments into a bag and looked up at the ship. "That's the best we can do without activating the drive."

Tom snugged the last fastener. "I guess my test run will be leaving the system."

"Don't you want to try a local test first?"

"My rent is due in two days and I spent those credits on the drive, so I have to leave tomorrow. If it doesn't work, I'll have to sell the ship anyway, so there's no point in paying for another month here."

"You're finally starting to think ahead." Marcus grabbed his tool pouch and jacket. "And if it doesn't work out, you can always come back."

"Yeah. Of course." The words felt like sandpaper on Tom's tongue. Coming home would signal utter failure. Next to Marcus, who he didn't begrudge for being good at what he did for a living, it would make him feel like a fool for having tried in the first place. He would make his venture work. He had to.

"I'm heading home," Marcus said. "Early start at work tomorrow." The brothers bumped fists.

"Thanks for your help, Marcus."

"Good luck. Let me know how it goes." Marcus heaved the small overhead garage door open and stepped into the night.

Tom gathered the rest of the tools they'd been using, securing them in one of the utility compartments in the ship's main cabin. He'd been stowing his personal belongings over the past few days, so there wasn't much left to pack. In the ship's tiny mess area, which was little more than a two-person eating counter, he'd already verified that the small built-in food rehydrator worked, and a makeshift sleeping bunk made of foam mats would serve him well enough.

Traveling out of the system made two of the standard features of his ship more important. Since his test of the breaker gun proved that it still worked, he'd leave it in place. At some point it would make sense to replace it with a more practical defensive weapon, but until then he'd load the standard impact rounds that came with the shuttle onto the firing rail magazine to arm the device. It was a poor substitute for a swivel-mount turret or auto-cannon, but pirates were a threat outside of planetary jurisdictions, and while they didn't normally bother small ships, it would be ready in case he needed to defend himself.

The other feature was the ion drive, which would be his only backup method of propulsion. Tom grabbed some cleaning brushes and solvent for the last task before his morning departure. Unlike the planetary engines, the ion drive was fairly new and less complex, and had fired properly during his orbital test. But cleaning each grid plate would give him extra peace of mind. Even though it was too slow for human interstellar travel, like the breaker gun, it was better than nothing.

If his tagalong worked the next day, he'd be on his way to a new off-world career.

10

The wait for the large ship to start its drive felt longer than the three hours Tom had kept his craft hovering near Copania's interstellar departure point, but he had to stay alert. His simple tagalong lacked most of the automated features found on pricier models, so when the freighter started its drive, he'd have less than a minute to manually start his own prelaunch sequence in time to collect the stray energy from its wake. If he missed it, it might be hours before another ship would be ready to leave.

Two star systems were well known for their industrial economies and relaxed commercial regulation. The Doulier sun had massive planets with dozens of resource-rich moons that supported businesses ranging from gemstone mining to agriculture, but they also had a reputation for unusual atmospheres and unstable terrain, and occasional reports of disappearing ships kept all but the most daring from exploring their frontiers.

The distant Feth system, with only a single barren planet of the same name, was renowned for its power-cell-charging industry, and because it lacked Doulier's colorful reputation, it also seemed like the safer choice for his first foray into the fringe systems. The navigation computer had determined that Feth was within the tagalong's range using the class C freighter's wake, but with his discounted kit drive, the trip would take at least fourteen days.

It was typical for several small ships to tag at the same time, but so far his was the only one nearby. Judging by its relative angle to his shuttle, the freighter would be traveling to a different system than he would, but that didn't matter to Tom. As long as at least one of his energy-collector panels was in the direct path of the exhaust wake, he could travel in any direction he wanted.

In most places tagging was legal and was used by anything from automated drones and delivery barges to personal shuttles and small commercial ships, but the method came with hazards. The large ships were mostly unconcerned with the tagalongs using their waste energy, but if one got in the way or otherwise interfered with the larger ship's navigation, it could find itself under quick attack. Government and corporate ships had both been rumored to cripple or destroy craft that interfered with their activities or disrupted commerce, and it wasn't worth testing those tales.

Another hazard was that a malfunction could leave him stranded far from any inhabited world or protected space where transmitting a distress call would be risky, since it also would be a signal to pirates that he was vulnerable.

A communication tone indicated an incoming transmission. "You still here?" Marcus's voice came through clearly, though slightly tinny.

"I'm waiting for the fun part," Tom answered.

"Take a look at this."

"I don't have comm imaging, remember?"

"Oh, right. Well, I just won sixteen hundred credits at the casino!"

Great. Not only was Marcus better than Tom was in school and more successful in his career, but he was also a lucky gambler.

"Send some of that luck my way, would you?"

"Let me know where you wind up, and try not to get into more trouble than I would." The transmission switched off.

Tom could use the ComNet—a slow but cheap form of relayed communication—to update Marcus on his progress, but he'd save any messages until he'd proven himself. The next time he'd talk with Marcus would be as either a successful entrepreneur or a broke pilot forced to come home in defeat.

The whole plan was exciting in a scary sort of way. The adventurer in him was thrilled at the prospect of discovering new places and people, but he'd already tasted some of the danger associated with flying his old ship. Without allies outside of Copania, he was vulnerable to any number of problems. If he couldn't find work and ran out of credits, or if his ship broke in a way that he couldn't repair, or worse, left him stranded somewhere, he'd have nowhere to turn for help.

There was no telling how much longer he'd have to wait, so with his ship's controls set to automatically maintain a relative position to the freighter, Tom headed back to check the cabin climate system. Travel in space typically required more heating than cooling, but as a mining craft designed for high-temperature service, his HF-T550 had a robust cooling system. He'd left it in place—not only because it was far too integrated into the ship's structure to completely remove, but because it also seemed to work. In contrast, the original heating system was designed only for short orbital trips, so he'd added auxiliary heaters for extended space travel. That system checked out except for a flashing low charge alert on one of the power cells. He dug in a utility compartment for something to unfasten the panel clips, but an alarm sounded in the cockpit before he could pull out a tool.

He dashed forward and hit a series of buttons on the taga-long controls to initialize its prelaunch sequence, and an array of counters began as the display showed a graphic representation of a compression field forming around the large cargo ship. This was it. If everything worked properly, he would be propelled to an interstellar speed that coincided with his taga-long's ability to utilize the exhaust energy. If it didn't, either nothing would happen and his ship would remain motionless, or he'd be in for a very short and uncomfortable trip that would abruptly send his craft tumbling through space.

With thirty-seven seconds left on the uppermost counter, he strapped himself into the pilot seat's six-way safety harness, his eyes darting between control panels as he monitored for any problems. The auxiliary counter hit zero, and the freighter disappeared in a cloud of green haze that threw out a wake of dim energy. The spherical wave dissipated into darker hues as it expanded from the exit point, and when it reached his ship, the tagalong's counter showed that it had begun collecting. Seconds later, the display flashed rapidly and the computer sensed the correct moment to engage the tagalong drive. With a sound like gravel scraping along the hull, his shuttle lurched forward. The viewscreens twisted the images of space into a dusky green, and a low vibration thrummed through the ship.

The instruments verified what the haze on his viewscreens told him—that he was traveling at interstellar speed—and he released the breath that he'd been unconsciously holding.

11

Daihn stared at the ancient stone writing as she waited for Uolo to collect his thoughts.

"Ah." He pointed to a short sequence of inscribed characters as he hovered over the tablet. "I think I've successfully translated these. They describe an area of space that I've cross-referenced to the Kala asteroid field."

Daihn's eyes shifted from the artifact to the historical specialist. "I expected a greater level of certainty from a respected scholar."

Uolo looked up at Daihn, and his voice stiffened. "Respected or not, we're looking at a form of communication that likely hasn't been in use for thousands of years. I never guaranteed certainty, only my most scrupulous analysis."

The confidence of his defense gave her some reassurance that he'd done his best work, and the edge left her voice. "The Kala field is vast."

Uolo refocused on the tablet. "It is, but the next sequence of symbols refers to locations corresponding to three stars." He moved to a data screen on the wall that displayed an astronomical chart. "The first is the Feth sun, the second is in the Toroniad system, and the third is an unexplored star in the Nestti region without habitable planets that is labeled only by its database identifier. When considered from the perspective of their collective plane, they form a nearly perfect equilateral triangle." He ran his finger along the screen. "The center of which passes through this edge of the Kala asteroid field."

Daihn raised an eyebrow. "This would seem to be an uncommon method of identifying a location."

Uolo kept his eyes fixed on the chart. "There's nothing common about these inscriptions, but it's a likely method of encrypting the location—if someone wanted to hide it."

"What has led you to believe that encryption was intended?"

"Nothing." He cocked his head. "Everything."

Daihn's impatience grew as she waited for the scientist to organize his thoughts. Uolo looked at her as if he was relaying something from memory. "It's just experience. I'm looking for the obvious within the unlikely."

"And does your experience suggest a specific location to search?"

"The field orbits the Kala sun, so without a more precise dating of the tablet, I can only estimate that the point is within an approximately ten-degree arc of the triangulated position."

Daihn looked to the symbols and held an unblinking stare. "Have you discovered anything more than a location?"

Uolo shook his head. "Nothing conclusive, but there are symbols that might indicate something of value was placed there."

Daihn turned to Uolo. "I hired you to provide an accurate translation. Is something located at these coordinates or not?"

Uolo stood straight and spoke as if presenting in a lecture hall, his chin lifted in a show of uncharacteristic confidence. "I've offered nothing more or less than my analysis of the materials you've presented to me, and I've given you my best interpretation. I'll instruct your crew on how to correctly apply the translation methods that I've used, and they should be able to continue searching the text, but from a practical perspective there isn't anything more that I can do to further the investigation."

The powerful chekt took a moment to search his expression for indications of deception. A search of the Kala system would have to wait until she had addressed more pressing matters, but it would come. "You have advanced my quest and fulfilled your obligations according to our agreement." She nodded to one of her silent furry crew members, who promptly handed Uolo a data chip. "Payment in full for services according to our contract. A bonus has been added for your diligence."

Uolo offered a respectful bow as a rumble and shudder rippled through the ship. A chime indicated that Daihn's presence was requested on the bridge, and her voice took on a confident edge as she turned to leave. "I will contact you if I further require your services."

⸺⬦⸺

THE *EMU JA'* was in isolated and empty space—a deliberate choice in order to avoid all normal transportation routes, but it was clear that someone had managed to track her. A bolt of energy flashed light onto the bridge and shook the ship again as Daihn took her elevated seat. "Report."

A human attendant turned to her. "Four Deca-class

armored fighters have formed an attack perimeter. Our defensive shields are holding at ninety-five percent."

The fighters were an outdated corporate model from a time before the factions had united. Their spindly Y-stabilizers puffed out dim bursts of white energy from each side of the small ships as they made tight maneuvers. The corporate alliance must have been desperate to hire mercenaries in an attempt to reclaim their ill-protected property, but the fighters were no match for the *Emu Ja'*. The attack was more likely intended to delay her until reinforcements could arrive.

By chekt standards, most of the species who made up the corporate alliance were barely civilized and perhaps even lacked the ability to recognize a more refined culture. Their leaders likely believed that the ancient tablet still belonged to them, but it wasn't the time to attempt a debate. If she didn't address the situation quickly, the fighters could inflict costly damage, and she needed to preserve her assets now more than ever.

"Target using primary weapons and fire."

There was no point in expending any of her more expensive secondary missiles without an audience to witness her display of prowess, but she was obligated to respond to the assault regardless of the intensity or level of threat that it posed.

A succession of quick blasts from twin forward energy cannons tracked one of the fighters until the target was struck, sending the damaged craft spinning away as the other ships retreated. The fighters would soon relay her location to a larger corporate force, so it was time to move. Daihn always had an escape destination plotted and kept her interstellar drive on hot standby for this kind of eventuality.

"Activate the interstellar drive."

Green haze washed over the viewing windows, and she

stepped from her elevated platform. Her next stop would be to gather supplies and hire a new key staff member to assist. It was time to accelerate her plans.

12

The tagalong system was completely automated during flight, so Tom had plenty of time to review information he'd downloaded before leaving Copania. Feth was not a spot for tourists or casual travelers. The infrastructure was built around the energy production industry, and nearly everyone on the planet worked either in the business or in a supporting field. He'd assumed the production method was associated with some kind of solar power collection, but the technical explanations he'd found had more to do with the planet's natural physics than any technology he was familiar with.

There was little information about any of the smaller settlements on the planet, but he'd found a corporate brochure for Eridia, Feth's only public spaceport. It was as close to a full-service station as the planet had and included indoor docking bays, parts suppliers, and mining outfitters. It was also the location of the administrative headquarters, which was run by a management team contracted by the energy cell companies. Hundreds of smaller privately owned outposts dotted the surface along energy transfer conduit routes, but most of the activity seemed to center around Eridia.

He also studied his ship's tattered service manual. It was always good to have a printed copy in case an ion storm wiped his soft data devices, and Tom preferred the feel of the weighty book to that of a data pad. The last random grease-smudged page he'd turned to was titled "Identification and Application", which explained that the HF-T550-1451 designation meant that the hauler was rated for "hot freight"—anything involving work in high-temperature environments, which certainly included the molten core of a planet. T550 meant that the ship was designed for normal service up to 5,500 degrees Celsius, and his was the 1,451st one built at the Finnji shipyard on Copania, a respected manufacturer in its day, but now little more than an abandoned factory. Some of the information was trivial, but they were details that a proud owner should know.

The closer he got to his destination, and the farther he got from home, the more he thought about Marcus's comment about his risky plan to arrive without any jobs already lined up. And the more he considered his lack of any solid work plan, the more he realized that Marcus was right. There wasn't much he could do about it during the trip though, since the compression field made outside communication impossible. He'd have to wait until he arrived to start his search.

But what he *could* do was get his tools and supplies organized better, starting with a couple of small bins that he'd cobbled together using pieces of an old wall panel that had come with the ship. They wouldn't win any handiwork contests, but he attached the functional boxes to the main cabin bulkhead and filled them with spare parts to reduce the clutter in the ship's built-in storage compartments. The improvement was a good start, but it wasn't enough to distract from his growing concern about finding work.

Tom wandered to the cargo area at the rear of his ship where the sound of interstellar travel was loudest. Maybe if he came up with some ideas for tasks that his ship was suited for, it would help him narrow his search once he arrived. The small rectangular room had no more than four square meters of deck space in total. Having gravity decking was a plus, since he could transport cargo that was sensitive to a zero-g environment, but whatever it was would have to be small. The space also had a lightweight strapping system installed, with anchors firmly bolted onto attachment brackets at six locations around the perimeter of the room. Tom reached down to give one of the straps a pull to check its strength. As he did, his foot slid a little as if he'd stepped on a slick of oil, then it jerked to a stop as it hit the edge of the next deck plate, but the floor looked completely dry. He pulled a rag from his pocket and dropped it onto the problem area to wipe away any unseen residue using his foot, but instead of flopping onto the deck as expected, it bounced up, then quickly settled on the deck plate next to it. Rags should not bounce. It was obvious that the anomalous deck plate wasn't working properly, and of course, it had to be right smack in the middle of the floorspace. It was normal for gravity decking to lose strength over its lifespan, and the plates required occasional recalibration. The service manual included the detailed procedure, but it added to the list of things to fix when he was in a safe location to take it apart, which was definitely *not* during spaceflight.

He hadn't had a practical way to test the decking on Copania, and it was probably good that he hadn't wandered around his ship during his test flight, or he might have been out of the cockpit when his engine failed. But the new problem made it clear that he needed to rethink his priorities. Instead of worrying about a job, he'd focus on making sure he got to Feth in one piece. The rest of the long trip would give him plenty of time to inspect every square centimeter of the deck—and anything else he could get to without having to take it apart.

—◦—

THE TAGALONG DISPLAY flashed a message and squawked an alert as he neared the Feth system. Two weeks of confinement in his small ship had felt like two months, and as happy as he was with its performance, Tom needed to get out, stretch his legs, and breathe planetary atmosphere instead of recycled air.

It hadn't been an especially comfortable ride. Aside from the quiet scraping sound that had accompanied him along the entire journey, the ship also vibrated most of the time. But since his ship wasn't designed specifically for travel at interstellar speeds, and the only mechanical problem he'd found aside from the failing gravity plate was a broken circuit breaker on the new heater upgrade, Tom counted it as a good trip.

Another squawk from the tagalong's console told him that he was about to arrive, and he strapped himself into the pilot seat as the computer prepared to allow the compression field that surrounded his ship to collapse. With a powerful jolt, the dusty green haze outside snapped into black, and Tom engaged his maneuvering thrusters to slow his remaining momentum.

13

There wasn't any obvious order to their arrangement, but at least a dozen ships floated in the designated interstellar staging sector for the Feth system. Arriving here assured that a ship wouldn't appear within any established in-system ferry routes or in the path of an orbiting satellite.

The planet hung in nearby space, and Tom rotated his shuttle eighty degrees on its longitudinal axis to match the planet's standard navigational plane. The ship shuddered, and a thrust stabilizer warning lit on the engine panel. The alert triggered the memory of his recent engine failure, and his body tensed. There was no way to access the stabilizer from inside the ship, and he didn't have any spare parts for that system anyway, so he eased the throttles forward, and the ship's engines responded. If he made it to the planet without having to call for assistance, the repair would be simple—as long as parts were available.

The ship rattled as a loud clank on the aft section echoed forward into the cockpit. Tom flinched at the sudden sound, and before he could process what had happened, another clank echoed. A tracer projectile ricocheted off the hull, sending fragments streaming past the ship. Without a line of sight to tell where the shots had come from, Tom jammed the thruster power to maximum and careened toward the planet, rolling the ship several times as more bright flashes came from behind and crossed his path. He twisted the shuttle into a corkscrew, and the engines groaned as two more streaks narrowly missed. A final ten-second dive straight for the planet's surface put him out of range of the attack, and the assault ended.

His hands trembled and his heart pounded. The staging area was in unclaimed territory—a holding area for private ships that was deliberately outside of planetary jurisdiction. That didn't mean the region was lawless, as corporate ships regularly patrolled open space to protect their interests between systems. But for the planetary authorities, strict boundaries existed for policing and protecting their borders. For the next twenty minutes, there weren't any more shots in his direction, but he kept his flight path erratic until he was in close range of what should be Feth's security zone.

Like all properly registered craft, Tom's ship transmitted identification telemetry when within range of a planetary control station so that automated traffic control beacons could guide him to the planet's surface.

"Craft Hff-Tee-5501451, state your destination."

It took him a moment to realize that the beacon was doing its best to pronounce HF-T550-1451—the default registration number his ship was transmitting. Whether it was because of a malfunction or simply a shortcoming with its language abilities, the beacon sounded like it was saying *Hefty*. While his ship was small, it was as strong and durable as any vessel in its class, and *Hefty* was a fitting name.

"Eridia Spaceport," he answered.

"Proceed on standard approach path seven at port velocity two point five and await further instructions."

The beacon didn't use navigational shorthand but gave clear and complete directions, since many species would use the port, and the authorities wanted as little chance for confusion or misunderstanding as possible. Most newer ships had systems that would set course automatically according to the beacon's simultaneously transmitted navigation data, but the verbal commands were always given for safety, and also for ships like Tom's that needed to be piloted manually.

His ship glided across the nightside of the planet where hundreds of energy-collector satellites moved in synchronous orbits, sending glistening streams of directed energy to charging stations on the surface. The flow of energy caused bright iridescent swirls to form around each pillar of light as it passed through Feth's deep cloud layer, and the entire upper atmosphere glowed with smooth ripples of orange and white.

"Craft Hff-Tee-5501451, slow to standard port speed point five for planetary atmosphere entry and proceed directly to coordinates twenty-three by eighty-seven of grid J, docking bay B-4. Enjoy your stay."

Tom made the necessary navigational adjustments, and his ship descended into the dusty atmosphere just as he entered the daylight side of the planet. The stabilizer warning light began flashing, and the malfunctioning part caused a jarring shake that grew more violent as he neared the surface. He tightened his grip on the control yoke.

"Come on, *Hefty*. Just get to the hangar, and I promise I'll get that stabilizer fixed."

As images of Feth completely filled his screens, another factor compounded the problem. The planet was big—more than twice the size of Copania, and his flight computer wasn't calibrated for the increased gravitational pull on the ship. As he operated the controls, his hands were pulled downward as if he were on a spinning carnival ride, and a powerful vibration resonated through the hull. Something in the cabin clanked onto the deck as another light on the nav panel lit—the proximity indicator for the port. He was almost there.

Gravity pulled him harder into his seat as he approached the station, but as the details of Eridia's structures came into view, he slowed the ship and the shaky ride subsided. With his ship out of immediate danger, Tom released some tension with a deliberate exhale.

Eridia was surrounded by a barren red-sand desert. The port consisted of a network of access corridors leading to assorted hangars and storage structures to protect its occupants from the planet's dusty winds, and even through layers of high-altitude dust, the sun made the air glow with daylight warmth.

The nav panel guided him to his assigned hangar, and the sky door slid open. He lowered his ship inside, and the *Hefty* landed with a hard clunk. As the entryway closed to shut out the hot dry air, the thrust stabilizer alert turned from amber to red, meaning it had just failed completely. He was grounded until repairs were made—and until he recalibrated the *Hefty's* flight systems for Feth's gravity.

14

The planet pulled at his arms as Tom secured the *Hefty's* systems. Leveraging himself on the flight control panel, he shoved himself up and managed to shuffle his way through the ship and down the loading ramp. Light from the dusty sky added a tint of orange to every space that wasn't artificially lit with vibrant green corridor markers, and a mosaic of stains that suggested it had been forming in layers since the station was built covered the hangar floor.

The lingering odor of stale engine exhaust in the small bay was familiar, but it mingled with the scent of the dry planet's unique mineral-rich sand to add a hint of muskiness, as if a damp forest were hidden somewhere beneath the dry, packed surface. The foreign sensations hailed his achievement at having arrived on a new planet and also tapped at his primal instinct to be cautious in an unfamiliar environment, especially after the unprovoked attack that had landed at least two hits.

He was only a few steps from the aft port quarter where one of the projectiles had left a dark gray streak that rubbed off easily. The other spot wasn't within easy view, but even if he didn't see any problems, there could be damage that wasn't visible.

Checking the rest of his ship would have to wait because the immediate concern was the powerful gravity that was making his legs ache. A busy eatery across from the access corridor entryway was the nearest place to sit, so he tapped the controls to raise and lock the hatch, then crossed the hangar to the bay doors, each step feeling like he had sandbags lashed to his legs and a pack full of deck plating strapped to his back.

The walls gently vibrated from the humming of ventilation fans, liquid distribution systems moving maintenance fluids to and from hangars, and ships across the complex arriving and departing. The framework that held the alternating clear and opaque corridor panels in place gave the impression of a temporary installation that had been pressed into lengthy service by continuous patching and overlaid weld rein-forcements.

Tom staggered across the walkway and into a large seating area with a full beverage bar along the interior wall. The room design made it useful as both a cafeteria and a saloon, likely out of necessity, since comfortable real estate would be at a premium on the hot planet. Light shone through a huge cres-cent-shaped transparent wall opposite the bar and made the space feel roomier than it was, though patches of dust that had accumulated on the outside dimmed the bright orange daylight. At the far end, a makeshift performance stage was bare except for a crooked banner above it that read "Magnifi-cent Jinaro."

Most of the room's patron species had been passengers on tours that Tom had piloted over the years, and a few looked his way as he entered. A number of the looks turned to sneers at the stranger who was obviously new to Eridia, but the regulars quickly lost interest and went back to their business. There wasn't much Tom could do about his hunched shuffle, but he put on his most casual expression and lurched to the nearest table. His legs shook from fatigue, and he allowed himself to be pulled into a chair with a thud.

The room was pleasantly cool, and his stomach rumbled as tempting aromas from foods that he'd never smelled before drifted through the processed air. Soft sounds of a peculiar background melody mixed with conversations that were being held in different languages—a mild overload to his senses after being alone in a small space for the past two weeks, but he couldn't leave until he'd rested his legs.

The bartender's brusk voice cut through the general commotion. "D'Nug, where are you? Customer at table five."

An uncommonly small but energetic alien rushed to Tom's table and presented him with a menu. "What to consume?" the server asked in a dialect that Tom guessed was local.

The selection list was short, but trying one of the native drinks might help him blend in and avoid a few stares.

"Bungen Ale, please."

The waiter hurried off without another word, and Tom had a chance to take a more inconspicuous look around. Ooranoans, vefulians, and knell traders drank, conversed, and laughed in their own particular way. A few humanoid aliens of an unfamiliar species played a card game in a corner of the room. They were dressed in surplus military uniform pieces either left over from the Transit War or stolen from conquered enemies. At a table near the bar, several humans in tattered work uniforms nursed drinks that had been served in tall glasses decorated with elaborate etchings. They seemed weary from some task or voyage that had taken its toll on their enthusiasm—either that or they had been satiated into a docile stupor by their meal. There was even a poorly dressed chekt, an unusual sight in itself, discussing something in earnest with a squat kethrether, who waved meaty limbs to highlight some point of conversation.

In most places, it would have been an odd mix of patrons, since most beings typically preferred to live among their own kind. It was widely considered to be the smarter choice, since cultural practices, not to mention odors and sounds made by certain beings, were often incompatible with dissimilar species and could lead to misunderstandings or even violence. But doing the smart thing wasn't always profitable, so the inhabitants of planets like Feth and places like Eridia tolerated those differences, usually in exchange for better business opportunities. And for those who chose a less-than-law-abiding lifestyle, the fringe settlements were the only options. With few laws, and infrequent enforcement of the ones that existed, it was easier for them to blend in.

These communities were considered to be more or less uncivilized by mainstream societies, but the unusual mix of inhabitants at each settlement created a kind of subculture of its own, with unspoken rules, standards of etiquette, and even new mash-up languages that resulted from trial-and-error interaction. The microcultures even gave residents a common bond, because when everyone is an outsider, they're all insiders.

The waiter returned with a mug of orange liquid. Tom sipped at the sour drink, and his mouth puckered involuntarily. He did feel a bit more at ease after several minutes, probably due to some intoxicating effect, but after half a glass he'd had enough.

Tom surrendered further to the gravity and slouched into his seat just as a nearby exterior door slid open. The planet's baked atmosphere washed over him as a human female not much older than him walked in, sweating through a silver jumpsuit powdered with desert dust. Her dark hair was pulled back in braids that kept it mostly away from her grease-smudged face, and she moved with a tired shuffle to the nearest seat at a table next to him. The waiter arrived almost instantly and hurried away after she mumbled her order, then the woman turned and looked directly at Tom.

"How did you get in here?" she asked.

He did his best to sound casual, but all Tom could manage was, "I'm, umm . . . What?"

"You're not wearing a gravity-assist suit."

"I . . . It's my first time here, so I was caught a little unprepared."

"My name's Kerra."

"Tom Sparker. Nice to meet you." Tom strained to offer his hand to shake, but his muscles were too fatigued to make a good show of it.

"Don't bother. Do you have eighty standard credits?"

"I think so. Why?"

The woman looked Tom up and down with a critical stare. "Wait here. I'll be back in a minute."

Staying put wasn't going to be a problem. He couldn't manage to shake hands, much less walk out of the place. It was better than his ship breaking or being shot at, but waiting for someone he'd just met to rescue him from gravity wasn't exactly a turnaround to his day.

Fifteen minutes later, Kerra returned with a folded bundle and plopped it onto the table in front of him. "Try this."

The wait had helped Tom recover his strength, and it only took a minute to unroll the dark blue jumpsuit and scoot into it. It was a good fit, but was stained with some kind of ship's coolant or actuator fluid. "Now what?"

She reached over and touched a panel on his chest, and the suit emitted a momentary hum. Gravity released most of its grip, and Tom straightened up in his seat. It was a strange sensation, as only the body parts covered by the suit were relieved of the strong downward pull. His head and hands still felt like they were weighted, but the rest of him felt fine.

"Thanks for that," Tom said with a relieved breath.

"There's a shop across the corridor. This was the only one they had in your size, but they discounted it because of the stains. You owe me fifty-five standard credits."

Tom dug into a pocket through an opening in the jumpsuit.

"I remember my first solo delivery here," Kerra said. "I'd forgotten to wear my grav-assist, and it took me nearly half an hour to get my suit on."

As Tom counted out the money, the waiter arrived and placed Kerra's food on the table before leaving in a rush.

"Let me buy your meal," Tom said. "It's the least I can do to repay you for your trouble."

"It wasn't any trouble. Drinks come fast, but it takes a while to get your food at this place. Sitting here waiting would have just made me hungrier." She began shoveling food into her mouth. "So are you in energy control or maintenance?" she asked through a mouthful of leafy stew.

"I don't work here. At least not yet. I mean, I'm looking for work now."

"Humph," she managed through more food than she could chew.

"I have my own ship," Tom said, "so I'm hoping to find shuttle transport work of some kind."

"You have a ship, huh? You a mechanic?"

"I have some background, but I'm not licensed or anything."

"Know anything about tagalong drives?"

Tom sat up a bit straighter. "I just installed the one on my shuttle."

"Yeah? Well, mine broke eight days ago. I just got in, and none of the port mechanics can get to it for at least three days." Kerra stopped chewing for a moment. "If you can figure out what's wrong and fix it before then, I'll pay you two hundred credits."

"I'd be glad to take a look at it."

"Okay, I'm going to eat and get cleaned up. Meet me at . . ." She dug in her suit pocket to look at her docking bay ID tag. "Docking bay A-23 in a couple of hours."

Tom took that as his cue to leave her alone while she ate, and he tripped over a chair as he got up to leave before managing to get his feet under him. He looked back at Kerra, who gave him a sideways grin as she continued chewing. He half waved and turned to leave as quickly as possible before he did something that made him feel even more awkward, or worse, something to make her change her mind about hiring him.

15

At the aft weapons station of a raider-class ship, twin crew members Loci and Dorn Malaris waved their arms in what was typical fashion for the duo. Dorn pressed his lips together as Loci took her turn in their argument over whose shot had hit the little mining shuttle first.

"I was supposed to get the first shot."

"But I hit it first."

"You lose because you broke the rules!"

A slim man wearing a combat jacket over a military-style jumpsuit stormed into the control center.

"I told you no games while we're in-system," he barked.

Dorn swiveled in his seat. "But it's boring here, Mius."

Mius leveled a two-fingered point at them. "Those launch charges are coming out of your pay."

The pair grimaced. The propellant wasn't overly expensive, but the fact that their pay would be docked added a dose of frustration to their already fidgety day.

"I've got a meeting with the commander of the *Emu Ja'* in twenty minutes and I don't want to make a bad impression.

With luck, we'll make a small fortune by the time we're finished here."

Loci's face lit in an excited grin, while Dorn remained sour. "How much is a fortune?"

"It'll be a lot of money. Just remember . . . all of my expenses get covered before you get paid, got it?"

Loci nodded eagerly, and Dorn rolled his eyes up as if calculating his potential pay. Mius turned to leave. "I expect the ammunition magazines to be refilled with standard rounds by the time I get back."

THE TRIP to the much larger ship took only minutes in his shuttle pod. Upon arrival, a saazu greeted him and made a wordless gesture to follow.

Mius had been aboard hundreds of ships, but this hangar was finished in materials more appropriate for a resort lobby than any working ship he'd ever seen, with walls covered in fine plasteel veneer and each piece of equipment clean and neatly organized. Every control panel and arched threshold was polished to a mirror shine, and the corridor that the small being led him through could have been mistaken for a walkway in a posh eatery. The saazu stopped and made a gesture toward a doorway. Mius gave a polite nod to his escort and stepped into the captain's lounge of the lavish *Emu Ja'*.

Daihn sat on a raised platform at the far end of the room, surrounded by masterpieces of culinary art that glistened with minute reflections of the room's azure light. Her earlobes writhed in ecstasy with each bite she took, as more saazu silently brought new dishes and removed empty serving platters. A polished blue defense mech standing in a far corner of the room caught Mius's eye. It stood like a suit of armor while in standby mode and probably served as Daihn's bodyguard. Mius had never dealt with chekt, but their reputation for ruthless business practices was well-known, as was their unfailing adherence to the terms of a contract.

"Enter and be comfortable, Captain," Daihn invited. She fixed her gaze on him, her silver eyes reflecting the ambient light like fine glitter.

Mius stepped closer, and a table holding a weathered stone tablet came within his view. It was etched with markings that he couldn't make out at a glance, and it seemed out of place in the clean surroundings. "I'm honored to be here."

"I am Exalted Daihn of the Chekt, and I offer you employment under the terms of the contract for which you have acknowledged receipt."

Chekt were notorious for getting straight to business, and it wasn't because they didn't enjoy being social. It was simply that, for them, discussing business *was* being social. It was a cultural peculiarity that business and pleasure were almost always intermingled, and it was widely assumed that chekt saw little value in anything but work and advancing their cultural status.

"It's a generous offer, and I'm happy to accept your terms."

"I am pleased," Daihn said with a tilt of her head.

Mius nodded toward the stone tablet. "Is that the relic?"

"It is more than a mere museum piece, Captain."

"It looks like part of it is missing."

Daihn stood and walked to the table as if she were gliding on ice, followed closely by a server carrying a tray of delicacies. She placed a hand on the etchings. "This half hints at a location, and according to my experts, it is very close."

"How close?"

She plucked a dainty confection covered with wispy tendrils from the serving tray. "If your performance proves worthy of your reputation, I will share those details in time."

Daihn placed the dessert in her mouth and seemed to swallow it whole as Mius took a step toward the tablet to get a better look.

"You will begin fulfilling your duties immediately. My resources are available to assist you according to our agreement."

"I'm looking forward to it."

Daihn returned to her seat as Mius stood for a moment in uncomfortable silence. "I'll get right to work, then." He took an awkward step backward as Daihn looked over her food choices.

"Understand that the terms of the contract will be enforced, Captain."

Mius stopped and gave her a fixed stare. His reply had a sharp confidence that could only come from a seasoned professional. "I'm here to make a profit, not back out on the deal."

Daihn looked up and met his gaze. "Excellent. I anticipate a fruitful collaboration."

Mius's quick turn and brisk march to the exit reflected his inner commitment. His first task was to fill Daihn's open contractor positions with competent and reliable crew, and he needed to make a good impression. It was the only way to gain access to her inner circle.

In less than two hours, Tom had gone from being an attack victim to having an opportunity for paid work, and it was a welcome change. He couldn't install a tagalong himself, but after helping Marcus install the one on his ship, he should be able to troubleshoot a broken one, and he wasn't going to turn down a chance at a job.

By the time he got back to the *Hefty* and finished a rehydrated meal, he'd gotten more comfortable with the strange freedom of movement the antigravity suit gave him. Since he had time before his appointment with Kerra, he crawled to the top of the starboard aft quarter that had been hit by the second projectile. The carbon streak it left made it easy to find the spot, but the impact didn't seem to have actually penetrated the hull, and it rubbed away easily with a swipe of his hand. A hull integrity scan would verify that there was no hidden damage—another unexpected expense—so the sooner he started to earn an income, the better. He scooted to the other side of the ship and slid down to drop onto the loading ramp. It took only a moment to duck inside to grab a dessert bar that he stuffed into his chest pocket, then he tapped the control to secure his ship as he hopped from the side of the ramp.

Tom chewed off a chunk of the bar as he made his way through the access corridor, then slipped the rest into the pocket of his jumpsuit before turning into an attached walkway. The corridor signage was sparse, and after passing entrances marked with "D" series docking bays, he backtracked to the main corridor. *Come on, Tom. Let's not get lost on our first day of actual work.*

As he turned the corner, a hoverdolly stacked with beverage cases sped down the sloping corridor, and he jerked his upper body backward barely in time to avoid a collision. The dolly operator, riding on the back of the cart as if driving an invisible team of untamed sled dogs, came so close that his face brushed against Tom's jumpsuit as he flew past. It wasn't the safest way to transport supplies, and the driver hardly seemed to be in control of the device, but Tom was there to take advantage of the lax safety standards, and the near miss was a good reminder to be extra careful.

With the way ahead clear, he continued to the "A" series walkway and stepped into the open door of bay A-23. Inside was a Thesine transport. One of the most common ships of its day, its cylindrical body was tipped with an oblate nose, and a dozen stabilizer fins ringed the lower third of its length. Twelve meters tall and nearly four meters in diameter at its widest, the ship had three levels. The large lower deck was meant for cargo, the middle level for living space, and the small upper cockpit had the ability to swivel on an internal gimbal to make planetary takeoffs and landings more comfortable, as the ship was typically vertical for both. Six different types of engines were modulated to accommodate the widely varying atmospheric conditions while on the Thesine home world, but during space flight, the exhaust from all engines blended to form a distinct violet plume that trailed more than twice the length of the ship.

The old craft looked to have been well-maintained, although several casing panels had obviously been replaced over its service life, and some of the stabilizer fins were red instead of the basic metallic gray of the rest of the hull.

"Hey there!" piped a voice from the other side of the ship.

"It's me, Tom," he answered as he craned his neck.

From the shadow cast by the loading ramp of her ship, Kerra emerged carrying a tool bag. She looked like a completely different person than the one he'd met earlier. Her clean silver jumpsuit reflected the orange daylight of the planet that spilled through the bay skylights, and her hair was freshly braided and neatly pulled back, forming a long ponytail.

Maybe he should have brought his own tools, since it was a paid job, but Kerra interrupted the thought. "I just noticed that the cover on her charge rod bay was loose, but they all looked okay, so I secured the panel."

"Her?"

"The *Damsel*. Some of the miners started calling it that, and it kind of stuck. The ship belongs to the miners' co-op, but I'm really the only one who's more interested in flying than in mining."

Tom nodded. "I've always liked Thesine design. Is the drive mounted internally?"

"Yes, the main drive panel is here." Kerra turned around and unlatched another access panel between two stabilizer fins.

The tagalong wasn't like Tom's. It was a professionally installed factory system, but all tagalong drives had the same basic components, and troubleshooting would still involve the same sequential process of elimination.

"Let's start at the top," Tom said.

After his rough start on Feth, working on a ship was something that felt at least a little familiar. He examined the controls in the one-person cockpit, then worked his way down through the control wiring harness and back to the docking bay floor, carefully inspecting each component and connection as he went.

After an hour, with Kerra watching every move, Tom stood holding a tuft of wire that looped from a ground-level access panel. "The discharge control wiring connections look like something chewed on them. I think the drive vented when it stopped receiving a signal from your navigation computer."

Kerra leaned into the compartment and examined the frayed wires closely as he continued. "It's actually a fail-safe feature that's supposed to keep you from flying into something if your nav computer fails."

A sudden rustling from the access port made Tom jump back as a small creature no bigger than his hand flew out of the compartment past Kerra and perched on a walkway railing just above them. It flew with a soft fluttering sound, using flaps of fleshy skin below its two arms like a Copanian bat, but this creature was mostly covered with well-groomed fur and had expressive eyes. It wore a tiny sling across its chest with a small pouch at its base, indicating an intelligence much higher than any bat or bird that Tom had ever seen. It also looked at him with what seemed like a permanent smile, though it was probably just a feature of the species.

"Ugh, kiks." Kerra stuck her head farther into the compartment. "Any more in here?"

"Kiks? What's a kik?"

Satisfied that it was the only one, Kerra backed out and wiped her hands on her suit. "They're harmless. It must have gotten in when I stopped to take on water."

"Not harmless to wiring though," Tom said as he pulled some of the strands apart. "I'll have to cut a bunch out, but it should be a simple repair."

"I have some patching wire in the cabin," Kerra said as she turned and walked up the boarding ramp into the cargo hold.

Tom turned his attention back to the small creature, which cocked its head as it silently fixated on him. It had small hands with articulating digits at the tips of its winglike extremities and feet that worked as grasping claws. After a moment, it startled Tom again as it suddenly hopped into flight and fluttered toward him. The creature managed to get a firm grasp on his shirt pocket as Tom stumbled back a step, and with a light touch, it reached in and carefully pulled a small piece of the dessert bar from its wrapper. The creature sniffed at the food and popped it into its mouth. It made a quiet squeaking sound, then pulled several more bits off and stuffed them into its satchel.

As Kerra banged down the loading ramp with the repair wire and splicing connectors, the kik leaped into flight and did a flying backflip before it perched back on the railing. Kerra ignored the creature, but Tom was still uncertain. "Are you sure that thing is safe?"

"They live in colonies inside the ice caves on Kala Prime. It's where I get water for the mine. They're really quite gentle, but they love to eat, so watch your food around them."

The creature sat on the railing and cooed softly as it snacked on bits of the bar from its bag.

"Is that where you live—the Kala system?"

"My family lives at the K2 mining colony. I'm here to sell some ore and get supplies, and I'm already more than a week behind schedule."

The highest quality deposits of pecrite ore to date had been found in the asteroid belts of the core systems, but wildcatters were always looking for new sources in the fringes. "Kala asteroid mining? I've heard of it, but I thought the operation went bust a few years ago."

"That was the original mine. We call it K1—a dismal failure." Kerra shook her head. "Most of the miners lost everything and had to go home. Fourteen families stayed to try again with K2. We make enough to survive, but even after a couple years, we haven't hit any really rich deposits."

Tom nodded. "So you're in it for the big payday."

She shrugged. "The thrill of striking it big keeps most of the miners going, but I just like to fly. I make transport runs to deliver ore and bring back supplies on return trips. We have smaller ships to make fuel cell and parts runs, but the *Damsel* is the only one of our ships that's large enough to make ore deliveries economical, so I need to get back as soon as I can."

"Are you leaving today?"

"I have to sell my cargo, and it's going to take at least a day for my power cells to fully charge before I can leave. Here." She shoved the repair wire and connectors at Tom. "I'm not paying you to complete the job myself."

Tom went to work on the cabling. Every few minutes, he checked on the kik, who perched quietly on the railing and watched him from a distance with apparent interest.

It took another hour to complete all of the delicate splices, and he called up to Kerra, who sat in the cockpit. "Okay, you can try powering the tagalong control system."

"Here goes!" piped Kerra, and a brief high-pitched whine ramped up in frequency until it disappeared into silence. "Self-diagnostic checks out. You just saved me at least two days." Smiling, she climbed down and tossed Tom a small roll of plastic chips.

Tom caught the bundle of credits, and for the first time since arriving in the system, he felt a little like he belonged. "Thanks for the work."

"All the businesses here will accept those, but make sure you spend them all at Eridia because they're not good anywhere else."

"I have a feeling that won't be hard to do. My thrust stabilizer went out just after I landed. Can you recommend a good parts dealer?"

"As far as honesty, they're all about the same, but I'd shop around if I were you. Some of the dealers specialize in certain parts and will give you a better price if they have a large supply in stock."

"I'll check around, then."

Kerra secured the compartment that held the new splices. "A potential buyer for my ore is stopping by here soon, and I need to get ready."

"All right, I'll head out. Thanks again for the work."

"Thank *you*, Tom. And best of luck to you!"

As Tom turned to leave, the kik fluttered behind and followed him to the docking bay door. He ducked slightly as it approached, but it hovered overhead and continued to shadow him as he made his way down the corridor and into an open shop court.

When Tom detoured from his route to check the prices of some food cases that were heaped in front of a shop, the small creature flew to perch on a beam near the clear dome that covered the area. It nestled up to a hanging support to watch the wide assortment of beings conduct business at the perimeter shops of the busy courtyard.

Tom spent the next ten minutes looking through a pile of discounted cases of nearly expired meal packs. Several days of food was well worth a few of his newly earned port credit chips, and he heaved one of the tattered cartons onto his shoulder before he headed for his rented bay.

THE RAMP of the *Hefty* clunked shut, and Tom locked himself inside for the night before he slid a meal pack into his food rehydrator. The blank viewscreens in his ship glowed dimly as the stove softly hummed. Without any windows, the only light inside the *Hefty* was generated artificially. The ship automatically changed the interior light intensity based on the time of day, and the lights were now low.

While he waited for his meal, he closed his eyes and fought the urge to doze. The stove timer chimed, and as he reached for the rehydrator door handle, something quickly climbed up his back and jumped from his shoulder.

Tom flailed his arms as the sensation jolted him fully awake. "Agh!"

The kik had hitched a ride on his suit and was now perched on the stove door.

"What are you doing here?" Tom demanded, as if the being had a complete understanding of his language. But the small creature just sniffed at the rehydrator door as if to ask for a bite.

"Get off of there."

The kik flew to a nearby shelf and sat quietly.

It took Tom a moment to calm himself, and because he was more hungry than annoyed, he took his food into the cockpit to get away from the creature. It followed closely, and as Tom sat, it perched silently on a nearby throttle lever. Kerra had said that kiks were harmless, but this one was at least being a nuisance. He gave up trying to get away and dug in, but after a few bites, he glanced at the creature, which was staring at his food.

"This is mine, but you can have the rest of this." He took the remaining piece of dessert bar from his pocket and held it out to the small being. It gingerly took the morsel and sniffed it before taking a bite, then stuffed the rest into its satchel. The kik stared at him for a moment with its permanent smile, then closed its eyes and sat perfectly still while Tom finished his meal. The food was a bit stale, but was still edible well past the expiration date stamped on the box. If he was careful, it should last for five or six days' worth of meals.

A few glances at the ship's indicator panels confirmed that the *Hefty*'s systems were all in minimum power mode and the power cells were charging. Tom was ready to turn in, but the kik was still asleep on the lever, and he was too tired to shoo it away. The creature was quick, and he'd probably end up chasing it around his ship for twenty minutes. There weren't any open panels for it to access wiring or anything delicate, so as long as it kept quiet and left him alone, he was fine with letting it stay for the night. Tom crawled into his bunk and slid the compartment door closed behind him.

17

The rumbling from a departing ship shook dust from the walkway dividers, and Tom paused on his way to the port's shipping office to take a look through one of the transparent corridor panels. Kerra's ship was leaving for Feth's staging sector, and he watched as the *Damsel* sped away from Eridia against the evening backdrop of the planet's dull orange sky. His business with her two days earlier was a solid start, but he'd need steady work to make a living, and so far all of the local contract postings had been for large freight hauling that he couldn't hope to fulfill with his ship. Docking fees on Feth were twice what they would have cost at home, and he'd already spent most of the credit chips that Kerra had given him on the hull integrity check and a used thrust stabilizer for the *Hefty*. The *Damsel*'s engine cluster formed its characteristic purple streak as it breached the upper atmosphere, and the ship disappeared behind the high-altitude clouds.

The office was nearby, and Tom made his way through the crowded room to check the postings board. Only one caught his eye, but as he moved closer to read the details, an ooranoan pilot stepped between him and the board. "What you doing?"

The grunted accent was thick, but the being's message was clear. "I'm just reading this to find out if I can bid on it."

The pilot sneered and peeled the posting from the board. "Go away, off-worlder."

The ooranoan was as much of an off-worlder as Tom, but a confrontation with the larger competitor wasn't going to help his situation, so he retreated to the exit without another word. It wasn't the first time other workers at Eridia had been less than friendly when it came to competing for jobs, but Tom had to keep trying. If he didn't find something in the next few days, he'd have to go home a failure. It was a thought he worked to avoid.

At least it was a quick walk back to the *Hefty*, so while it was frustrating to be unemployed, it never took him long to confirm that status. He tramped up the ramp and plopped himself in front of the stove to start the rehydrating cycle for a bowl of expired vegetable root stew. The aroma filled the cabin, and in moments the meal was ready to enjoy from his comfortable pilot chair, which had become his favorite place to relax.

The kik fluttered to the control panel and perched on one of the throttle levers. It had been completely quiet that first night and seemed content to mostly watch Tom as he went about his daily routine, so Tom had let his guest stay. Whenever he left the ship, the tiny creature would fly out to do whatever it was that kiks did during the day, but it was always waiting for him when he returned. It would flutter from atop the hull or a nearby ceiling beam and enter the ship again when Tom lowered the ramp. He couldn't be sure if the creature liked him or just stayed for the morsels that he gave it, but whatever the reason, it was nice to have some company. He held out a piece of his meal, and the kik stuffed it into its satchel. "Which is it, pal? Are we friends, or are you just camping out here for the food?"

Hearing his own words made him sit up straight. *Camping.* If he set up camp in the open desert, he could avoid the steep port charges and extend his stay. It would be hot, but it might buy him enough time to find steady work, and he could always come back to Eridia if it didn't work out. The outdoor temperature would be cool and comfortable in the morning. That's when he'd make his move.

⋯ ◇ ⋯

THE NEXT MORNING, Tom gesticulated in every way he could think of to indicate that he was leaving and that the kik should fly away, but it simply smiled as it watched the one-way game of charades from its perch on the starboard engine throttle lever.

"Listen, I'm taking off. So if you want to stay here, now's your chance."

The kik stared at him with wide eyes. Tom didn't have a clue as to whether or not the little being knew what he was trying to communicate, but he'd already checked out with the port authority, and if he didn't leave in fifteen minutes, they'd demand another day's port fee. He tapped the engine ignitors and eased the *Hefty* through the sky door, then nudged the yoke and headed for the open desert. The kik fluttered to the copilot seat and perched on the backrest, staring intently at the forward viewscreens.

An energy conduit connecting distant outposts made a thin, lonely stripe across the horizon. Tom flew a few passes over the landscape for a radius of five kilometers, but except for the remnants of an abandoned escape pod several kilometers to the east, now half buried by blowing desert silt, there was no sign of anything but wilderness. The region was mostly flatlands with occasional rocky outcroppings rising from the hard-packed dirt. It wasn't an ideal place to camp, but if he stayed fairly close to Eridia, he could walk to the station and save on hourly docking charges. He made a wide sweeping turn to the south toward a formation of large rocks about two kilometers from Eridia that would offer some shade and might also shield the *Hefty* from any desert windstorms.

Fine sand swirled around his shuttle as it touched down, and as Tom powered off all but the solar-charging and water-generation systems, the ship went silent. It was the hot season on Feth, and while the *Hefty* had a first-class cooling system, it would take energy to run, and he was on a budget. Supplementary solar chargers would keep his ship's power cells charged enough to operate the water reclamator and condensing systems, and although the latter would collect moisture slowly in Feth's arid climate, he should be able to generate enough water to keep an ample drinking supply on hand. An onboard shower would be out of the question, but he'd be visiting the spaceport daily to look for work and could wash up there as needed.

Food, however, was a problem. He still had some provisions that he'd brought with him from Copania to supplement his case of expired meal packs, but most supplies on Feth had to be shipped in and were sold at a premium. Even if he rationed his food, he could only afford to stay another fifteen days or so. Overall, the desert plan would buy him some time, but it was far from a permanent solution.

18

Time dragged out in her private communication room as Daihn waited for a transmission from the Grand Council of her home world. They had granted a brief audience for a review of her petition to advance her cultural status according to Kahr, the chekt code of conduct—a system of social laws that had been followed by her people for millennia. It defined standards for intellectual precision and rules of professional conduct, provided guidelines for application of strength, and outlined a canon of combat etiquette. It often conflicted with more widely accepted standards of right and wrong, but the moral code was the foundation of chekt society.

It was unusual to have technical trouble with a transmission of this type, but a show of impatience would reflect badly on her. The ship's internal comm system activated, and Daihn's communications operator interrupted the silence. "An external connection has been established, but they're still having a problem with audio. Native language mode is unavailable."

"Begin communication," Daihn said.

Tiny plasma sparks jumped from the pedestal-mounted holoimager, and Daihn uncrossed her arms. A brief hum preceded the appearance of a holoimage of nine miniature, green-skinned figures, each wearing a robe representing a slightly different hue of native chekt soil.

"Exalted Daihn," one of the figures said. "Your conduct as reviewed by this council is satisfactory."

The shrunken figure tapped on a data pad, and Daihn bow-curtseyed as protocol required. "My desire for the ultimate status remains."

The tiny being's answer came quickly. "The Supreme must commit all to Kahr." It was a loosely translated but common quote from the code, and also its only reference to qualification for the long-vacant position of Supreme ruler of her race. The council alone decided what behavior proved mastery of the complex set of rules and standards—and ascension to the position. Until a Supreme was chosen, the council's rule on all matters was final. "You have not demonstrated such distinction."

The pronouncement stung. Her incident with the freighter was only one of a recent string of victories and accomplishments that demonstrated her precise application of her people's code.

"Your petition for advancement is denied. We encourage your continued pursuit."

The tiny figures bowed in unison, and the holoimage flicked off. Daihn spun on her heel and paced across the room. She'd built a personal fortune through cunning business transactions, exercised her dominance over lesser rivals, and demonstrated her respect for the long-established tradition of fully exploiting a contract, yet the council still deemed her unworthy.

Before leaving the chamber, she paused to consider her current pursuit. There *was* a prize that would prove her worth beyond dispute and guarantee her rightful ascension to the throne, and circumstances had presented an opportunity for her to win it. But if a seven-thousand-year-old legendary treasure had been easy to locate, it would have been found long ago.

Hiring Ketsa had been an error. The inexperienced freighter captain hadn't possessed the skill or resources necessary to acquire the clues that she needed. But Captain Mius's reputation for organization as well as his connections with other mercenaries were well-documented, and those resources would yield results. Achieving success was only a matter of time.

19

Mius piloted his small shuttle pod high above the outlands of Eridia on the way to his rented bay. He had plenty of business connections from the old days, but none of them were in this part of space, and the selection of contractors in the Feth system was dubious to say the least. Outlaws and people of questionable character left him short on hiring the needed weapon specialists and transport ships.

As he slowed to port speed, something caught his eye near a large outcrop of rocks on the border of the wilderness near the Feth dunes. He grabbed a monocular from its holster in an overhead visor and discovered that a small ship had landed in the dangerous area. It also appeared to be deliberate, as a canopy and tables had been put up. It even looked like someone had set out a lounge chair in the shade. Whoever was there was either more dangerous than the local threats or an unwitting traveler in serious jeopardy. He circled his quiet craft above the formation and reduced his altitude to get a better look. The setup didn't look like one that a mercenary or any kind of fighter would use, and there was no obvious defensive mechanism nearby. Not only was there a lounge chair, but also someone appeared to be sleeping on it. Maybe it was an elaborate trap to lure would-be rescuers, but it was more likely someone who didn't know any better.

His military training would make Mius a poor choice as an ambush target, and the prospect of helping someone in need outweighed any concern he had for himself. He set his shuttle down on the opposite side of the outcropping to maintain a tactical advantage in case the scenario was a trap. Then he grabbed some weaponry before heading into what was a hostile place even under the best conditions.

WILDERNESS CAMPING WAS quiet and gave Tom plenty of space to work on his ship, but the heat was intense during the day, and the cold nights forced him inside just after dark. If he let the ship's interior cool off in the evening, he could stay inside his well-insulated craft the next day without feeling the effects of the desert climate. But most of his work was outdoors, so he spent the hottest time of day under a shade canopy that he'd set up on the starboard side of the *Hefty*. The climate control at the spaceport was part of what travelers paid for, but he could put up with the heat and lack of other conveniences of Eridia for the money that he was saving.

The cool early morning hours were best for working on projects like the ore pod door mechanisms. A few days of tinkering had gotten the starboard pod doors freed and working, and he'd hammered most of the caked-on magma slag from the walls on that side. After a thorough cleaning, the pods would eventually make good storage compartments, or maybe even cargo space, depending on the job.

By late morning, Tom would usually be on the walk to Eridia to look for work, with the kik either fluttering nearby or clinging to his pocket. Once they got to the port, it would sometimes come inside, but it typically waited for him outdoors. In spite of its dense fur, the heat didn't appear to bother it, and it managed Feth's gravity without any noticeable issues. The creature seemed happy to be living with Tom, who enjoyed its quiet companionship. It also reminded him of Kerra, his only other friend in that part of space.

On the fifth day at his new home, Tom strayed from his usual morning routine to relax in a worn but comfortable lounge chair he'd salvaged from one of the scrap heaps at the port. The combination of rationing his food and acclimating to the planet's intense heat was taking its toll on his energy, and he needed a rest, especially since he'd stayed up late the night before to dismantle the *Hefty*'s gravity decking system for a maintenance calibration. The procedure revealed that the problematic gravity plate in the cargo area was only the first of many that were close to failing. Worn foil-clad proximity switches were the culprit, and since they would be costly to replace, Tom had spent hours dismantling the tiny mechanisms to find a cheap way to refurbish them instead of incurring another expense that he couldn't afford. He'd managed to get most of them working properly, but the extra step turned what should have been a simple job into a major project, with components still scattered on a portable workbench near the base of the *Hefty*'s loading ramp. The weather was good, and without any current job prospects, he wasn't in a hurry to reassemble the complex system.

The desert breeze made his makeshift canopy flap as the kik

napped on one of the support poles, and as the late morning heat bathed the terrain, Tom dozed off in the relaxing warmth.

<hr>

A LOUD SNAP and clang against the hull of the *Hefty* woke Tom so abruptly that he reflexively sat up, but he was quickly turned sideways as his lounge chair was lifted and slammed against the hull of his ship. Thick metal cables had enmeshed the *Hefty* and most of the surrounding portable furniture in a kind of slipknot web. The mechanism had sprung out of the sand, along with a beacon that emitted a wavering high-pitched squeal. Tom twisted around to get upright in the jumbled mess that used to be his campsite, but he was too tangled to maneuver easily. He struggled to get a good look at the beacon just as a creature nearly as tall as his ship emerged from behind a large boulder. It lumbered to the wailing device and silenced it with a delicate touch, then turned its attention to the parts table that hadn't been captured by the metal web and picked up a component to study it more closely.

"Who are you? What's going on?" Tom squawked.

The creature turned its head toward him and evaluated Tom with a long stare. It was larger than any sentient being he'd ever seen, and its mass seemed to prohibit it from moving quickly. Its appendages were thick and meaty, and its head swiveled slowly with each step it took. On Copania, it would weigh upward of a ton, and on this planet much more. Its pale skin was covered with sparse dark fur, and it had only simple rags covering parts of its body. The creature lumbered to him, and Tom gasped as it wrapped one massive hand nearly halfway around his body, squeezing him tightly. With its other hand, the creature easily freed him from the entanglement and drew

Tom's face close to its own. The creature's warm breath made Tom's skin crawl as he dug at its powerful grip, but his left arm was pinned to his body by the huge fist. The being huffed a low growl and sniffed at him. Tom's face contorted as he put all of his effort into a vain pull at the giant fingers.

Exhausted and trapped, Tom stared at the creature with wide eyes, but the being's attention was drawn away by an unseen distraction. Its head swiveled as it searched for the source of a low-pitched thrumming sound that began to course through the area. Its intensity grew exponentially, and after only a few seconds, Tom could feel pulsating waves beating against his body. The creature recoiled and released his grip, allowing Tom to fall back into the tangle of cables, and a helmeted man walked from around the rear of the *Hefty* pointing a bulky device at the creature. The beast swung its head back and forth as if trying to shake away the sensation, then retreated behind the boulder from which it had emerged.

After another minute, the pulsating stopped, and the man took off his protective helmet. The slicer rifle that hung from a bandolier across his shoulder and the modified military-style sidearm left no doubt that he was trained in combat. "You must be new here."

Tom struggled to clear his senses after the ordeal. "Yes, um . . . Thank you."

"Sit up and relax. You fell for the oldest trick on the planet. Most of these outcroppings have sand traps set up around them."

"What . . . Where did that thing come from?" Tom asked.

"Tokchuk. Thousands of them live in caverns too deep and dangerous to explore."

"Tokchuk," Tom repeated, still dazed.

"I'm Mius. What's your name?"

Tom worked to collect his thoughts. "Tom Sparker. Why the trap? I wasn't bothering it."

Mius waved a hand at the terrain. "You see much wildlife around here?"

"Wildlife?"

"They use these nets to catch food."

Despite the midday heat, a chill washed over Tom. "What was that you used to chase it away?"

"Sonic cannon."

"I've never seen a weapon like that."

"They're expensive. But you're not allowed to kill tokchuk."

Tom's head began to clear. "Even in self-defense?"

"Not for any reason." Satisfied that the threat had passed, Mius finished powering down the device. "When merchants first got here they fought them, but once they realized the natives didn't have anything they wanted, they made a treaty. In exchange for the right to do business on the planet, they gave the tokchuk components to make traps, rudimentary electronic systems, and other gadgets. They have an intense curiosity for the technology, which is quite advanced by their standards. It was a cheap deal for the merchants."

"But I've been here for a week, and the trap just sprang now."

Mius shifted the full weight of the bulky weapon onto its shoulder sling. "I didn't say the merchants gave them *good* tech —just good enough to satisfy the tokchuk. The vibration from my ship touching down probably set it off, but a gust of wind or a herd of roaming greblo would have tripped it eventually."

"So they're allowed to attack us . . ." Tom's voice lowered in volume mid-sentence. "But we can't hurt them?" A headache was building, either because of his encounter with the creature or from the device Mius had used.

"The politics of this world are a lot different than on . . . Copania?"

Tom nodded. "Yes, Copania."

"I recognize the accent." Mius hooked his helmet on a belt clip. "As long as they don't bother the energy stations or space-ports, they can do what they want. Killing one of them could trigger another war."

Indeed, Tom was learning that many things were different on Feth. The locals had seen that he was camping, but nobody had warned him about the danger. The harsh reality that allowing him to get killed would simply eliminate him as a competitor had never occurred to him. He'd gotten lucky this time, but the planet was starting to feel much less hospitable. He should have done better research on the fringe systems during his trip instead of fiddling with shelving or browsing his maintenance manual, and it was a mistake he'd make sure he didn't repeat.

"Why aren't you in port?" Mius asked, looking like he already knew what Tom's answer would be.

"Um . . . I can't afford it." Tom glanced around and made a quick survey of his campsite. The fleeing tokchuk had tipped the worktable over, and the components were scattered.

"I was on my way to Eridia and saw you camped out here. You didn't look like you belonged, and I hate to see anyone snuffed out because of a mistake like this."

"It seemed like a good way to save credits. I've been looking for a job for the past seven days but haven't had any luck."

"Oh? What kind of work are you looking for? Is this your ship?"

"Yes. I can haul heavy, but I'm limited to small cargo. At

this point I'd be willing to consider anything that would pay enough for me to stay in port and allow me to put a little money away." Focusing on work helped Tom shake the memory of the attack.

"Heavy, huh? What's your payload weight capacity, adjusted for Feth?"

"Nearly twelve tons."

For the size of his ship, it was a lot of weight.

"Ah." Mius nodded as he looked over the *Hefty*. "Converted mining craft. Good. I know someone who might be willing to give you a contract to haul T16 energy cells."

Industrial energy cells were extremely heavy for their size and would be an ideal payload for a small ship like his. "I'd like that."

"The job doesn't pay full cargo rates, but for someone like you with low overhead, there'd be a nice profit margin if you're willing to work for it."

"That's fine with me. I'm ready to work."

"All right, let's get your ship untangled so you can get to port."

Mius pulled a welding cutter from a utility pouch and sparked a brilliant blue laser from its tip. He made quick work of the thick metal cables while Tom gathered the parts that had been tossed from the table and shoved the furniture and tarps into his ship.

"Follow me in," Mius said as he tucked the cutter back into his pouch. "I have a leased bay that can hold both our ships. After I take care of some quick business, I'll take you to my employer."

Tom pushed the crumpled canopy tarp farther into the entryway to make a path to the cockpit. "I'll be right behind you."

It was a lucky break that Mius had shown up, and now Tom had a lead for a contract job—the only one he'd gotten since he arrived. He powered up his thrusters, and as soon as he saw the ship rise from the other side of the rocky outcropping, he lifted off and followed. The small passenger shuttle was a custom craft designed to interface with a large raider or interceptor-class vessel, and was state of the art compared to the *Hefty*. If his employer paid Mius well enough to afford those kinds of craft, this could be a great opportunity.

With his gravity decking system still in pieces, he was only able to follow using thrusters, but the fancy shuttle wasn't in any hurry.

———◦———

THE OLD MINING ship moved slowly, and Mius reduced his speed so it could keep up. Rescuing the eager young shuttle pilot was a fortunate turn for both of them. The best way to solidify his professional relationship with Daihn was to produce results, and Tom would make an excellent addition to the employment roster.

20

Mius's small shuttle was comfortable and quick, and it didn't take long to reach Feth's interstellar staging sector. Tom spent most of the trip reading through the proposed hauling contract, which included specifics regarding delivery timelines and payment, along with vague references to "standard contractual penalties."

"I'm sure I can haul the weight," Tom said, "but I can only carry three or four cells at a time."

"That's fine. She needs someone to make supply runs from each of the one hundred and fifty-five independent energy suppliers that she made deals with. The small companies only produce two or three cells a month, so it makes sense to hire someone like you with a small ship."

Tom nodded. "And a larger freighter would charge more."

"She didn't get rich by paying full price," Mius said.

"Will I have to load and unload myself?"

"You might have to load at some locations, but you'll have grav-assist gear to help. The *Emu Ja'* dock crew will always unload, record, and store the cells. Don't ever try to do that yourself."

"Got it," Tom assured him. That many power cells could meet the needs of a small fleet of ships, but he didn't want to ask any questions that might raise doubts about his willingness to take the job. If they were planning a settlement operation or a deep-space trip, it wouldn't be that unusual to stockpile them. And while the contract might have offered low pay by Feth system standards, it was very generous by Copanian standards. The job would take about a month to complete, and he could make enough profit on the contract to support himself for six months or more, even while paying premium docking rates at Eridia.

Mius nodded toward the tactical raider they were approaching. "That's my ship. The *Celestial Blue*."

It was Tom's first chance to get a good look at some of the ships that were in the staging area, which ranged in size and design from medium freighters and survey ships to large cruisers and combat vessels. The *Celestial Blue* was as sleek and polished as any ship he'd ever seen. Its mirror-reflective blue exterior made parts of the ship seem to vanish and reappear as they passed, and he could identify two deck levels as well as a full-scale interstellar drive system. The ship also had two custom docking alcoves. The port-side shuttle was nestled in its place, and the one they were using would fit into the starboard side to blend stylishly with the shape of the hull.

"I've never seen anything like it."

"It was custom-built by an organization to help safeguard their business interests in a distant system. It was my payment for an expensive job I did for them a long time ago."

Tom craned his neck for a final glance at the *Celestial Blue* as the *Emu Ja'* came into full view. The formidable ship had curved lines that would have made it seem elegant if not for the myriad heavy weapon ports and armor retrofits that gave it a fierce look. It was an attack-class light cruiser with five decks and a standard crew of more than seventy. He'd studied the design in school but hadn't seen one until now, and as far as he knew, it was built and used exclusively by the chekt. Its large bay doors slid open as their shuttle approached, and the small craft pushed through the static energy barrier of the air-retention field. They landed among a variety of passenger transports and automated salvage drones that took up nearly a quarter of the large hangar's floorspace. Mius tapped a button, and both of the shuttle doors swung up. "She's expecting us, so we'll head straight over. It's never good to keep a chekt waiting."

He was only in the landing bay of the ship, but it was already apparent to Tom that no expense had been spared in its construction. Every detail exhibited quality materials and workmanship, and he'd never seen a docking bay floor clean enough to see his reflection.

As a tour guide, Tom had encountered most of the known sentient species, and he'd observed that chekt were meticulous. Everything about them, from the way they dressed to their choice of words and even the company they kept, seemed to be calculated and deliberate. The opulent yet functional design of the expensive ship perfectly reflected those characteristics.

Tom was also keenly aware of the foul temperament that many chekt possessed and their unusual hierarchy and code of conduct that was not only unforgiving but could also be unabashedly violent. A contract wasn't something they took lightly, and penalties for defaulting could be severe. But this was his only job opportunity at the moment, and since he intended to completely fulfill any agreement he made, he'd take the risk.

Mius led the way through the hangar and into a main walk-way. Although Tom couldn't read the chekt signage that was neatly etched into the corridor walls, he was able to understand some of the spoken language. However, since it included subtones that couldn't be heard, much less pronounced, by humans, he could never hope to hold even a basic conversation. Without an interpretation device, his ability to translate was limited to words that contained no subtones, which most people who were familiar with chekt guessed to be more than half the words in their language. But the name *Emu Ja'* seemed fitting to Tom, since loosely translated it meant "most worthy."

He followed Mius into the opulent lounge where Daihn sat at the head of a large table placed in the center of the room. Two fur-covered creatures of a species Tom didn't recognize sat working at computer consoles built into the walls of the chamber.

"Ah. Enter and be comfortable," Daihn said as one of the furry beings promptly got up and left the room, the door sliding closed behind it.

"Thank you, ma'am," Tom said.

"I am Exalted Daihn of the Chekt. Mius has informed me that you possess an adequate transport ship and are agreeable to the terms of a delivery contract."

Daihn glanced at the other crew member, who promptly stood and walked to a control console to begin working on something.

"Yes, ma'am. I should be able to complete the job on schedule."

"Then you will begin tomorrow. Mius will instruct you further, and you will report to me for final payment when our agreement has been fulfilled."

If a chekt was satisfied after a properly fulfilled contract, it was possible to receive a bonus and an offer to extend employment.

"Yes, ma'am."

As they turned to leave, the door opened, and the furry crew member entered the room again. Without a word, it began preparing a beverage for Daihn from a console near the door.

"I trust that Mius has counseled you regarding the fulfillment of our agreement," Daihn continued.

Tom paused and turned to answer.

"I . . . intend to honor our agreement. I'm ready to start tomorrow."

Daihn had already returned her attention to the furry crew members and didn't acknowledge his reply. Mius gave Tom a nudge, and they continued out of the room. "Make sure you do a good job," Mius said as the doors slid closed behind them. "Chekt don't treat those who default on contracts very well."

"Don't worry. I got the message."

21

After carefully sorting through all of the parts for the fourth time, Tom stared at the gravity decking components he'd laid out on the table in the *Hefty*'s main cabin. The gravity coil—the part the tokchuk had picked up—was missing. It was too large for him to have overlooked it when he'd gathered his scattered belongings, so the creature must have taken it when it fled from Mius's sonic device.

Without his gravity decking in service, Tom's cargo would be damaged in transit. T16 energy cells were much too heavy to properly support using only a strapping system, not to mention the damage the shifting load could do to his ship. The *Hefty* would fly but could only travel at minimal port speed— far too slow to make deliveries from the planet to the *Emu Ja'*.

The gravity coil was a precision component that would be expensive to replace—if he could even find one on Feth. But unless he did, he wouldn't be able to start work the next morning, much less fulfill the rest of his contract with Daihn. That was bad. He'd been clearly warned to neither deviate from the terms of the deal nor default on his agreement, and he didn't want to find out what would happen if he did.

If he asked Mius for help, he'd risk appearing incompetent, and Daihn might cancel his contract. Or worse, if he couldn't fulfill his obligations, she might be glad to let him fail and confiscate his ship as a penalty. She might even reward Mius for providing the opportunity. Without knowing more about either of them, it wasn't worth taking the chance.

The only sensible thing to do was check the port shops for a suitable replacement, so he grabbed a couple of meal bars and stuffed them into the chest pocket of his jumpsuit before he set off. With only a few credit chips left, he'd need to either find a real bargain or work out a payment plan. And as far as he knew, there were only two shops at Eridia that might sell what he needed.

Although the port never seemed to be very busy, there was a regular stream of activity during the day. The shops had enough business to profit, and there was always a ship or two undergoing repairs in one of its forty-six hangars. It was definitely a working settlement, more concerned with function than aesthetics—or cleanliness for that matter. But the commercial vibe was also relaxed enough for Tom to feel at ease in the port after his short time there.

The first shop looked promising. It had a modern storefront with lots of new components on display, and signs boasted that the shop could supply any needed part. It wasn't busy, so the shopkeeper was able to quickly pull up an inventory list. He ran his finger down the data screen and stopped at the line he was looking for. "Yep, I can order it for you, but you're looking at ten or twenty days before my next delivery."

"Don't you have anything in stock that will work, even as a temporary fix?"

The man shook his head. "If the coil isn't matched perfectly to your system, it'll burn out your deck plates."

"Can I just replace the gravity system?"

"Sure. I can have a new unit here in ten or twenty days."

Tom shook his head and fought off the urge to make a sarcastic remark. "I'll have to keep looking."

"Try Mypwig's across the corridor. He sells a lot of used gear."

"All right. Thank you." Tom exited and headed across the walkway. If Mypwig's didn't have what he needed, he'd be out of options.

As Tom entered the shop, the first thing he noticed was the giant, sparsely furred being standing at the counter. This tokchuk had much darker fur than his attacker, but it held what Tom was sure was his gravity coil as it conversed with the shopkeeper. He completely forgot himself in the moment. "Hey, that's mine!"

The creature turned to inspect its accuser, though Tom couldn't tell if the tokchuk had understood him.

"If you have a disagreement regarding ownership, take it out of my shop," the shopkeeper said. "Half of my stock was destroyed the last time someone had an argument, and I still have bloodstains on the racks."

The shopkeeper pointed toward the door and muttered something to the tokchuk in a language Tom didn't recognize. The being turned its head and snarled at Tom before it lumbered out of the shop. As he followed the dark gray mass, Tom had both a desire to fight and a compulsion to run, but there was nowhere for him to go. Once they reached the corridor, the creature planted its feet and stared at him as it snarled again. Clearly it understood that Tom had just ruined its transaction and wasn't happy. Tom mustered as much courage as he could, but his voice cracked and squeaked.

"That's mine!"

The creature answered with a roar loud enough to get the attention of everyone in sight. Tom felt his legs beginning to buckle as the creature took a step closer.

"Ugar key lem!" shouted a voice from somewhere to Tom's right. That caught the creature's attention, and it seemed to calm slightly. Kerra walked up between them and continued. "Malik touk tei. Amna soik lim na' cha." Kerra gestured toward Tom.

The being studied her, then looked at Tom. "Loikcha," it groaned as it held up two digits.

"Soik!" Kerra almost screamed.

The creature studied Tom for a moment, then blinked in agreement. "Mala."

At that, Kerra grabbed one of the meal bars that was sticking out of Tom's pocket and gave it to the creature. It gently handed her Tom's coil, then turned and slowly lumbered away, vibrating the station's decking with each step.

Tom leaned against the shop window and slid to the floor as the rush of adrenaline faded. "What just happened?"

"She wanted both of your meal bars, but I talked her down to one."

Tom watched the creature continue down the corridor. "She?" he squeaked.

"Yeah. They're much quieter than the males. And easier to negotiate with."

"So you traded for it? But the coil's worth twenty cases of meal bars."

"She doesn't know that," Kerra said with wide eyes and a

slight grin. "And a gravity coil wouldn't be much use to her, even if she knew what it was."

"I think you just saved my life."

She reached for Tom's hand to help him up. "Good, then you can buy me dinner with all the money you just saved."

22

The nicest eatery in Eridia was a dimly lit lounge draped with tattered fabric wall hangings. Despite Feth's dry climate, the thick red material filled the place with a musty odor. Tom and Kerra sat at a comfortable corner table and finished their meals.

"Where did you learn to speak their language?" Tom asked as he pulled a piece of spiced flatbread from a basket.

"I grew up helping my father make deliveries to K1, so I learned Tok when I was pretty young. You can get good deals from the tokchuk if you know how to negotiate with them—as long as you don't mind how they got whatever they're trading."

"I wish I'd known their language a few days ago. One of those things nearly killed me."

Kerra shook her head. "No. They'll get loud, but there's no way a tokchuk would harm anyone in port. It's part of the peace agreement."

"Not here. It was a couple of kilometers out in the desert where I was camping."

"Camping? You can't camp in the desert, it's way too dangerous!"

"I wish I'd known that before I did it."

Kerra leaned in. "By the moons of Doulier! What happened?"

"I got caught up in some kind of net trap, and one of those things grabbed me. I bet you could have reasoned with it."

Kerra slowly shook her head. "That's not likely. They're docile when they're in port, but the rules are different in their territory. It probably would've just ignored me."

"I don't know what would have happened if a guy hadn't come along and saved me."

"What guy?"

"His name is Mius. He showed up right after the trap sprang and chased the tokchuk away, then he offered me a job. You're looking at a cargo ship pilot with a contract for a hundred and fifty-five scheduled deliveries."

Kerra's eyes widened. "Ooh, that's wonderful news, Tom. Congratulations."

"I would have been in trouble if I hadn't gotten my coil back. It'll take me most of the night to reinstall it, but I should be able to start my first run in the morning."

"Then we both have good news," Kerra added. "But I'll tell you later. You can show me your ship, and I'll treat us to a bottle of suchet to celebrate." Suchet was a sweet, nonintoxicating dessert beverage made with cultured olf milk that was a favorite during Copanian festivals and holidays.

"All right. Is there a good shop nearby?"

"There's only one that sells suchet. It's just across the corridor."

They scooted out of their seats and left the waiter a few credit chips. It had been the best dinner Tom had eaten since he got to Feth, but it wasn't because of the food. It felt good to see Kerra again, and he was excited to show her the *Hefty*. They stopped at the food shop, and Kerra bought a bottle of suchet that had been on the shelf for so long that the shopkeeper had to wipe a thick layer of dust from the label. With his last credits, Tom bought two black dessert pastries topped with ushua honey, and they headed for Mius's hangar.

When they arrived, Kerra paused at the entrance. It was a deluxe space with full amenities.

"*This* is your hangar?"

Tom led the way past Mius's shuttle. "It belongs to Mius. He offered to let me use it since he had extra room."

"Nice. He must have some real money to be able to afford it. What does he do?"

"He's a contractor liaison to a chekt ship that's out in the staging sector."

"If he needs an ore hauler, let me know."

"I think he's looking for engine techs and weapon specialists right now, but I'll let you know if that changes."

Tom lowered the *Hefty*'s ramp. "This one's mine. It's a decommissioned magma-mining ship." He nodded toward the aft compartment. "I've got a small cargo hold." He stepped up the ramp and motioned to his right. "And the bulkhead separates the dual cockpit from the main cabin."

Kerra followed, eyeing the heavy deck plating. "And gravity decking?"

Tom nodded. "A safety feature for working subsurface. It's one of the few advantages of an industrial craft, and it should be great for hauling high-mass energy cells, too. I can dial up the intensity in the cargo space to hold them down like a magnet."

She peeked into the storage closet and glanced around the main cabin. "You rebuilt all of this yourself?"

"I overhauled all of the critical systems, and installed the tagalong with some help, but most of the secondary systems still need to be updated."

"I bet you'll find lots of work once you get established."

"That's what I'm hoping." Tom wrenched at the drink stopper. "So tell me your good news." The bottle opened with a pop.

Kerra looked back into the hangar, scanning the area that was still visible from inside the *Hefty*. "Let's close the hatch first."

Tom reached into the cockpit and tapped the ramp control to seal them inside the ship, the kik fluttering in at the last moment.

"Oh!" Kerra yelped.

"It's okay. It's been staying with me."

"That's strange. I've never heard of a kik wanting to be around humans."

"It might not be the human company." Tom nodded toward the creature, which already had both hands full of crumbs from a leftover meal that sat on the galley counter.

"That explains it."

Tom rummaged through a storage compartment above the stove. "So why all the secrecy?"

"Well, I have to be careful, but we've found a good vein of ore at the mining colony. A *very* good one," she whispered.

"That's great," Tom said in a slightly louder whisper.

"But I have to keep it quiet. It's dangerous to have something that valuable, and we don't have much to defend ourselves with if someone wants to take it. A lot of the miners would die fighting to keep what they've worked so hard to earn."

"I won't say anything."

"I know you won't. I was just so excited that I had to tell someone."

Tom pulled out a pair of handled metal cups. "I guess K2 is turning out better than K1, huh?"

"Actually, we were about to shut down the operation, but shaft seven hit a vein of ore that was shallower than the test cores showed."

"Is this the kind of strike that makes you all rich?"

Kerra shook her head. "No, but we should make enough profit to keep the mine going for quite a while. I'm heading back tonight to load up the best ore first, and a freighter is going to deliver some mining equipment in twenty days. That's when I'll get a tag back here with armed guards to cash in."

"But why bring the best ore first? Won't that attract attention?"

"It sure will, but bringing in a quality shipment of any kind is going to attract attention. We want to make as much as we can as fast as possible."

Tom placed the mugs on the counter. "Good thinking, I guess."

Kerra filled the cups with the frothy Copanian drink. "Once we get paid for the first load, we'll be able to hire a professional security team to help with the rest of the ship-ments." She set the bottle down and raised one of the mugs. Tom took the other. "To our success," she said.

"To success," Tom repeated, and they each took a drink.

The kik fluttered to the wet cork on the counter and sniffed at it before licking the residue off, which formed foamy bubbles at the edges of its mouth.

"So, do you already know how much the ore is worth, or do you have to wait until you have a buyer?"

"The market will determine the price, but so far it looks promising. We've never hit anything that looks this good, but we know of some others who have. That's the reason we're being so cautious."

"Did they get robbed?"

"Killed. Almost all of them." She took a long drink as the sobering thought lingered in the air, then held out her cup. "How about another for the road?"

23

After an all-night gravity decking coil installation, the *Hefty* was working as well as it ever had, and Tom settled into a comfortable routine of making four to five deliveries a day, including the time it took to clear lading documents and wait his turn to dock at some of the busier charging stations. He'd finally achieved a measure of independence and financial stability, and the next time he passed the Eridia communication office, he'd send Marcus a ComNet message to let him know of his success.

After being on the job for fifteen days and completing sixty-one deliveries, it was time to treat himself to a small luxury. Working prior to his first run of the morning, he tightened the final attachment brackets of the new food dispenser that secured it to the main cabin decking. It used standard energy cells to produce food and drinks, and it fit nicely in the *Hefty*'s galley. The time-saving addition would allow him to make his own Kushi tea, a local blend of herbs and tree roots that he'd gotten used to. It would hardly be called tea anywhere else, but the murky brew helped him wake up for early morning starts. He'd been drinking tea and water since he arrived, since the only other popular options at Eridia were Bungen Ale or Stellar Dagart. The Bungen Ale he'd tried on his first day had made him slightly nauseous. The gooey, frothy mixture was an intoxicant with a sour taste and pungent odor, and the beings who regularly drank it smelled like a damp cellar. Stellar Dagart was a highly regarded beverage that was manufactured off-world, and it glistened when poured from its small but elegant shipping flask. At several hundred credits per portion, only the wealthier residents indulged. It wasn't something that Tom considered trying, as it was a known narcotic and appeared to also be highly addictive.

A second benefit of his new device was its ability to produce basic food cubes. The bland pieces of homogeneous gelatin were barely palatable, but with the eventual addition of a secondary module he'd be able to use artificial flavor programs to approximate the tastes and aromas of the foods they were modeled after. A few taps on the control panel produced a hot cup of tea, which he took to the cockpit to prepare for his first run of the day.

The uneventful trips back and forth from the planet to the *Emu Ja'* had become routine, and he'd passed the time pondering ways to spend his new income. A holographic entertainment suite small enough to fit into the main cabin would be nice, but some kind of special seat for his furry companion might be more considerate. He looked to his right, where the kik sat on its usual perch atop the copilot backrest. It appeared content, and since Tom didn't know what other options a kik might prefer, the entertainment suite seemed like a better idea.

ORANGE DUST BLEW OUTWARD from his landing site as Tom lowered the *Hefty* onto the hard-packed desert next to the small remote outpost on the opposite side of Feth. He rummaged for a data pad while the kik watched. All of his pickups and deliveries had been prescheduled by Mius, with payment automatically credited to his account at Eridia after each delivery was received aboard Daihn's ship—and his credit savings were growing fast. The only daily changes that Mius made were the delivery coordinates, as Daihn seemed to prefer changing the holding location of the *Emu Ja'*. On one occasion, her ship had exited interstellar travel right in front of him just as he'd arrived at the rendezvous point, but it was always at the specified location on schedule. Punctuality was a hallmark of the chekt, and Tom never had to wait to deliver his cargo. She was honoring the contract to the letter, so whatever business she had that required her to travel so much wasn't any concern of his. All in all, business was great.

Tom found his data pad and hopped up, but the kik didn't follow as it usually did. "You staying here?"

The creature just shuffled a few steps sideways and continued staring at the viewscreens.

"Fine with me. This should only take a few minutes."

A light arid breeze puffed over him as he tramped down the loading ramp. Above ground, the remote station was little more than a few weathered shacks connected to a larger storage shed by a shade-covered walkway. A surface energy conduit approached from somewhere over the horizon to intersect with one of the buildings before continuing into the desert in the opposite direction. Only one other shuttle was at the outpost —a dirty ship covered with deep dents and tagalong panels that looked more beaten up than the rest of the craft.

It was normal for an attendant to meet him upon arrival, but the place looked deserted. He pulled on one of the shed door handles, but it was locked. The attendant might have been down in the tunnels that ran through the underground sections of the charging station. That's where the energy collection system was housed, and if there was a problem, that's where repairs would be made. He headed for the next shed, twisting his head as he scanned the area, and as he rounded the corner, he plowed right into a man coming from the opposite direction. It felt more like running into a padded wall than a person, and Tom bounced off the large man into the metal sheeting of the structure as his data pad flipped into the air.

The towering stranger leaned over and picked up the pad that skidded to his feet, then pointed it at Tom as if it were an extension of his index finger. "Well, it's about time you got here. We've been waiting since midday. I have a mine to run, you know."

Tom regained his balance as the rich baritone voice echoed off of the shed walls. "Huh?"

"Shek Windham, here to pick up six fully charged B10 power cells. I expect you'll get right to loading us."

Tom shook his head. "You've got it wrong, friend. I don't work here. I'm here for a pickup myself."

Shek looked down at Tom's pad. "Chekt pickup, eh?" He stuck the pad out toward Tom. "Well, you'll have to get in line, then. I've got mining equipment that's running low on power. I hope you're more careful at your job than you are running around this place. Chekt aren't the friendliest sort, you know. Have you seen anyone else around here? I'm in a hurry."

Tom accepted the pad and patted off some dust he'd collected from the shed wall. "I just landed. The attendant must be below working on something."

The door on one of the other buildings popped open with a creak, and a vefulian stepped out, wiping her slender blue hands on a rag. "My apologies if you've been waiting long. I had to fix an emergency leak. No sense having a power station with no power, eh?"

Shek took a few steps toward her and extended his lading pad. "We *have* been waiting long, so the faster you get us loaded, the less you'll have to listen to me complain about it."

The attendant took the pad and hustled off toward the larger storage building without another word. Shek followed while Tom waited in the shade.

One constant on Feth was the daytime heat. The days were always bright, too, although the dusty atmospheric haze probably blocked most of the sunlight that would have otherwise made it to the surface. A breeze ruffled the shade canopy that was reminiscent of the one he'd set up in his wilderness campsite, and the memory instinctively made him crane his neck to check on his ship. But the *Hefty* sat peacefully next to the commotion that was happening at Shek's ship as he loaded his cargo. After a few loud mechanical clunks and several expletives from the miner as he attempted to get his freight hatch closed, the vefulian returned to Tom.

"Sorry for the delay."

The dirty shuttle fired its engines. Tom offered his pad and had to raise his voice to be heard over the loud ship. "I understand, but I have a schedule to keep, so I'd appreciate it if I could get loaded soon."

A blast of hot exhaust from the miner's vessel hit them as the glassy-voiced worker replied. "I already have your cells ready in building two. This way, please."

As the shuttle rose up and away from them, the roaring whine faded. Tom wasn't sorry to see Shek leave, but he had to admit that the impatient customer had been right about one thing. Daihn would be watching his performance, so he had to make sure he completed all of his deliveries for the day. His contract made it clear that it was his responsibility to resolve any delays or risk not getting paid, and the wait had already put him behind schedule.

As THE *HEFTY* rounded the starboard side of the *Emu Ja'* and entered the docking bay with his first delivery of the day, a flurry of activity surrounded a luxury yacht that was docked in the center of the hangar. It was only about twice the size of the *Hefty*, but it was obviously a top-of-the-line model with all available options. Finished in dull black with silver trim, it looked brand new, aside from several fresh blast marks streaked across its hull in diagonal slashes that had turned the finish into a rusty gray. It was the kind of ship that only planetary executives and corporate officers could afford, and it looked out of place among the utility craft that surrounded it.

Tom set his ship down, and after lowering the loading ramp, he leaned against the hatchway and watched as the short, fur-covered workers examined the yacht's exterior features and moved items out of the fancy ship. The quiet and hardworking beings comprised more than half of the crew aboard the *Emu Ja'*, but they seemed to have little interest in interacting with him or any of their human coworkers. They just silently went about their tasks, and on the single occasion he'd tried asking one of them a question, it simply stared at him momentarily before returning to its work. As usual, by the time Tom's loading ramp was down, two of them were already heading to the *Hefty* with a gravity-assist sled to unload his cargo.

"Hey, Tom!" Mius walked into the main hangar from the central corridor.

"Hi Mius." Tom was getting close to the halfway point in his contract, and he took advantage of the face-to-face opportunity. "Hey, I was wondering if you knew of any jobs I could get once I'm finished with these deliveries."

"Well, there's usually work to be found for a reliable contractor. If Daihn doesn't need you, I'll make sure you get a good referral that should help at Eridia."

"I appreciate your help, especially setting me up with this contract. It's the best job I've ever had."

The commotion around the yacht increased, and Tom nodded toward the workers. "I've been wondering about them. What are they called?"

"Saazu. They have a kind of social contract with the chekt."

"They don't say much."

"No, but they're hard workers, and Daihn trusts them."

Tom motioned to the yacht. "What's all this about?"

"Daihn's latest . . . acquisition."

At that moment, several saazu walked out of the yacht carrying stretchers with what appeared to be dead occupants draped across them. Tom wasn't sure how to react. He looked at Mius as if to ask a question but couldn't get any words out.

"Never mind about that," Mius said. "It's none of our business. Just unload and get set for five more deliveries today. Daihn wants to move up the schedule."

Tom nodded and went back inside the *Hefty* to wait for the saazu to finish unloading his cargo. His excellent job situation had suddenly turned sour. Until now, he'd stayed focused on his work, but he couldn't dismiss what he'd just seen as simply part of a job, and he didn't want to be involved with whatever was going on. As soon as he fulfilled his contract with Daihn, he'd get as far away from her as he could and find a different employer.

24

Just before sunrise the next morning, an alert sounded, and Tom swiped at his small nightstand looking for an alarm button that wasn't there. The blare was coming from his ship-to-ship communication system. With a stretch, he hit a button on the comm panel.

"Hello?" Tom groaned.

Mius's strident tone crackled through the *Hefty*'s worn comm system. "Tom, get your ship up to the *Emu Ja'* with the next delivery of power cells. We're moving out of the system earlier than scheduled, and Daihn wants them aboard before we leave."

"Okay, I'm on my way."

The channel switched off, and Tom jumped up to start the prelaunch sequence before getting his morning tea. Protocol for early deliveries was to preload the night before, so getting underway took only minutes. The kik was already awake and perched on the copilot seat, and in a few minutes the dull orange sky on his viewscreens turned to black space.

With the *Emu Ja'* moving out early, his business situation

was uncertain. If Daihn decided that she already had enough energy cells, she could exercise her option to terminate his contract. And after the yacht incident in the docking bay of her ship, cutting his lucrative deal short would be a welcome development. The other possibility was that she would suspend the contract, and he'd be obligated to resume deliveries at a later date, which would prolong his business relationship with her.

As he arrived at Daihn's ship, the increased activity in the loading dock confirmed that something big was happening. Maintenance crews packed equipment in containers, and saazu scurried about carrying test gear and data pads. The *Celestial Blue* was docked diagonally across the hangar, leaving just enough room for the *Hefty* to squeeze into the last of the floorspace. The crippled executive yacht had been moved into the far corner of the bay, its blast scars as fresh as they were the day before when the stretcher-bearing saazu had removed its crew. Tom lowered the ramp in time to see two saazu towing a gravity-assist sled in his direction.

Suddenly the *Emu Ja'* shook fiercely, almost knocking Tom from his feet and sending several robotic cargo lifts crashing to the bay floor. Another slightly smaller jolt shook the ship again as workers scrambled to stations at the edges of the bay, strapping themselves into seats that held them tightly. The *Emu Ja'* was under attack. By the sound and feel of it, it was a bombardment that could only come from a well-equipped military unit or corporate ship. As the rocking continued, Tom stumbled to a view port to confirm his theory. It was a heavy diadu class destroyer used by large corporate alliances as part of a commercial fleet to protect company assets. Its flattened teardrop shape dwarfed the *Emu Ja'*, being at least four times its length and twelve times its volume.

Several more quick blasts rocked the ship before green haze

replaced the blackness of space. Daihn had engaged her interstellar drive, taking Tom and the *Hefty* along for the ride. It was unlikely that the diadu would try to follow, as its mass made it slower at interstellar speeds. Diadus typically used ambush tactics to overpower and cripple ships before they could escape, but the tactic hadn't worked this time.

He headed down the nearest corridor that led to the liaison office. Hopefully, Mius would know what was happening and where they were going.

If not for the hue and texture of altered space outside every porthole and viewing window Tom passed, he wouldn't even know that they were traveling at interstellar speed. The *Emu Ja'* was equipped with the latest in passenger comfort stabilization, which made this trip, wherever it was taking them, a smooth ride. A steady stream of workers made their way through the familiar corridors as if it were an ordinary workday. As he approached the office, Mius appeared from an intersecting corridor and held a hand out to stop him. "Looking for me?"

"Where are we going?" Tom asked.

"We had to leave sooner than planned."

"I see that."

"It seems the corporate interests took exception to Daihn capturing that corporate yacht."

"Is Daihn at war with the corporations?"

Mius pressed his lips together for a moment. "According to her, she had every right to take it, and do a half dozen other things that have them fighting mad."

"But how will I get back?"

"You're just going to have to wait until we're out of this. If Daihn wants you to finish out your contract, she'll make sure you get back to Feth."

His doubts about the morality of Daihn's actions were

growing, and his involvement with her had put him at higher personal risk, especially if a corporate force found him aboard her ship.

"Listen, Mius, I've been having second thoughts about—" Tom was interrupted by an alert that indicated the ship would be exiting interstellar at any moment.

"I have to get to the bridge," Mius said as he headed up the corridor. Tom instinctively followed. The bridge would be the best place to find out what was happening, and accompanying Mius at least gave him an excuse to be there.

"Mind if I join you?"

Mius glanced at Tom. "As long as you stay quiet and out of the way."

Tom nodded. "I didn't realize you had bridge duties."

"Daihn finds my military expertise useful, so I agreed to assist when needed."

The hazy green disappeared from the passageway portholes as they rounded a corner to enter the bridge. Both saazu and human crew worked busily at stations all around them as control consoles hummed and chirped. Several open communication channels echoed overlapping conversations that created a steady stream of vocalizations and static throughout the room. A deep sea of giant asteroids lit by a distant sun filled the viewing windows, and Tom guessed at what he was seeing.

"Holding at tactical position one relative to Kala settlement," said a human crew member.

They were near the K2 mining colony, and right now Kerra would be there. Daihn relaxed in her command chair overlooking the scene. "Ah, Captain, are the necessary ground teams prepared?"

"They're awaiting orders," Mius said.

"Instruct them to begin the operation at the main refinery.

They are to report immediately when they have secured the facility."

Mius walked to a communication console alongside the wall of the bridge. "Acknowledged."

Whatever Daihn's reason was for being there, whether justified by chekt code or not, the miners were in serious trouble.

"Mius—" Tom started.

Mius held up a finger and interrupted. "Stay out of the way."

Tom had no choice but to comply, and watched as the troop transport headed through the asteroid field toward K2. Several missiles launched from the colony in an effort to ward off the attack, but they were quickly destroyed by the transport's energy weapons before the ship disappeared into the crevices of the giant rock. Daihn had probably kept the *Emu Ja'* at a distance in order to protect it from any defensive weapons the colonists might have, though it was difficult for Tom to imagine that the miners had anything that would pose a serious threat to the huge attack cruiser.

An incoming call from the ground troops sounded on one of the communication channels, distorted by live weapon fire and explosions. "We're encountering heavy resistance inside the secondary hangar. We're going to need ammo packs and a supply of class four explosives."

Eating a spoiled raqtle egg would have made Tom's gut feel less queasy than hearing the sounds of combat in the background of the transmission. The miners were fighting, just like Kerra had said they would.

"Team Alpha is requesting supplies at zone two," reported the comm attendant.

Hopefully Kerra wasn't near the battle. Even if she

wasn't his only friend within a hundred light years, the idea that he was involved with the attack, however remotely, made Tom feel he needed to say something, and he whispered to Mius. "Why are we attacking the colony? I can't be part of this."

Mius paused at his console and looked at Tom, but instead of answering, he just frowned for a long moment.

"Ah, Tom," Daihn said, looking in his direction. "Do you have something that you wish to discuss?"

With all the commotion on the bridge, Daihn couldn't have heard him whisper to Mius.

"No, ma'am," Tom said.

"But you object to our activities."

Tom searched for the right words to get him out of the situation. "I'm . . . no, I meant . . ."

Daihn turned to the forward window. "You will ferry supplies to our troops on the surface of the mining asteroid immediately."

It wasn't a request. Daihn had the contractual right to change his delivery cargo and destination at any time.

Tom exchanged a glance with Mius. They both knew that the *Hefty* didn't have a chance of making it to the colony through the miners' defensive fire. Without having to be told what to do, two armed saazu immediately appeared at Tom's sides and nudged him off the bridge.

It was the worst situation he'd ever been in. Panic would only make it more difficult for him to find a solution, but knowing that didn't stop his mind from racing as his silent escorts took him to his ship. It didn't feel at all like Daihn was sending him on an actual mission, but more like sending him out for target practice—as the target. And how had Daihn heard what he'd said to Mius anyway? There was so much noise and activity on the bridge that he hadn't even been sure Mius could hear him.

A utility cart guided by a saazu worker blocked the corridor at the next intersection and forced Tom to stop until it passed. The worker paused and exchanged looks with each of his guards several times as if they were conversing, then continued down the cross-corridor. Tom's adrenaline-fueled thoughts coalesced into a realization. It had always appeared to him that saazu didn't talk, but if they were able to communicate using the same subtones as chekt, it would explain why they seemed to know what Daihn wanted without being ordered. Saazu crew members had filled the bridge and could have easily reported his comments to Daihn.

The saazu finished their exchange and nudged Tom forward. His options weren't good. If he tried to escape, Daihn would destroy his slow ship immediately. If he did as he was instructed, there was little hope of making it to the colony. And even if he somehow managed to make it through the defensive fire and succeed in delivering the supplies to the surface troops, he would be assisting in the defeat and possibly the deaths of the miners—maybe even Kerra herself.

They turned the next corner to enter the docking bay and crossed to where the *Hefty* sat, already reloaded with ammunition and explosives. His escorts stood at the ramp of his ship as Tom walked aboard to start the prelaunch sequence.

⸻ ✦ ⸻

DAIHN RELAXED in her position overlooking the bridge. "Captain, prepare to deliver the requested supplies to our ground forces in your ship, should the shuttle pilot fail."

"I'll get to it right away," Mius said.

Expressing opposition to the actions of an employer warranted severe penalties, and Daihn was less forgiving than what was permitted by Kahr. The small craft would help her secure the mining operation, and she would destroy it as it returned, unless the miners' defensive weapons did the job for her. Tom's cargo was minuscule, and under the right circumstances, even the destruction of such a small ship could benefit her quest for improved status.

25

The kik perched on the backrest of the copilot seat, staring intently at the forward viewscreen as the *Hefty*'s engines warmed up. The obvious options—running or hiding—were both out of the question. Daihn would easily find him if he tried to hide in the asteroid field, and his ship couldn't maneuver quickly enough to avoid being blasted if he tried to run.

With the saazu guards still watching from the docking bay, Tom lifted the *Hefty* from the deck and accelerated toward the battle. While he slowly weaved into the asteroid field and put distance between himself and the watching *Emu Ja'*, his mind raced to come up with a plan that could get him out of the situation, or at least survive the miners' defenses. He needed more time to think, but he also needed to maintain the appearance that he was carrying out Daihn's order.

His hand trembled as he feathered the controls to give the high-powered engines barely enough throttle to keep them from shutting down. They were built to run best at full power for transporting heavy cargo, but moving the ship as slow as possible would give him more time to come up with a plan. Unfortunately, his reduced speed also made him an easy target for defensive fire from K2, and the *Hefty* wasn't made for quick maneuvering. So maybe trying to buy time was a mistake. He jammed the throttles to full, and the ship lurched forward. The faster he got to K2, the more he would narrow the window of time the colony weapons would have to intercept him.

But halfway to the settlement, the small red flame of a tracking missile's engine appeared on the *Hefty*'s center screen, and it was intended for him. His chest tightened, and he fought to take in shallow breaths. The *Hefty* wasn't nimble enough to evade the weapon, and he had no chance of outrunning it. The red flame grew larger on the screen as it accelerated, and he had only seconds before the missile met him in open space.

The kik fluttered from its seat to the forward console and hopped up and down on a small control panel.

"Hey!" Tom scolded reflexively.

It was jumping on the breaker gun controls. *The breaker gun.* There might be a way to save them from both the missile *and* Daihn, but there was no time to think through the details. He had to act. With a shaky hand, he flipped the safety cover on the trigger as he nudged the flight controls with the other. The nose of the ship adjusted to point directly at the incoming missile, and an alarm wailed in the cockpit. He pulled the trigger, spraying railgun fire at point-blank range. Tom squeezed his eyes shut, and the missile detonated with the loudest sound he'd ever heard.

26

Echoes from energy weapon fire made the walls vibrate as Kerra ran through the cylindrical utility corridor. A quick glance into each attached workroom had so far failed to locate her mother. Several miners ran toward her from the opposite direction. "Kerra," one of them panted over the rumbling. "We can't hold them for long. Is your ship ready?"

"I'm on my way there now." The attack had been sudden, and she'd been sleeping when the alarm klaxon began to wail. Her ship was needed to evacuate others, so she didn't miss a step as she rushed into the main hangar and ran aboard the *Damsel*.

She stopped at the top of the loading ramp where her mother, Winnet Aramine, was already onboard supervising workers as they secured containers of ore in the cargo compartment. Kerra's mouth hung open. "I've been looking for you." Her eyes drifted to the crates. "What are you doing? Where is everyone else?"

"We need this ore to trade," Winnet said. "I told the others to come, but they insisted on fighting."

Having so much prime ore stored for quick loading was suspiciously convenient.

"Trade to who? How did you get this loaded so fast?"

"I'm always prepared for contingencies. You should know that."

Kerra glanced back at the tunnel entrance, where flashes of light from the firefight were brighter than they had been a moment earlier. "They'll have to use one of the other ships." Kerra scrambled up the ladder to the cockpit and frantically flipped switches. "We need to go now, or we won't have time to escape before they get to us."

Winnet called from the deck below. "We're ready here, Kerra. You can take off."

Kerra ignited the engines. The ship lifted off and tilted toward the hangar door, which barely had time to open wide enough before the *Damsel* reached it.

Invading troops stormed into the hangar, and several energy bolts from handheld fire made glancing blows on the *Damsel*'s hull. Kerra's whole body tensed, but they were moving with speed, and they made it through the hangar doors before their attacker's aim improved. Once she crested the jutting rock wall that mostly concealed the settlement complex, the engines flared into a bright violet streak, and the ship pushed away at full power.

More shots flashed by the *Damsel*, this time from the attack shuttle that had landed at the far end of the settlement. The shots didn't connect, and Kerra heaved the controls to turn the ship in as tight of an arc as possible to escape toward the opposite side of the asteroid, then farther into the interior of the field—hopefully out of sight and reach of their attackers.

27

Daihn watched the small fireball erupt where the mining shuttle had been. Debris-filled tufts of explosive energy spinning away confirmed its destruction, and she tapped the comm panel on her armrest. "Captain, proceed with the substitute delivery. Report when you're on the surface."

Mius answered from aboard the *Celestial Blue*. "Taking off now."

◦

FRAGMENTS OF ROCK and metal slowly ground against each other as they floated next to a large asteroid. The slight gravitational pull of the massive body held on to several dozen medium-size pieces that had been splintered from the surface. There was no hint of ordered activity, but amid the bouncing boulders was the battered gray hull of the *Hefty*.

Tom woke to the sound of rock scraping against the hull and a cockpit filled with flashing indicator lights. His shoulders throbbed where the seat restraints had dug into them, but he didn't seem to have any serious injuries. Most of the ship's systems were offline, and his port and aft viewscreens flickered as they threatened to fail at any moment. He could make out enough detail to know that he was in the light gravitational influence of an asteroid, along with metal debris and countless chunks of rock. It was hard to tell how much of the wreckage was from the missile and how much was from his own ship, but several pieces of his upgraded nav antenna floated amid the rubble. The explosion had thrown his ship away from the direct path between the *Emu Ja'* and the mining colony, apparently into a collision with one of the asteroids floating between the battling forces.

An alarm sounded. He couldn't hear the cabin air system as it struggled to maintain pressure, but the whine from escaping air was growing. A breeze rushing into the cockpit from the main cabin left no doubt that his ship was leaking air from somewhere in the cockpit. He grabbed a handheld emergency light and began a frantic search, but the problem area was easy to spot. At the nose of his ship, next to the forward viewscreen, air was rushing out of a crack nearly ten centimeters long. He lifted the copilot seat and rummaged for a tube of repair caulk in the storage compartment. A large blob of the clear substance quickly made a temporary seal, turning white to indicate that it was curing. He couldn't tell what damage had been done to the exterior from where he was, but at least he'd relieved the strain on the cabin air pressure system, and the alarm stopped.

Tom's intention had been to destroy the missile with breaker gun fire just before it hit his ship and fool the *Emu Ja'* into thinking he'd been destroyed in the explosion. His timing had been a bit late, but at least he'd survived the attack, and floating with the asteroid might provide some camouflage. The

Emu Ja' maintained its position, giving no indication that Daihn was aware of his survival, but he couldn't power up any major system without risking detection.

There was no sign of the kik. Hopefully that was because it was hiding and not because it was injured, but Tom didn't have time to look. He had a new problem. The *Celestial Blue* was approaching quickly.

Instead of coming for him, it passed within two hundred meters and continued on its way to the mining asteroid. With luck, Mius would overlook the *Hefty* in a rush to get replacement supplies to the colony after his own failed attempt. But for now, Tom could only watch helplessly from his drifting ship as flashes of light bombarded the settlement. Even if he could get his communication system back online, he wouldn't dare send any messages for fear of being detected.

Ships fled the colony asteroid. Among them, an engine cluster ignited and streaked away from the battle trailing a violet plume. Since Kerra's was the only Thesine ship he knew of at the colony, it was a good bet it was the *Damsel*. There was no way to know if she was piloting it or if someone else was using it to escape, but it was good to see, nonetheless.

The explosive flashes on the mining colony dwindled, then finally stopped. The battle was over, and the troop transport was returning, followed by the *Celestial Blue*. If they noticed him, he would be taken back to the *Emu Ja'*, where he would again be subject to Daihn's wrath. Or worse—they might just blow up his ship on their return trip. The troop ship passed him, but a small jet of accelerant from Mius's ship confirmed Tom's fear. He had launched a magnetic drift mine, and as the *Celestial Blue* passed, the *Hefty*'s port-side viewscreen flickered and went dark. There was no reason to use elaborate energy weapons or a missile to destroy an easy target, and drift mines were inexpensive. The mine would attach itself to the ship and direct a focused charge through the hull. Not even the *Hefty*'s thick armor could protect it from that kind of blast. Tom's stomach muscles cramped as he watched the *Celestial Blue* return to the *Emu Ja'*, the aft viewscreen flickering as the mine clanked onto the hull. It would be only seconds before it did its job.

28

Seconds passed as Tom rifled through a storage compartment in a vain effort to find one of the emergency pressure suits he kept onboard. Even if he was protected from the vacuum of space, the suit would do nothing to protect him from the blast. But his racing mind insisted that he do *something*. As more seconds of frantic searching ticked by, his thoughts began to shift from fear to curiosity. The mine hadn't detonated. *Was it a dud?* As he processed the lack of an explosion, an area of space near the *Emu Ja'* warped, and a diadu appeared out of an interstellar cloud.

A sudden and fierce barrage of blue and white energy rained onto the chekt cruiser. The fire splashed across its hull as it lurched and returned its own volley, which was little more than a delaying tactic. Daihn couldn't hope to win a head-to-head fight against the destroyer, but it would buy her time to initialize another interstellar trip. After less than twenty seconds of fiery exchange, the *Emu Ja'* had again disappeared in a cloud of green mist.

The diadu sat in space like a cat that had pounced but come up without its prey. Tom held his breath as he watched, hoping the regulators either wouldn't notice him or wouldn't care that he was there. His ship was loaded with military-grade weapons and supplies, which was more than enough evidence to prove his involvement with Daihn. The massive ship moved toward him, and Tom steeled his nerves, but the diadu passed the *Hefty* and headed directly for the scene of the mining battle. After a brief pause at the settlement asteroid, the destroyer continued past the colony and slowly turned toward open space.

There were still no signs that the mine was active. If it hadn't detonated by now, it probably wasn't going to, but he needed to make sure. And the sooner, the better.

—◆—

THE KIK APPEARED JUST as Tom found and pulled out one of his pressure suits, and it fluttered into the other one that still sat in the storage compartment.

"Glad to see you're okay. Stay there and you'll be safe until I get back."

The kik pulled a bit of food from its pouch as Tom activated the suit to seal it inside. Satisfied that his own suit was secure and properly sealed, and that his tool belt was firmly attached to his utility harness, he lowered the cabin pressure and opened the emergency hatch above the lounge. A slight hiss released the remaining air pressure from his ship, and he pulled himself up into open space.

His suit's thrusters nudged him to the port side where the mine had induction-clamped itself to the hull. He'd have to disarm the weapon before attempting to remove it, and while the procedure should be simple enough, it would take time. A careless move could cause the explosive charge to detonate.

Using a fastener wrench, Tom gently removed several bolts and attached them to a magnetic strip on his sleeve. Perspiration beaded on his forehead, and a drop floated onto the clear facepiece, partially obscuring his view. As he loosened the final bolt, his hand slipped, and the wrench slammed into the side of the mine. A wave of fear coursed through him, but the bomb sat silent. He slowly slid the access panel from the outer shell, but nothing inside resembled any type of explosive device. Instead, it held only a clear-walled cylindrical tube that contained something wrapped in a cloth rag. The mysterious payload was obviously not meant to explode, but then why use such an odd method of transporting . . . whatever it was? He carefully removed the cylinder and secured it to his work belt before moving to the front of the ship, where the nose was splattered with black streaks. He'd waited too long to pull the breaker gun trigger, and while the hardened tip of the missile had been deflected, the blast itself had dug dozens of deep gouges into the tough pecrite. There wasn't any way to tell how much the hull had been thinned in those areas, but the crack that he'd sealed from the inside looked much worse on the outside. He pulled a dispenser tube from his tool belt and carefully smoothed a thick layer of vacu-putty onto the outside of the crack, filling it the best he could in the zero-gravity environment. The sealant would bond to the repair caulk that he'd already applied inside the hull via the slight opening of the crack and should hold well enough to get to a repair port. But it was obvious that the entire front section of the ship was badly damaged, and he wouldn't be able to risk traveling at interstellar speeds until permanent repairs were made.

Before returning inside, Tom surveyed the rest of his ship.

While the ion drive and planetary engines seemed to be undamaged, the top of the tagalong housing and one of the energy-collector panels had been crushed. He had no way to tell if the drive would still work, but it didn't matter. Even if he had an interstellar wake available, the ship wasn't in any shape to try to use it. His upgraded antenna array was missing, but the *Hefty*'s factory systems used their own internal antennas, so he should still have at least basic functionality.

He lowered himself back through the escape hatch and slowly pressurized the ship again. After the *Hefty* had a breathable atmosphere, he removed his suit and released the kik from its protective enclosure. The creature fluttered to perch on the stove handle and cocked its head as it watched Tom take the cylindrical package to the table in the lounge. Inside the wrapping were two small standard power cells that would fit his food dispenser and a handwritten note that read:

Nice trick. Stay low for a while.

Why would Mius help Daihn attack the mining colony, then risk infuriating her by helping him? The *Emu Ja'* probably wouldn't have been able to see the mine launch, but Mius had still taken a chance. Whatever the reason, Tom was grateful.

He couldn't try to contact any survivors at the settlement to get permission to land, since a signal over the comm system could give him away to any of Daihn's forces that might still be there. The miners might have planned an evacuation rendezvous for the ships that had gotten away, but he had no way of knowing where or when it might occur, and the miners would probably consider him a threat anyway and try to blast him again. The only option that made sense was to set a course for the next available port and stay as inconspicuous as possible until his ship was repaired.

The navigation system required a reset to get it back online, and a quick search of the database showed that the closest settlement was Koyla Center—a large, privately owned, public-access spaceport with its own security force. It might take months to reach it using only the ion drive, but he didn't have a choice. The fuel cells would keep his beverage and food cube dispenser working for at least a month, and in addition to the emergency rations that he kept onboard, it would be plenty to last both him and the kik until they arrived.

The ammunition charges from the *Emu Ja'* were common rounds that could be sold without attracting attention and were probably worth several hundred credits. Combined with the money he'd saved, it might be enough to get his ship repaired. The explosives would have value to the right buyer, but they could be tricky to sell without getting into more trouble, so it would be smart to get rid of them when he had a chance to do it safely. Since the *Emu Ja'* would be able to recognize the *Hefty*, some cosmetic alterations would be a good idea as well. With a new look, it would be easier to follow Mius's advice.

⬥

TOM SAT BACK in his pilot seat as he finished a meal. More than a day had passed, and the *Hefty* still drifted in the field of debris. He'd gotten all of the critical systems back online, and the others could wait until the ship was moving again. Fragments of rock bumped against the hull as he gave the kik the last morsel of his lunch. It had clung to the pocket of his coveralls as he'd worked, but he didn't mind. It was because of the small creature that he'd been able to save them both. It obviously possessed intelligence of some kind, but he couldn't be sure just what kind or how much. Had it deliberately suggested that he use the breaker gun, or was its behavior purely coincidental? Without a way to communicate such a complex question, he'd probably never know.

He engaged the thrusters and oriented his ship toward Koyla Center. When the navigation computer verified that they were on the correct heading, he shut down the thrusters and engaged the ion drive. Energy collectors would fuel the slow drive during the monthslong trip, and his path would be far from any established route, so it was unlikely that he'd encounter anyone along the way. Since there was little more for him to do but wait for the ship to gain speed, he increased the ion drive power to maximum and sat back. The kik fluttered to a throttle lever and stared at the forward viewscreens as the *Hefty* slowly accelerated.

29

Daihn tapped her fingertips together as she stared at the mysterious stone tablet. Several saazu examined the artifact while others entered data into workstations. Her eyes moved to Mius as he walked into her lounge carrying a data pad.

"We got a good amount of ore," Mius said, "but there was no sign they'd found anything else. I thought the tablet markings said the Oraca was located within the richest pecrite vein."

"They suggest that the Oraca is hidden near something of great value in the Kala field, but perhaps the miners did not find the most valuable deposit."

"Is it possible that the translation is incorrect?"

"Perhaps. The inscriptions are ancient and difficult to decipher."

Mius handed her the data pad. "Several small craft, including a Thesine cargo ship, escaped during the battle. We didn't have time to go after them before the diadu arrived. If they found something in the asteroid, it's possible they took it with them."

"Inform our associates in the Jobjon Syndicate that we require their assistance," Daihn said. "Triple the standard bounty."

He gave a nod. "Where do we go next?"

"Have your sources revealed any new information about the location of the tablet's companion piece?"

"Not yet."

"Report any findings, regardless of how trivial they may seem."

"Understood." Mius left the room at a brisk pace.

Daihn stepped to the table and ran her hand over the attachment point on the end of the stone. Even if they were misreading the markings, a curious detail of the Kala field supported the idea that it was special. An asteroid field of its type and age should have a much greater number of smaller asteroids moving at unpredictable speeds and trajectories within it. But the small fragments had been cleared, and the larger ones were stabilized. No one would carry out such a massive undertaking without a good reason. It was obvious that the Kala system still held secrets. Whether they were the ones she was looking for remained to be seen.

30

Kerra gently pulled on the ship's controls to avoid an asteroid, and the *Damsel* responded. She could have used autopilot if she'd skirted the edge of the field, but manual control gave her something to focus on, and flying among the asteroids made her feel like the ship was better hidden. The relative quiet of her ship's small but comfortable cockpit gave her a chance to reflect on the attack. Outlaw raids on mining colonies were a known threat, but the swift assault on K2 was faster and better organized than what she would have expected from pirates. Whoever hit them must have thought the miners had something more valuable than pecrite ore.

From behind the pilot seat, Winnet crawled along the ladder that led to the cockpit hatch. "How far are we from Dag?"

Kerra's hands didn't leave the controls. "Not long. Maybe another five minutes."

"Good, it's crowded in there."

"There'd be a lot more room if we'd taken more people instead of cargo."

"We're going to need that ore, Kerra. How do you think we'd survive without something to trade?"

It was easier for Kerra to change the subject than get into an argument. "Is the hangar big enough for us to land vertically?"

"No. The docking bay is small, but they have gravity decking."

The last time Kerra had landed the *Damsel* horizontally, she'd sheared off one of the stabilizer fins. But given their current situation, she'd gladly trade a couple fins plus the backrest of her pilot's seat for a good hiding spot. "I'll just feel better once the ship is out of sight."

Winnet leaned forward and squinted as she scanned the field ahead of them. "Don't get too comfortable. The Jobjon have better scanning tech than is generally known, and they've turned their bounty-hunting sideline into a featured service."

"The syndicate? Is that who attacked us?"

Winnet shook her head. "I don't think so. They would have found us already. But if whoever it was figures out we got away with a load of premium product, they're going to be looking for us." She looked at Kerra. "And professional trackers would be the quickest way to find us."

"Sounds like a lot of trouble just to get some ore."

Winnet pursed her lips. "Did you even look at our cargo? It's all grade five. Six containers."

Kerra kept her gaze forward, but her eyebrows turned down sharply. "No. I was busy trying to keep us from getting blown up."

Winnet made another quick scan of the asteroid field.

"Let's just hope they don't realize what we have before we can sell it."

Kerra suppressed a sigh. They'd barely escaped K2, and all her mother could focus on were credits. "All right, I'll let you know when we're on approach."

Winnet rejoined the other miners, and Kerra focused on the rocks in her path. A few more sweeping maneuvers brought them within view of their destination.

The Dag distillery sat on a nearly spherical eleven-hundred-meter-diameter asteroid that drifted near the edge of the field. Only a few dim marker lights gave away the outline of the building's structure against mottled gray patches of what looked like fine sand coating the asteroid's otherwise cracked brown surface. The hangar looked barely long enough to accommodate the *Damsel*, which would make bumping into something on the way in more likely.

"We're on approach to Dag," Kerra shouted through the ladder hatch. "Everyone strap in."

She tapped a control on her comm panel. "Dag Control, this is the *Damsel* from K2 on approach."

The response came quickly. "Welcome, *Damsel*. Keep it nice and slow. Our landing bay isn't very big."

"I'll try not to dent anything. *Damsel* out."

Kerra maneuvered the ship to lie parallel to the asteroid surface, then eased it into the low-ceilinged landing bay. The space doors closed, and she gently lowered the ship onto stubby auxiliary landing struts. Her ship settled with a groan, and the engine whine diminished as their power drained.

Kerra called back to the cargo hold as she waited for the bay to pressurize. "Mother, we're secure."

She shut down her ship's systems and made the crawl to where her passengers were waiting to disembark. Kerra was the only one who wasn't eager to get off the ship, so instead of lining up with the group she grabbed a cold drink from a food storage unit.

A green light on the wall panel signaled to the miners that it was safe to open the cargo bay door. Winnet was first down the ramp, searching for their host among the dockhands entering from a maintenance doorway. "Kerra, come here. I want you to meet someone."

Kerra tromped down into the roughly excavated hangar with her drink in hand. A damp coating covered the walls, giving the space the feel of a large, artificial cave. Perimeter lighting reflected hints of green from a liquid that ran in tiny rivulets along the gray rock and disappeared beneath the top-quality gravity decking. Winnet stood near the ship, embracing the arm of a slightly shorter man with slick black hair.

"Kerra, this is Tanger Ellis. We used to work together before K1."

"Welcome again, Kerra," Tanger said with a kind voice. "I hope you didn't scrape your ship getting in here. Our facility wasn't built for anything as big as the *Damsel*."

"Sorry to take up so much room."

"I'm glad we could accommodate you. Our delivery ships are all small tagalong vessels."

"Tagalongs? How do you make deliveries from the middle of nowhere with tagalongs?"

"We cater to several trusted customers who pick up their orders, but mostly we use a central interstellar drive generator that sends out a dozen shipments at once. Since we only deliver to major ports, they get a tag back when they're finished. It's a very economical setup."

Kerra gave a slight nod. "Clever."

"Your mother and I have some business to take care of.

There's a small lounge attached to the commissary at the end of the hangar. Please make yourself at home."

———◦———

AN HOUR LATER, Winnet had joined Kerra at a table in the small commissary for a drink. The edges of a transparent wall made an airtight seal where it was embedded into the rock of the asteroid, which gave the sense that the six-table seating area extended into the hangar.

"You did what?" Kerra stared at her mother with her mouth open.

"We had to borrow some money from Daihn. It was the only way to make sure shaft seven kept going long enough to make it pay. Firkis just got a little behind on the payment schedule, that's all."

"But the miners voted to stop drilling before going into debt."

"If I'd allowed that to happen, we could have lost everything."

"We *have* lost everything. K2 is destroyed, and we probably have a bounty on us."

"I just sold that ore to Tanger for enough to get K2 going again—or better yet, to find another place to mine."

"Another mine? We nearly got killed and you want to do it again?"

Winnet glanced around the room. "Keep quiet. You should be grateful you have a job and a place to live."

Kerra scowled. "And what about the people who died defending K2?"

"I told them to leave with us, but they ignored me."

Kerra kept the volume of her voice low, but not its intensity. "They didn't know you'd made a deal with Daihn!"

Winnet picked up her drink and stood. "They should have listened to me."

Kerra glared at her. Winnet leaned across the table and softened her voice. "Besides, if it wasn't for them fighting, we would never have escaped ourselves." Without waiting for a response, she turned and headed for the landing bay.

The situation made Kerra burn inside. She had become an unwitting party to her mother's scheme, and there was nothing she could do about it, at least not at the moment. Since the *Damsel* was the property of the colony, she couldn't leave without permission, and for better or worse, Winnet was leading their group. Kerra would keep pushing as much as possible to help anyone who might still be alive at K2, but she had to wait until her mother—or at least enough of the other miners—were ready to return before the issue could be forced.

31

Tom sat at his eating counter picking at bits of the gelatin cube from his food dispenser as he imagined flavor program possibilities that didn't taste like a cube of gelatin. He was only two days into the trip and had a good supply of other rations, but he'd decided to occasionally switch to the synthesized fare for some variety.

The ion drive's energy collectors kept it running with enough power left over to keep life-support systems online and maintain the planetary engine cells, and he'd have to accelerate for at least a month before starting the deceleration process. It was tough knowing he'd have to start slowing down at the halfway point, but ion drives used real speed instead of compression field technology. His velocity would increase to maximum at the middle of his journey, and then he'd have to reverse the thrust. Otherwise, he might overshoot Koyla Center and have to spend days or weeks backtracking.

Until then, his main job was to keep from going stir-crazy. He took the leftover bits of his meal to the cockpit, where the kik perched atop the copilot seat staring at the forward viewscreen. "What's so interesting out there? It's just a lot of black space."

The kik looked at Tom's leftovers, then returned to its viewscreen monitoring.

"You don't want it either, huh? I don't blame you." Not wanting to waste the food, Tom scraped the last bits into his mouth and set the empty plate on the copilot seat.

He was relying on the navigation computer to guide the *Hefty*, but with all the damage his ship had, it would be smart to perform manual calculations to double-check for accuracy. He'd record his location on a simple table at several intervals using x-, y-, and z-axis coordinates and compare them to the navigation system's data as it was displayed.

He grabbed a data pad from the floor and switched it into freeform mode. With the stylus, he drew two vertical lines and crossed them with two more horizontal lines. He headed the first column with an X, and for the first time, the kik fluttered over to perch on his arm. Tom paused to see what it would do next. It stared at the pad, then gently took the stylus from Tom's hand with its wing hands and drew an O in the center of the hand-drawn grid. Keeping its attention fixed on the pad, it handed the stylus back. Tom took the stylus and placed an X in the second column heading. The kik took its turn and placed an O in the third column heading space, blocking Tom's attempt at three X's in a row. Tom made an X in the bottom right corner, leaving the kik an opportunity to win. It placed an O in the bottom left corner to make three in a row, then jumped up and did a backward flying somersault while chittering and squeaking. It knew how to play tic-tac-toe.

The kik tapped on the screen, and Tom cleared it to draw another game board. This time he won the game, but the kik reacted in the same happy way with a flying backflip. They played several more games before the kik flew onto a throttle lever and pulled a snack from its satchel.

It was the first time Tom had had any intelligent interaction with the small creature, and watching it enjoy playing the games made him smile. Despite his situation, he didn't feel alone.

32

The loud bang and violent jolt startled Tom awake, but it was the sobering drop of air pressure that made him jump out of his bunk and scramble to the bulkhead that separated the cockpit from the rest of the ship. The rush of air escaping from the nose of the ship was deafening. He pulled at the hatch, loosening it from the scrap of wire that held it open, and slammed it shut to isolate the leak.

The cabin pressure pumps worked at full output to restore normal air pressure as Tom peered through the small circular viewing port in the hatch. The repair had failed, and the crack had turned into a half-centimeter wide vertical hole. The communication and navigation panels had gone dark, and the cockpit gravity decking was offline. Wires sparked and debris floated throughout the room that was now in a complete vacuum, but the cockpit hatch seal was holding.

It was then that Tom saw the throttle levers, and a wave of panic washed over him. The kik always slept on a throttle lever. He quickly scanned the ship, dashing back to the cargo area, then returning to the main cabin, where he flipped seat cushions and knocked over tool bags in his search, but it wasn't there. It had been in the cockpit.

The bulkhead hatch could only be opened after depressurizing the main cabin. His hands shook as he grabbed a pressure suit, and was struggling to get his legs in when a faint glow from the hatch window caught his eye. With most of the suit still on the floor around his ankles, Tom leaned closer and looked through the port.

A glowing, egg-shaped energy field, bristling with animated aqua-blue light, floated past the window. Inside, the kik was upside down and looking at Tom with its permanent smile. The egg rotated slowly until the kik was upright again, then the small creature pulled a piece of food from its satchel and took a bite.

Tom stared at the odd scene with his mouth open, then finished putting on his suit. He used the aft cabin environmental controls to reduce the cabin pressure and opened the bulkhead door with a hiss. The slow aerial spin of the kik-filled bubble turned into a gentle roll as it left the cockpit and the main cabin gravity decking pulled it down and across the floor.

Tom turned his attention to the opening in the nose of his ship, which looked worse as he inspected it more closely. The ion drive controls were located on the far edge of the console and were still intact but offline. He pulled himself into the pilot seat and strapped in. A quick reset of the breaker powered the engine panel back up, but while it indicated that the ship's steering controls worked and the ion drive was still functioning, he couldn't risk additional stress on the hull, so he shut the drive down. If the hole in his ship spread beyond the cockpit bulkhead he'd be out of compartments to pressurize.

After only two days of accelerating, they were still traveling far too slowly to reach Koyla Center before running out of supplies. That left only one option—send a distress signal and hope that someone friendly would receive it. The unsettling prospect of broadcasting his vulnerability made his stomach churn. But if he did nothing, their fate was certain.

The communication console was wrecked, and he'd need to gather tools before he could work on repairs, so Tom unstrapped himself and floated back out and onto the functioning gravity decking in the main cabin. He secured the bulkhead door, and when the main cabin pressure was restored, he slid out of his suit.

Tom went to where the kik still sat in its energy orb and crouched to get a better look. "What is that?"

The kik pulled a tiny device from its satchel. It had controls on it that were too small for Tom to see clearly, but the creature tapped at them, and the field of energy snapped off. It stuffed the object back into its bag before fluttering to the galley and perching on the stove handle.

"You're full of surprises."

The kik stared at him as it pulled another morsel from its pouch.

33

Kerra and her mother walked with Tanger as he pointed out various areas of his distillery and explained the delicate process of making Stellar Dagart. He gestured to the bottling machine at the end of a long conveyor. "It takes thirty stages of distillation to make it safe to drink, and even then it packs a real kick."

Kerra wrinkled her nose. "So the slime just oozes out of the ground?"

"The quality of the raw liquid near the surface is low, but the good stuff is only a few meters beneath the rock and runs in small channels."

"How did it get into the asteroid?"

"My technicians think it's the result of an electrostatic breakdown of trace minerals embedded in the rock, probably from a freak magnetic storm at some point in the asteroid's history. There are probably more like it in the Kala field, and I have a survey team looking for possible locations."

"That's so ambitious!" Winnet said.

"Right now we can process enough liquid to make forty cases a day, but that doesn't keep up with demand."

"Why don't you just start another plant on Dag?" Kerra asked.

"I'm planning to, but we've been so busy trying to keep production up that I haven't had a chance to get the building process started. Plus, we're careful with how we get supplies delivered. Not many people know our location, and we want to keep it that way."

"Yeah," Kerra said. "It seems like someone with some heavy firepower could clean you out pretty quick."

"We're prepared for that. But you're right, if someone wanted to take the place badly enough, we couldn't stop them. Of course, beyond any product we have on hand, the only way to get real value from the distillery is to operate it, and raiders aren't known for their manufacturing expertise."

Winnet took a step closer to Tanger and held his shoulder. "I think it's wonderful that you're doing something in business, Tanger."

It was unusual for her mother to give anyone so much attention unless it was to manipulate them, but she'd already sold him the ore, so it seemed pointless. Kerra's lip curled at the behavior, but she tried to hide her reaction by picking up one of the fancy bottles of glistening liquid. "Is the finished product a drug of some kind?"

Tanger half shrugged as he raised an open palm. "I like to think of it as a recreational beverage."

"And," Winnet said, "I've heard it's one of the most popular around."

An alert chime sounded, and Tanger looked at a data pad. "You'll have to excuse me for a while. There's a ship coming in for a special order pickup."

Winnet took a half step to her side but left only enough room between her and the conveyor so that he was forced to brush up against her. "We'll wait here for the tour to continue."

Tanger gave her a sideways look as he scooted past, moving with a graceful limp he'd acquired during the Transit War.

Winnet picked up one of the Stellar Dagart bottles to examine it more closely. "Maybe we should be in manufacturing instead of mining. What do you think, Kerra?"

Kerra sat on a shipping crate. "I'd like to get back to K2 and find out if anyone is still there who needs our help."

Winnet ignored her and instead tugged the cap from the bottle to sniff at the odorless product.

Kerra leaned against the housing of a rumbling conveyor and folded her arms. Arguing was pointless.

34

Mius carried the fresh memory of the attack on the miners as he walked across the hangar of the *Emu Ja'* toward the *Celestial Blue*. Daihn's troops had killed at least a dozen, and although he hadn't pulled any triggers this time, he felt no less responsible. By the book, giving Tom a chance to escape was an unwarranted risk, but he had to do something to remind himself that he wasn't a bad person.

Loci and Dorn were playing a hologame at a table in the lounge. The *Emu Ja'* had a small shop that sold assorted sundries and convenience products, including an odd assortment of the portable entertainment devices. They bounced to their feet when Mius entered.

"Loci, make sure those engine maintenance diagnostics get done today."

"When are we getting another payday, Mius?" Dorn asked.

"There's no big money yet, but I'll give you your regular wage tomorrow."

The twins exchanged excited glances and hurried to the engine room.

Daihn had provided Mius an onboard suite, but he preferred the modest quarters aboard his ship. As a combat veteran, he was accustomed to a simple lifestyle that made it easier to adapt to changing circumstances, and the luxuries that Daihn found appealing would only distract him. Docking the *Celestial Blue* in the hangar of the *Emu Ja'* was restrictive, but given recent events, it was a safer place for the twins, and it was also the best way to stay close to Daihn. If she was somehow successful, he had to be ready to act. The exhausting internal struggle that raged within him between his sense of duty and his personal code of ethics would be for nothing if he failed in his true mission.

35

Tom reached up to scratch his nose, but his hand only clunked into the clear face shield of his pressure suit, reminding him that although he was inside the cockpit, he was also working in the vacuum of space. He moved carefully to avoid rubbing his suit against any of the twisted metal brackets that jutted from beneath the flight console as he assessed what remained of the comm system. The circuitry was wrecked, either broken into small pieces or missing completely. Even if he'd had the expertise to fix it, he didn't have any replacement parts. Sending a distress call would be impossible.

As he stared at the mess of components and wires, a slight trembling shook the console, and he crawled out to find a ship approaching. Someone had found him. As the larger craft slowed its advance, a massive bay door opened. Were they pirates who had detected him while on a random patrol of their territory, or had Daihn sent a mercenary to search for him? Judging by the age and condition of the ship, it was probably a junker of some kind. That would be better, but then they might want to claim his broken ship as salvage and abandon him on some convenient planet or space station.

Bright lights from the larger ship's bay brightened the *Hefty*'s viewscreens as the gaping mouth of the bay door enveloped Tom's ship. He scrambled back into the main cabin and secured the cockpit bulkhead door. By the time he pulled himself out of his suit and unzipped the kik from its suit, they were inside the strange ship and its huge bay door had closed.

A few clanks and jolts later, automatic docking straps had secured the *Hefty*. Tom watched the viewscreens from the main cabin through the small window on the bulkhead door. The hangar walls looked ancient, but the area was neatly kept. Modern tools and parts were stored on workbenches along walls that had been painted or covered in a patchwork of finishes and materials that spanned the ship's service life. The bay was lit with updated floodlights that showed what looked like a hundred years' worth of stains on the deck, and an escape pod that was strapped down in a far corner looked about as old as the ship's bulkheads. There were no bins of twisted metal structures, damaged engine cores, or any other type of wreckage that he would expect a junker to be carrying. If this wasn't a salvage ship, it might be an antique cargo ship of some kind, although the particular design wasn't anything he'd seen before.

A light above one of the hangar entryways lit, and the airtight door swung open. Two men stepped through and approached the *Hefty* as Tom forced himself to take a deep breath and relax a little with the exhale. At this point their rescuers—or captors—were going to get inside, and he had no way to fight, so he'd try a friendly approach.

Tom lowered the ramp, and the kik flew out quickly and hovered above him. In spite of its grungy style, the hangar didn't have any odor that would betray its age, though occasional clunks and whirs from ancient control mechanisms echoed across the large area. Tom painted on his friendliest tour guide smile and raised a hand in greeting, but before he could say anything, a tall gray-bearded man who carried a small sidearm barked at him. "Stay where you are."

Tom froze as the men continued their approach. The shorter man dismissed the threat. "Don't pay no attention to him."

"Who are you?" Tom asked.

"Well, that's some kind of thank you," the bearded man growled as he stuffed his sidearm into a jacket holster.

The kik fluttered down and did a flying backflip in front of the shorter man. "Hey, little fella."

Tom looked between the two men. "I'm . . . thank you. How did you know where I was?"

"Fernius told us to look for you on this course," the shorter man said. "So here we are. I'm Joss, and this is Orni."

"My name is Tom Sparker. Who's Fernius?"

Joss studied Tom for a moment. "That's who we work for. You hungry? We've got a couple of hours before we'll get to Koyla Center."

"I don't understand. How did you know where to find me?"

The two men exchanged glances. "I already told you," Joss said. "Fernius sent us."

The kik landed on Joss's shoulder. "C'mon little fella. I've got some of those bitter twists you like."

Tom followed, still unsure. But the men had just rescued him, and the kik seemed to trust them. Maybe Fernius, whoever that was, would give him straight answers. At least they were taking him to Koyla Center, where he'd hopefully have repair options for his ship.

———◆———

As they approached, Koyla looked more like a small city than a typical fringe spaceport. It was constructed in the terminator zone of a large barren moon, which kept the station in perpetual twilight. The complex looked like it had been built over a long time period, with additions made from of a variety of materials in different styles that formed a mostly enclosed network of buildings. They landed in an open area, which meant that the moon had an artificially generated atmosphere.

The private landing field was large enough to accommodate the salvage freighter with room to spare for several smaller craft. It even had two private hoverpuck lanes adjacent to the well-kept field, presumably as entertainment for guests of the administrator. Joss led Tom and the kik through the nearest doorway to the facility and down a short hallway to the administrator's office. He opened the door, and the kik fluttered in.

"I'll leave you here," Joss said as he walked off. "I have work to do."

Tom followed his flying companion into an octagonal room. Its walls were covered with wooden shelves from floor to ceiling, and they were packed with a wide assortment of colorful curiosities, most of which Tom couldn't identify. A pyramid-shaped piece of wobbling gelatin hovered over a plain black disk as it slowly spun, a speck of light traveled along a winding track that had been formed into a sphere that would fit in his palm, and a boxy device fitted with an impossibly complex assortment of spinning gears and reciprocating pistons operated with quiet precision to perform some unknown task. Muffled sounds of station activity made their way through the walls into the otherwise quiet room.

At a large desk in the center of the space sat a squat being who appeared to be a human-pyer hybrid. His facial skin folds were less pronounced than those of the long-lived race, and his ears resembled a human's more than the tiny stubs of his other parent. Tom was ready to find out who his rescuers were and what it was going to cost him for their help.

"Welcome, my friend!" the man said with a mild pyer accent. The kik did a double midair backflip and landed on the desk. The rotund man looked up at Tom.

"And welcome to you as well. My name is Fernius Poh. I'm the owner and chief administrator of Koyla Center."

"I'm Tom Sparker, sir. Thank you for sending help. We were in a lousy situation."

"You're most welcome. Joss tells me that your ship is badly damaged."

"I was trying to make it here for repairs."

"The mechanics will perform an evaluation, and we'll find out what options are available."

Before Tom could ask any questions, Fernius turned his attention to the kik. "It appears that you have had some adventure, my friend."

The kik twittered and squeaked for several moments, and Fernius nodded as he listened. "Yes, yes good. Very good. This is valuable information. Daihn, you say? Yes, most important. And attacked K2, possibly looking for the item we all seek."

Tom watched in silent fascination.

When the kik had finished, Fernius leaned back in his chair. "You've done well this time, my friend. What is it you ask in payment?"

The kik chittered.

"Are you sure? It's a low-quality item and hardly reliable."

A single squeak from the kik prompted Fernius to open a desk drawer and take out a tiny object, which he handed to the small being. "This was well-earned."

The kik hung it from its neck like a bizarre necklace, and as it chittered and squeaked again, a tiny voice spoke from the device. "*Mine thanks very much*," it translated.

Tom looked between the kik and Fernius as their interaction revealed more of the small being's intelligence. Fernius turned to Tom. "Thank you for taking such good care of my friend."

"How did you know where to find us?"

"The Pfonas shield automatically transmitted a distress signal directly to me when it was activated."

Fernius looked at the kik and nodded. "A very fine choice to accept it as payment for your previous venture."

"So . . . the kik works for you?"

"I employ many eager and talented beings on a contractual basis. I value knowledge, and I'm willing to pay fairly for information that satisfies my curiosity. My friend and his colleagues bring me news and interesting facts from time to time. His species is intensely curious, which is a quality that I appreciate more than most."

A young man about Tom's age banged through the door to Fernius's office using an overflowing box of wire cables like a battering ram. "Where do you want this?"

"Put them here so I can review them. And be careful."

The man staggered up to Fernius's desk and plopped the box down, its fibers tearing a bit along a corner seam as it hit the desktop.

"I must return to business now, Tom. Let's chat again

soon. Risul, please help Tom find accommodations at a reasonable price."

Tom couldn't find any reason not to trust the friendly hybrid proprietor who had not only rescued them both but also answered some questions about his small, winged companion. "Thank you again, sir."

Risul opened the door, and the kik flew out ahead of them.

"I'm Risul. You new around here?"

"Tom Sparker. Yeah, my ship needs some work so I'm going to be here a while."

"Ever do any target shooting?"

"I haven't in a long time."

"We practice about once a week. You can join us if you want."

Tom was learning how important it was to have friends in the fringe systems. Koyla seemed like a hospitable place so far, and Risul worked for Fernius, so it might be a good opportunity to get to know some locals. "That sounds like fun. What do I need?"

"I'll let you know when our next match is. We always meet at the recreation center late in the day."

"That'll be great."

"I have to haul more junk to the old man's office." Risul nodded toward the end of the corridor. "If you follow this to the end, there's an information desk on your right. They can set you up with a room."

Tom gave a nod. "Thanks, Risul."

Risul turned and walked in the opposite direction. "Welcome to Koyla, Tom. I'll see you around."

Tom looked at the kik, who fluttered just ahead of him as they made their way to the information desk. "So you've been able to understand me this whole time?"

"*Understand me normal wires*," the tiny device translated. It obviously was an imperfect piece of technology, as Fernius had warned.

"Well, now you can tell me your name."

"*Hamburger Popsicle*."

"What?"

"*Hamburger Popsicle*," the device repeated.

Tom stared at his friend as he walked. "There's no way I'm calling you Hamburger Popsicle."

36

Energized after his first full night of sleep in days, Tom made his way through one of the busy corridors that led to the administrator's office. A message from Fernius had said there was news about his ship, and Tom was eager for the update. His sidekick fluttered alongside as they made their way through the maze of corridors that made up Koyla Center.

Station workers, mechanics, and even tourists filled the walkways. Species from all over the known systems were represented here, as well as a couple that looked like they must have come from places beyond the seventeen civilized suns. Small courier bots wheeled or tracked along their assigned routes, and more complex mechanoids—more or less resembling the organic life forms who made them—mingled with the crowd of station patrons. It was the first place outside of Copania that Tom had seen crowds, and it felt more sophisticated than Feth. The large, tidy walkways and huge buildings of the central complex made Koyla Center easy to navigate, and they included every type of business a spacefaring society could want. The mix of used parts and surplus technology shops, along with retail outlets offering modern gear and entertainment services imported from the core systems, made it the kind of place where a shop owner or service technician could settle in relative comfort.

His companion fluttered ahead of him as they entered the office filled with curious objects. A transparent crystal sat in a dirty box on the desk in the center of the room. It appeared to be etched with a three-dimensional geometric pattern that resembled some type of ship. Fernius looked up from his paper-work. "Good morning and welcome, Tom."

The kik landed on Fernius's desk. "And you as well, my friend."

"Good morning, Mr. Poh."

"Fernius, my lad. Just call me Fernius."

"Did they have a chance to look at my ship?"

Fernius's eyebrows furrowed. "Yes, indeed. The damage to your tagalong drive is mostly cosmetic, but your hull is badly damaged, along with several of the cockpit systems. I'm afraid it will be quite expensive to repair."

"I wasn't sure if a pecrite hull could even be repaired."

"Possible, yes—but expensive. You might do better to purchase another ship. Perhaps something easier to operate and maintain?"

"I can't afford another ship, but if you're interested, I have a supply of ammunition that I'd be willing to trade, and I could work off the rest of the cost."

Tom's sidekick tapped on the translation device, and it emitted a burbled squeak.

"You see?" Fernius nodded toward the tiny device. "I cautioned you about that." He pulled a tiny pouch of tools from a desk drawer and set it on the desktop. "Take these, as well. I'm sure you'll manage repairs."

Their winged friend jumped into flight and hovered in front of Fernius, then chirped something to him before settling onto the tabletop to dig into the tiny tool pouch.

"Mmm, it's possible that you're correct, my friend. Yes, quite possibly a good idea."

"What's a good idea?"

"I'll gladly purchase your munitions supply, but their value is minimal compared to the cost of the needed repairs. And I do have need of someone to help maintain the grounds, but I might be willing to accept something else in trade."

"I don't have much, sir."

Fernius opened his arms. "Look around my office, Tom. What do you see?"

"It looks like you have a big collection of . . . things."

"Yes! My collection. This represents only a small portion. I've gathered tokens of remembrances and souvenirs of found knowledge from across the galaxy." He pointed to a door behind him. "I have entire storage rooms filled with wondrous fascinations and simple items of days long past."

"It's very impressive."

Fernius waddled across the office to one of the shelves. From between a flask that contained dark residue from some kind of evaporated mixture and a small wooden box filled with tiny jumping specks of light, he picked up a tubelike object only a few centimeters long and held it up for Tom to see. "Did you know that there was once a race of beings that lived beyond the Lothan Expanse who used only small puffs of air as a method of communication?"

"I didn't know there were *any* civilizations beyond the charted systems."

Fernius gazed at the object for a moment as if reliving the memory of its discovery, then gently placed the item back on its shelf. "Many of these items are relics of ancient civilizations or simple devices of ingenious engineering. Some are mere souvenirs, but nearly all of them have one thing in common. They are unique items and contain or represent knowledge that I alone possess."

"I don't think I have any knowledge that would be worth trading."

"Quite correct! But as my friend here suggests, you may be able to acquire some information that I would consider extraordinarily valuable."

"What kind of information?"

Fernius drew closer to Tom. "Are you aware that Daihn of the Chekt is searching for something?"

"I know she attacked the K2 mining colony. I assumed she wanted the ore."

"She seeks something far more valuable, and I believe it may be hidden in the Kala field."

The idea of encountering Daihn again sent a weak shiver through him, and Tom shook his head. "There's no way I can compete with Daihn."

Fernius furrowed his brow again. "You should avoid any contact with her. It's information that I want, and obtaining it will require an inconspicuous approach. I need someone to go to the Kala asteroid field to locate a person of interest and bring me a discreet method of contact."

Tom's sidekick squeaked and chittered again.

"My friend has vouched for you, so I'm willing to repair your ship so you would have full use of it. A lien would be placed on ownership of course, and I'd require either the information or full payment through employment or acceptable currency."

It was quite an offer. "But why me? I mean, I hardly know anything about the Kala system, and my ship sure doesn't have any special abilities that would help find someone in an asteroid field."

Fernius gave a gentle smile. "Your ship has *you*."

Tom's eyes narrowed at the obvious statement. "Well, yeah. But how does that help get what you need?"

The shorter being held Tom in his view for a long moment. "Those details only come with acceptance of my terms."

Accepting a job offer that presented unknown risks was not appealing, especially an offer from someone he'd only met a day before. The only risk for Fernius was the loss of the repair cost, which did demonstrate some trust in him, so his fluttering friend must have given a glowing recommendation. But Tom had already stumbled into enough dangerous situations to be wary of any offer that he hadn't taken time to carefully consider. It wouldn't take long to find himself in trouble again if he didn't develop a more cautious instinct.

"I appreciate your confidence in me, but I'm not sure I'm ready for something like that. Would it be all right if I slept on it?"

Fernius gave a nod. "The quest presents danger, indeed." He leaned closer. "Think on it."

37

Tom sat in a booth in one of the restaurants at the port that was much newer, cleaner, and busier than any at Eridia. Orders were placed by remote menu stations and delivered through a cylindrical hatch that rose from the tabletop, then disappeared seamlessly into the surface. A sanitizing array that dropped down from the ceiling played a happy tune as it cleaned the table after each patron was finished, leaving the smooth surface sparkling before zipping upward again. The only odors in the brightly lit diner were those of the prepared food, which were mostly pleasant except for a plate of dustworm cheese ordered by a member of a quadruped species that Tom had never seen before. The dish had a fungal aroma that almost made him gag. Fortunately, the being ate ravenously, and the odor dissipated with the vanishing meal.

His flying companion sat on the table and observed the patrons as they went about their eating and fraternizing.

"You must have given me a good recommendation for Fernius to offer me a job. Thanks for that."

His friend just blinked at him as he chewed on a piece of thick flatbread.

"What do you think I should do?" Tom asked.

"*Eat fish sticks.*"

"I mean about Fernius's offer. It sounds like you've told him lots about me, but I hardly know him. Should I do it or stay here and work off the repairs?"

"*I'm with you. Stay now or go french fry,*" the translator squeaked.

"I'm not sure what that means, but I think it's a vote of support." Tom took a last gulp of his drink and stood. "Let's take a look at the ship."

It was a short walk to the repair center, but there wasn't anyone at the service counter. The *Hefty* was visible through an open doorway, so Tom stepped into the service bay. It was his first time inspecting the damage since Orni and Joss had rescued them, and it looked worse under the bright lights of the mechanics bay. He crouched low in front of the nose and ran his fingers along the inside edge of the jagged crack. "What am I thinking? We nearly got killed out there."

"*Bang snap breaks ship.*"

"That's right. Why would I want to go back to the same place we just escaped?"

"*Scary travel smarty think.*"

"If you're saying that it's time I played it safe, I agree."

38

Tom dragged the floor-cleaning unit into the storage room after a long day of getting commercial bay fifteen ready for its next stage of remodeling. The station job Fernius had given him was as a low-level maintenance tech, but so far he'd had only janitorial duties. It was no more tiring than putting in long hours for the tour company back home or spending weeks getting his ship ready to fly, and he had little responsibility compared to those jobs.

He made his way through the maze of corridors to his cabin after his first day as a Koyla employee. Repairs on his ship had begun, so he couldn't stay onboard the *Hefty,* but room and board were included in his employment contract. It was a reasonable deal. In eight months, his bill would be paid and he could look for safer transport work. The door slid open, and Tom dropped into a chair, exhausted. The small living quarters were simple but included double bunks and a work desk. There wasn't much storage space, so he'd left anything that didn't fit into his large duffle locked in storage compartments on his ship.

His winged friend was already eating his evening meal.

"*Working nicer flying fixing?*"

"They're working on it."

Tom motioned to the small translator necklace. "I wish that thing worked better."

"*Understanding mine better than not.*"

"I guess I can't argue with that." He heaved himself up and crawled into the lower bunk. "I'm going to get some sleep."

"*Sleep chocolate resting.*"

Tom rolled onto his side. "Goodnight, Hamburger Popsicle."

THE NEXT MORNING, Tom started his workday by stripping the old waxy buildup from the floor of one of the restaurant's storage rooms in preparation for refinishing. The noisy machine was heavy and awkward, but by midday he had all but a small section completed. For his ten-minute break, he sat on a utility box and leaned against the wall that separated the room from the dining area. Muffled voices of restaurant patrons talking and laughing barely overcame the prominent buzzing of the storage room's old lighting system.

He cracked open the door to get a look at the activity, and the voices poured into the room at full volume. Travelers of all sorts ate, drank, and laughed. It reminded him of his first visit to the café at Eridia, except that now he wasn't a part of it. Working as a laborer wasn't anything like the success he'd had in mind when he set out from home. His only consolation was that Marcus wasn't there to see it.

Tom stared at the crowd. The galaxy was a dangerous place, but Mius had risked a lot to help him, and Fernius had been fair and accommodating. Then there was Kerra. The times he'd felt happiest since he left home were when he was with her, and working at Koyla was only keeping him from finding out what had happened to the *Damsel*. After just two days, the plan to safely work off his debt was quickly losing its appeal.

Tom let the door creak shut and stood to continue his work. He grabbed a mop handle that leaned against the wall and froze mid-pull. The obscure maintenance position was exactly the kind of job that he'd left Copania to avoid. Now, instead of flying, he was back to working for another employer with rules and hours and schedules. He returned the handle to its position.

Years of working a safe job back home had barely been enough to get him off-world, and although he'd had mixed experiences since then, it seemed like the only times he'd really accomplished anything—whether it was buying his ship, getting his first contract, or even traveling someplace new— were the times he'd taken risks and faced uncertainty. Sure, he'd been shot at, nearly eaten by a tokchuk, and sent to his supposed destruction by a chekt, but he'd survived. Maybe some luck was involved, but it was also possible that he was learning to survive—and maybe someday even thrive—in the fringe systems where all of the excitement seemed to be.

Tom patted dust from his clothes and strode toward the storage room door. He could hide at Koyla in safety for months while he saved for repairs, but if Fernius had a way for him to pick up where he'd left off, he'd take his chances. Now that he'd had a taste of success, he was ready for more.

Tom knocked and slowly opened the door to the administrator's office. "Excuse me, Fernius?"

Fernius sat at his desk poring over data pads as he glanced at a monitor that displayed an animated three-dimensional spreadsheet of some kind. "One moment."

Tom waited patiently in the doorway as he examined the strange objects on the shelf next to him. A clear bubbling liquid circulated like syrup within a sealed cube-shaped container that had no obvious source of energy to power the motion, and on a nest of hairlike bristles next to it sat a faceted gemlike sculpture that reflected red light from somewhere in the room. Fernius paused his work. "How may I help you, Tom?"

Tom crossed the room to the chairs in front of Fernius's desk. "Well, sir, I've been thinking about that information you want."

"Information. Yes, it can be valuable."

"I've been . . . If you still think I could get what you want, I was wondering if your offer still stood . . . about paying for the repairs."

Fernius's eyes narrowed in typical pyer fashion. "Have a seat, Tom."

Tom sat and Fernius leaned back in his chair. "What's caused you to reconsider my offer?"

Tom searched for the right words before he answered. "I left Copania because I wanted to live more on my own terms. That didn't work out like I expected, but at least I was out there trying."

"And you're dissatisfied with your work here?"

"Yes, sir. Well, no . . . not exactly. It's not you or your station, it's just that I feel like I've given up, and I don't like it."

"This quest is dangerous, Tom. Are you certain that you're up for it?"

Tom looked at the floor, then back at Fernius. "I'm certain that I'd rather live dangerously than feel like I'm wasting my life in safety."

Fernius studied him for a moment. "Then you will need more information." He waddled a few steps to an oddity-filled shelf near his desk where two clear flasks sat next to each other. One was filled with oily purple liquid, and its twin was empty. He picked up the full flask and poured it into the other, whereupon the syrupy fluid turned green. He set the newly emptied flask back in its place, and the shelf began to click. Sounds of spinning gears and mechanical locking mechanisms echoed for a moment, then the shelf slid out like a drawer. Inside sat a stone tablet with alien inscriptions. "This item was delivered to me from a reliable source, and I have confirmed that it was made more than seven thousand standard years ago. It is part of what I believe to be a multi-section guide of sorts."

"Guide to what?"

Fernius's eyes glistened. "The Gashon Oraca."

Tom slowly nodded, hoping for a more detailed explanation.

Fernius read the confusion on his face. "An obscure legend tells of an ancient race of beings who possessed a device that was capable of transchronolinear conveyance, and I believe this is what Daihn is looking for."

Tom squinted. "Translinear . . ."

Fernius gave a patient shake of his head. "The Oraca allows the user to communicate with those in future time periods."

Tom studied the markings on the tablet as Fernius continued. "The one who possesses the Oraca would have the ability to gain knowledge from further points on our timeline and use it to great advantage in the present. Until recently, I had no evidence that the legend had any merit, but this object suggests that it may in fact be real. The markings don't translate from any known language, but I believe it indirectly refers to the Oraca." Fernius pointed to an edge of the tablet. "You can see that the edges have attachment points indicating that at least two other pieces were part of the original assemblage. Without those, it may be impossible to produce a contextual translation."

"So you want to find the people who made this?"

"The individual who sent this artifact to me was able to decipher a few symbols that refer to a Guardian who protects the Oraca. That is who I want to find."

"Wouldn't it make sense to just ask that person to find the Guardian?"

Fernius's eyebrows peaked and his face softened as he put a palm on the tablet. "Shortly after my associate sent me this arti-fact, I lost contact. Sadly, I may never hear from him again."

It was clear that Fernius didn't want to go into detail about the loss of his source, but it highlighted the dangers of what Fernius was asking Tom to do. "I still don't understand why you want me for this. You have a ship with a crew and plenty of other resources."

Fernius leaned in and narrowed his eyes. "You have friends among the miners of the Kala settlement."

Fernius knew more than Tom had realized, and at this point would obviously know about Kerra and probably the rest of his experiences on Feth. By comparison, Tom knew little about his rescuer and current employer, but so far Fernius had been helpful and accommodating without asking much of him in return. Tom nodded. "I know one of them."

"It's likely that survivors from K2 have taken refuge at a

small factory within the field, and my source believed that the Guardian may be among the workers. A bold presence from any of my ships might cause the Guardian to avoid contact, but you may be able to use a more discreet approach."

Fernius leaned closer and lowered his voice to a near-whisper. "Time is also an adversary. I must know how to retrieve the Gashon Oraca before Daihn does, and you are my most expedient resource to gain access to the information I need. Bring me a way to contact the Guardian, and I will accept it as payment for the repairs to your ship."

Tom ran his fingers over the shallow etchings on the stone artifact, then looked back at Fernius. "I didn't realize anyone lived in the asteroid field except the miners."

"There are few, but since Daihn is looking for the Oraca in the field, I assume she believes it to be there. It's logical that the protector is close to that which it protects."

"But why would this Guardian help you find it after protecting it for so long?"

Fernius's expression shifted into a solemn frown. "Because it may be the best way to prevent misuse of the Oraca. Before my friend went missing, he relayed his belief that the Guardian is dying."

Tom nodded as a moment of silence passed.

Fernius picked up the flask of green liquid. "If we can convince the Guardian to give us the Oraca, I may be able to keep it hidden from Daihn, who would undoubtedly use the device for selfish personal gain."

"Hidden in your private collection."

Fernius smiled widely and softened his words. "What better place?" He poured the green fluid back into its original flask, causing the mechanical sequence to reverse, and the drawer slid closed. "On a small asteroid, a private outpost refines a popular beverage. I will place an order, and you will retrieve it for me. While you're there, locate the Guardian and obtain a secure method of contact."

It obviously wasn't a listed settlement, and that was yet another reminder of how little Tom knew about the fringe systems. The location was very close to the K2 colony, and he could have easily made it there if he'd known about it.

"There are undoubtedly many who know of the quest that is underway," Fernius said in a stern whisper. "Do not discuss your mission with anyone."

Tom ran his hand over the nearly invisible seam of the hidden drawer. "When will my ship be ready?"

Fernius's lip turned up in a satisfied grin. "I'll expedite repairs."

39

Tom made his way down a narrow corridor that led to the recreation center as his companion fluttered next to him.

"Okay, you have to admit that Hamburger Popsicle is kind of a mouthful. Do you have a nickname that I can call you?"

"*Liking Refrigerator Freezer.*"

"I meant something shorter. You know, easier."

"*You telling talking name.*"

"All right. What about Flyer?"

"*Better Hamburger Popsicle.*"

"Okay, that was just my first try. Let's see . . . I don't like Ham or Pop."

"*No ham-pop.*"

Tom ducked under a low shop sign that hung from the corridor ceiling, and his sidekick performed a backward aerial flip to maneuver under it as he flew.

Tom snapped his fingers. "I have it. How about Flip?"

His partner chittered while performing a double midair backflip.

"Do you like it?"

"*Naming is Flip grand!*"

"Flip it is, then. Let's grab something to eat on the way."

———◦◦◦———

TOM AND FLIP arrived at the packed recreation center with a bag of spiced pastry flakes. The perimeter of the large circular room housed several types of target simulators, each with a small group of players huddled around it. A cheer erupted from one of the groups each time a contestant swung a digital launcher or pulled a firing trigger. Several five-seat tables were concentrated near the middle of the room, each filled with players engaged in card games or some other noncomputerized amusement.

"Tom, over here!" The familiar voice was Risul's, who stood at the entrance to a side hallway.

Tom weaved around two tables where patrons sat at digitally enhanced board games. "Hi, Risul. What are you playing?"

"Not here. We have to go to the old factory. C'mon."

Risul turned and started down the hallway.

Flip fluttered toward the gaming tables. "*Watching round play tacking tick dough.*"

"All right, I'll see you back at the room." Tom turned to catch up with Risul. "What's down here? It looks like all the action is back there."

"All you can get there are simulations. The best pragging is in the old section."

"Pragging?"

"How's your marksmanship?"

"Like I said, I don't get much practice."

"Well, you'll get some today."

At the end of the walkway was a door that opened into an abandoned warehouse. Outdoor air circulated through large missing sections of wall, and a cool breeze met them as they entered. At the far end of the huge building, a small crowd of people stood holding some type of long-barreled rifles. Risul shouted as he quickened his pace. "Hey, wait for us!"

"You haven't missed anything," one of the players said. "The next ship isn't due for another ten minutes."

Risul got to the group first. "Everyone, this is Tom." He gestured to the group. "Tom, meet the Star Reachers."

Tom gave him a sideways glance. "Star Reachers?"

A lanky female alien that reminded him of the waiter at Eridia answered. "It's what they call us fringe system folk on Nanadet. That's my home planet."

Risul peeled off his thin vest and set it on an old storage box. "We wanted a name for our informal pragging team. If you're not happy in the core and travel to distant stars to get away from home, you're a star reacher."

Tom reflected on the description. "I guess that's not far from the truth though, right?"

Risul chuckled. "Well, it's not a very original name, but we're not trying to impress anyone, really."

"Unless a pragging tournament comes to Koyla," added the Nanadet native.

Risul exhaled. "Nieda, nobody wants to travel to Koyla for a pragging tournament. They're too busy betting on mech battles in the core systems to bother with us."

Someone in the group saw something through one of the small windows. "Early arrival!"

Everyone's attention turned to the sky, and rifles pointed

into the twilight. A freighter arrived in a cloud of green, and the players started shooting.

Tom panicked. "Risul, what's going on?"

"Pragging, Tom. First hit gets the pot of credits. I'll take the next round, and you can borrow my gun for the round after."

"I'm not shooting at any ships!"

"Relax. We only use splash rounds. No damage. I've pragged in a lot of systems, but some of the best players are here at Koyla Center."

"Splash rounds . . . don't do any damage?"

"It's a pastime among spacefarers. It isn't technically legal, but everyone knows it's harmless. Sometimes you get lucky and the pilots play along, diving and twisting to make it more challenging. But other times a spoilsport will get annoyed, so be ready to run if a ship heads our way."

It was now apparent to Tom that he'd wasted a lot of money on Feth paying for a hull integrity check, since the attack rounds had just splashed off the hull in powder form as intended. He passed when his turn came and instead watched the players argue about whose shot had hit first. Instead of a long rifle, one of the players in the second round used a small handheld sidearm. Lots of spacers carried some kind of self-defense weapon, and the unpredictable nature of living in the fringe systems made it a sensible precaution. He'd already had a close call with the tokchuk in the desert and was lucky that Mius had shown up when he did, but there was no telling when he might need to defend himself again. Hopefully he'd never need to use it, but it would be good to have some protection at the ready.

THE NEXT MORNING, Tom browsed the aisles of one of the local armories until an attendant approached. "Can I help you find something?"

"I've been thinking about getting some kind of sidearm for self-defense."

"All of that is over here," she said, motioning to the other side of the shop. Tom followed her to a wall where new and used weapons were displayed, with several exotic models locked inside cases.

"Are you looking for a pocket weapon or something holstered?"

"I'm not sure, really. I want to have something that's reliable and easy to use."

"Let's start with this." She removed an energy-based weapon from a display case and placed it on a padded mat.

"This is an R80-S20, and it's our most popular sidearm. It's the one you see most of the freighter crews and security teams carrying."

Tom picked up the weapon, which was comfortable to hold.

"It uses standard S20 energy cartridges, which are good for 200 shots. Eight hundred credits and worth every bit."

"Eight hundred is a little out of my price range. Do you have anything for around two hundred?"

"All right." She nodded toward the opposite end of the display case. "Let's look at our used stock." She took a few steps and removed a slightly larger weapon with a worn finish.

"This one's a different setup. Projectile based, eight-round capacity, and uses T4 ammo, which is getting hard to find, but it comes with an extra full magazine. It's also slightly less accurate than anything energy based, but for personal protection it should work fine, and I can take two hundred for it."

Tom held the weapon, and although it was heavier, it felt more balanced than the first. "Does it come with a holster?"

"Let me check in the back."

The gun had obviously been carried a lot, but the wear seemed cosmetic. The saleswoman returned with two holsters. "I have two used ones that will fit. One is a shoulder sling, and the other is a hip holster with a drop. I'll throw either one in as part of the deal."

The shoulder sling looked almost new, but it was tight across his chest, and the strap rubbed on his arm. The hip holster was worn but comfortable. It also made it easy to reach the weapon in a hurry. "I'll take this one."

"Okay. C'mon over here, and I'll get you cashed out."

⸻ ◈ ⸻

It felt strange to wear the sidearm as he walked to his room, but Tom also felt a bit more secure. It wouldn't help in a space battle, but it was something that might give him an edge in a face-to-face situation. A tokchuk might think twice before grabbing him if he fired a shot or two into the ground.

He was about to open the door to his room when Risul called to him from down the hallway. "Tom, did you get the message?"

"I just got back. What message?"

"Your ship is fixed. Fernius says it's being charged, and you can go to work when you're ready."

"Is it still in bay 12?"

"I don't know, but they'll tell you at the service counter."

Tom waved to his new friend. "Thanks, Risul." He opened the door to his room, and Flip jumped into flight. *"Ship is fixing flying!"*

"I guess I'm the last to find out. Let's go see it."

They made their way to the maintenance section, where a line of customers waited at the service counter. Tom was eager to see the new repairs, so while the attendants weren't looking in his direction, he entered bay 12 through an employee side entrance.

The first full meter of the *Hefty*'s nose had been replaced. It was a bright blue color, as he'd requested, and was completely smooth. The repaired surface was reassuring to the touch but was also a reminder of the real dangers he was about to face. As he ran his hand along the repaired section, a mechanic walked around the side of the ship, wiping thick gel from his hands onto a rag. "Is this your shuttle?"

"Yes. Did you do the work?"

"I did the grinding before the pecrite base layer. It took the guys five passes with the plasma caster to get the thickness right and two more to add the color. Should be good as new now though."

Tom looked at Flip and hit the control to lower the ramp. Flip zoomed in before it was completely down, leaving no doubt about his enthusiasm. *"Ready going flying."*

"Not too fast, partner. I want to get some charts of that asteroid field, and I still have to get my things from our room and check out."

They were returning to the Kala system with a clear mission—two missions, really. The pickup for Fernius was an actual order placed to supply one of his shops, but without knowing what type of situation his covert assignment might lead him into, he wanted to be as prepared as possible.

"Waiting mine your checking here."

"All right. I'll be back in about an hour."

After stopping at a navigation shop to download charts,

Tom returned to his quarters and scooped whatever personal items he'd placed on the desk into his duffle. A partially eaten piece of dried fruit sat on the top bunk, and he grabbed it to give to Flip.

He paused and looked around the room. Koyla Center might be the last safe place he'd be for a while. He slid his hand to his sidearm. Its use would be limited, but being better equipped was part of being better prepared. He also had Fernius's backing and the ability to communicate with Flip—as uncertain as that could be. Then there was the possibility of finding clues to Kerra's whereabouts, and that thought pushed aside the last of his nervous tension. He was ready.

40

The steady stream of freighters that stopped at Koyla made it easy to catch a tag, and Tom and Flip were soon on their way back to the Kala system. The order pickup would be easy, but he needed a way to find the Guardian using only a general location in an asteroid field. Fernius had warned him against sharing details with anyone, which seemed like sage advice, considering some of the individuals he'd already dealt with, so he and Flip would be the only ones to know about their covert assignment. Maybe he'd be able to sniff out clues by talking with the refinery workers, or there might be a separate settlement nearby that he could search. He looked at Flip, who was intently staring at the viewscreens. Flip was as keen an observer as anyone, so maybe he'd notice something useful while they were there. And, of course, any leads to Kerra or the miners might give him ideas—and possibly help him find her, too. He'd only have the time it took to pick up the shipment, maybe a few hours, but hopefully that would be enough to gather the information Fernius needed.

THE TAGALONG SOUNDED its destination alert, and Tom strapped in as the computer counted down. The compression field released, and the *Hefty* dropped into normal space right into the edge of a battle.

Two nimble single-pilot space fighters orbited a Thesine transport, and even in the dim light from the Kala sun, Tom could make out the gray and red stabilizer fins that unmistakably belonged to the *Damsel*. Kerra's ship returned laser fire from two midship-mounted defense turrets, but the *Damsel* was no match for the agile fighters, so it was only a matter of time before she would be crippled.

Tom looked to Flip as though he might have a suggestion as to what he should do, but Flip only stared at the battle with interest, no doubt taking mental notes for Fernius. One of the fighters scored a flat hit on Kerra's ship, and a stabilizer fin flew off, along with a splash of sparks. Tom winced at the blast and hit the comm panel. "Kerra, what's happening?"

"Tom? Is that you?"

"It's me. How can I help?"

"I'm not—" A volley of fire from one of the fighters raked across the *Damsel*'s comm antenna and disrupted her transmission. "—from the surface."

The *Hefty* was even less of a match for the attackers than the *Damsel*, but Tom wasn't going to stand by while they tore Kerra's ship apart. He engaged his main engines and pointed the *Hefty* toward the battle. There was no way his ship could maneuver fast enough to track the fighters, so he kept the *Damsel* out of his direct path and hoped one of them would cross his line of fire. If he anticipated it right, he could score a hit and at least help even the odds in her favor. He'd also draw fire to the *Hefty*, which should be able to withstand it better than Kerra's ship.

Tom flipped off the safety on the breaker gun trigger and waited, his stomach tightening each time one of the small ships scored a hit on the *Damsel*. It took a few moments for one of the fighters to maneuver into his narrow targeting field, and he adjusted his aim to fire directly into its flight path. A second before the ship reached the center of his targeting display, Tom squeezed the trigger and unleashed a stream of railgun fire. The rounds hammered across the hull of the aggressor, and it spun into a starboard roll away from the battle. The other fighter quickly targeted Tom, and bolts of energy raked across the hull of the *Hefty*. Tom pulled his ship into a slow curved path to try for a shot at the second fighter, but its nimble counterpart had already recovered and splashed another volley across his hull, this time hitting his starboard engine exhaust port. The engine sputtered, and the ship lurched. His flight controls fought him, and the *Hefty* headed straight for the distillery asteroid.

Fortunately, maneuvering to defend against the attackers had relied on technique instead of speed, so the *Hefty* wasn't moving very fast, but Tom killed power to the main engines to prevent another uncontrolled spin. He held the flight yoke with a white-knuckled grip. "Hold on, Flip. I'm not sure how hard the surface is."

Flip gripped the back of the seat tightly. "*Asteroid crasher.*"

The thrusters wailed as they slowed the ship, and by the time they reached the surface, their speed was the equivalent of a fast run. Tom fought to keep the nose of his newly repaired ship from digging directly into the surface as they hit the asteroid with a hard bounce. He cringed as the ore pods plowed fifty-meter-long furrows into the surface, blasting compacted dust into space until the *Hefty* ground to a stop.

Without any appreciable gravity holding it in place, the ship began to float upward, but a quick adjustment to the thrusters held it against the surface. As it sat motionless, the *Hefty* was now an even easier target. But instead of coming for him, the fighters continued their attack on the *Damsel*.

After a few more hits by the raiders, a brilliant flash of tangerine light shot into space from somewhere on the asteroid. The powerful bolt of energy passed through the continuing battle, missing any mark. Then a second blast caught both fighters in perfect alignment and destroyed them with the single shot, spraying brief showers of energy into space ahead of the scattering debris from each ship. Whoever had fired the weapon was either a master marksman or had been incredibly fortunate to catch the ships one behind the other. Either way, the battle was over.

Kerra's voice crackled through his comm panel. "Tom, are you okay?"

"I'm grounded, but in one piece. How about you?"

"We're headed back now to check for damage. Can you get to the distillery building?"

"I don't know yet. Let me check."

"I've already cleared you with the docking center."

Tom eased the thruster controls, and the ship responded. "I should be able to get there using thrusters."

"We'll see you there. It's good to see you, Tom."

Tom looked at Flip, who gazed intently at the image of the distillery through the starboard viewscreen. Between them and the structure, wreckage from a crashed ship jutted from the asteroid's surface. "You okay?"

"*Buckling safety shaking.*"

Tom strained to make out details of the wreck on the

viewscreen, but there wasn't enough light to see anything clearly. "It looks like we aren't the first to crash land here."

"*Busted cracking smack.*"

"Let's get inside and find out how bad the damage is."

Tom lifted off and moved just above the surface until he arrived at the bay door. It was small, and with the *Damsel* landed horizontally, there was only enough room left to fit maybe two more ships the size of the *Hefty*.

He set down on the gravity decking and shut down power to his engines as he watched the bay door close and waited for the *Hefty*'s external sensors to tell him that the bay had been pressurized with a stable atmosphere. The hangar was located partially underground, and dark green slime seeped from the rock that made up the lower half of the walls.

"You ready?" Tom asked Flip.

"*Liking friendly flyer female.*"

Tom hit the control to lower the ramp and stepped out, followed by Flip, who flew to the highest part of the bay to watch. A group of people were exiting the *Damsel*, and Kerra weaved her way across the bay to get to the *Hefty*, followed by an older woman who craned her neck as she searched the hangar for something or someone.

"Tom!" Kerra took him by surprise as she flung her arms around him.

"It's great to see you, too," Tom said. "Are you all right?"

"We're fine."

The older woman caught up with Kerra. "I see you know each other."

"Mother, this is Tom Sparker. We met on Feth a while back. Tom, this is my mother, Winnet."

"Pleased to meet you," Tom said.

"Did that crash do any damage?" Winnet asked.

"I don't think the landing did, but one of those blasts hit an engine."

"Tanger will sell you parts if you need any," Winnet said. "I'm sure I can get him to give you a discount."

"Tanger?"

She scanned the hangar again, expecting that their host would arrive soon to check on them. "He's the owner of this entire facility and the reason we're safe."

"Tom had something to do with that too, Mother."

"I wish I could have done more," Tom said, "but my ship isn't built for fighting."

The echoing clank of a heavy door from a far corner of the hangar drew their attention, and Tanger made his way to them with his slight limp. The rhythm of his gait was almost elegant in spite of his handicap. "Everyone in one piece?"

Winnet looked in his direction and motioned to him. "I appreciate your effort, Tom," she said, "but it was Tanger who saved us."

Tanger reached the small group and Winnet held out her arms to give him a quick embrace as she continued. "Although you could have shot them sooner."

"We had the pulse cannon set up to protect the refinery, and it took a few minutes to get it aimed in your direction. I tried a warning shot before we got it completely swung around, but the Jobjon aren't easily discouraged."

"It was fast enough," Kerra said. "All we lost was a stabilizer fin." She looked at Tom. "Tom, this is Tanger Ellis."

Tom shook his hand. "Thank you for your help. Why were they attacking?"

Kerra glanced at her mother before answering, and Tom sensed the tension between them. "We were going back to K2, but Daihn has put a bounty on any of the miners who escaped the attack."

"I'm sure she wants the rest of our ore," Winnet said. "Some people are never satisfied."

Daihn might have actually been looking for clues about the Oraca, but Tom heeded Fernius's advice and kept that information to himself.

"Well, we're all safe now," Kerra said with a sideways look at her mother. "Tom, I'd love to catch up, but it's going to take some time to check out the *Damsel*. Let's talk in the morning."

"That's a good idea." Tom turned toward the *Hefty* and gave a nod. "I don't know how bad the damage is, and the sooner I get a look at it, the better." He looked at Winnet and Tanger. "It was good to meet you both."

"Likewise," Tanger said.

Winnet and Tanger continued their discussion as Kerra returned to her ship, and Tom glanced up at Flip as he headed to the *Hefty*. "You coming or staying out here?"

"*Eating sooner hungry?*"

"Not until I check the damage, but you go ahead."

Something smoldered from the engine exhaust vent as they approached the *Hefty*.

"Well, it was great having a working ship for half a day."

"*Good ship reason breaking.*"

"You're right. I'm glad we came back. It's just that I seem to spend more time fixing it than I do flying it lately." He looked back toward the *Damsel*.

"*Liking friendly female?*"

"Of course I like her. She's a friend." Tom tramped up the ramp. "Let's get to work."

Flip fluttered inside and headed straight to the food

cupboard as Tom dug out a tool bag filled with fastener wrenches and driver bits. If something was still burning in the compartment, it would be better to get it out instead of waiting until the next morning. He wasn't looking forward to the added repair work, but the situation did offer one odd benefit. Now he had an excuse to spend more time at the refinery, and that meant more opportunities to find a way to contact the Guardian.

41

The next morning, Tom got an early start on the *Hefty*'s repairs. Getting to whatever was smoldering had proven to be too much to tackle the night before, and he still hadn't been able to reach the underside of the engine. Flip perched nearby, watching with great interest as Tom unfastened components one at a time to make room so he could reach the hidden area. The last of the obstacles required him to hold a wiring bundle to keep it from flopping down into the open space at the bottom of the engine compartment while he unfastened its attachment clip.

"Flip, would you get the medium fastener tool for me?"

Flip hopped into flight and picked the appropriate tool from a tray, then dropped it into Tom's free hand.

"Thanks. I should have this off in a sec."

He pulled a small, burned cylinder from the housing. It still smoldered a little, and Tom held it at arm's length to avoid the sour fumes. "The problem seems to be with the firing initiator."

"Part is stinky waffle."

"I hope Tanger has one that will work, or else we'll be grounded."

Kerra bounced up to the ship, carrying a small bag. "Good morning!"

Tom put the burned part on the deck and wiped his hands on a rag. "Something smells good."

Kerra wrinkled her nose. "Better than whatever you're cooking."

"The firing initiator is fried."

"I brought you some breakfast. They have a small selection at the commissary, and these looked good."

She held up the bag of freshly baked pastries, and Flip hopped over to get a good sniff. "*Mmm, tasty sticky smelling.*"

Kerra stared at Flip. "Did you just say something?"

"Kerra, this is Flip," Tom said.

"*Eating thanks snacking.*"

Kerra blinked. "I'm . . . speechless."

"I was surprised, too." Tom pulled a pastry from the bag. "These look great." He took a bite and handed a piece to Flip. "Any damage to the *Damsel*?"

"Aside from the missing stabilizer fin, just a few scrapes and burn marks."

Kerra pulled out a thin wafer with icing and they all ate for a moment. The pause in conversation gave Tom an opportunity to switch the topic. "Kerra, about the attack on K2 . . . I want you to know that I couldn't do anything to stop Daihn."

"You were there?"

"We were on the *Emu Ja'* when she attacked, and we almost got killed because I questioned what she was doing."

"There's nothing you could have done, Tom. Daihn's troops tore through the place."

Tom chewed on the doughy treat. "I don't understand why

she attacked the colony. She's cold, but outright stealing doesn't seem like her style."

Kerra's expression cooled. "The truth is that my mother borrowed some money from her and couldn't repay the loan on time."

Tom nodded. "That explains it. Have you been back there yet?"

"Yesterday was the first time we tried to leave Dag since we got here. The comm channels have been quiet, so if anyone else survived, they're not advertising it."

"*Please yummy bread again?*"

Tom handed Flip another piece of pastry, which he promptly stuffed into his satchel.

Kerra glanced at Flip. "And how did you find out it could, um . . . talk?"

"Well, we made it to Koyla Center where I got the *Hefty* repaired and Flip got a translator. Then Fernius gave me a job picking up an order here."

"Who's Fernius?"

"He owns and operates Koyla Center."

Kerra gave a nod. "Well, I'm glad you got away okay."

"We barely did." He looked around. "I wish I'd known about this place sooner. It would have saved me a lot of trouble."

"I didn't know about it myself until my mother told me after we escaped from K2. I guess Tanger's been trying to keep its location a secret, but ever since the attack, there have been lots of mercenary ships roaming the asteroid field."

"Maybe it's time to go someplace safer."

"We have to find out if anyone needs our help on K2 first, and my mother wants to salvage any equipment that's left."

"When are you planning to try again?"

"Maybe in a few days. How about you? Are you returning to Koyla soon?"

"Tanger said that production is slow, so I'm going to have to wait until he can fill my order." He nodded toward his ship. "Plus, I can't go anywhere until I make repairs."

"At least you found another job at Koyla."

Tom popped the last bit of pastry into his mouth. "Jobs like this are going to bankrupt me if I keep having to fix my ship."

"Maybe your luck will turn around soon." She held out the bag with both hands. "Here, have another."

42

Tom sat in the pilot seat while Flip took a midday nap on a throttle lever. Tanger had one of his workers looking through their parts stock to find a firing initiator that would work with the *Hefty*'s engine, so Tom had some time to work on his covert assignment. The Guardian had to be very old to have protected the Oraca for so long, so it made sense that it would be an alien. But only a couple dozen workers lived on Dag, and as far as he could tell, they were all human. The only unexplained thing he'd seen since he arrived was the shipwreck on the surface, and that's where he'd start his search.

Kerra's voice came through the comm panel. "Tom, are you there?"

Tom tapped the control. "I'm here."

"How about some lunch? My treat."

"I can't turn that down. See you at the commissary."

Tom hopped up and made his way to the small eating area at the other side of the hangar, where Kerra waited for him.

"At least everything is a quick walk around here," Tom said.

Kerra nodded and looked around. "It feels a lot like home to me, although it would be nice to live someplace with open sky someday."

They made their selections at the food counter before taking seats at the table nearest to the hangar.

"Did you notice the wreckage on the asteroid surface?" Tom asked.

"It's a crash site from some old ship. Why?"

"I was just wondering how it got there."

She shrugged. "Tanger said it was already here when they built the distillery."

"I think I'll go take a look at it. Want to come along?"

"I can't. I'm having the stabilizer fin replaced."

"Are you sure? You never know what you might find in an old wreck."

"I don't like space-walking." She gestured and made a face like she would vomit. "But you go ahead and have fun."

＊◦＊

TOM WORE a pressure suit and an old pair of gravity boots that he'd borrowed from the refinery equipment closet as he entered a small airlock next to the docking bay door. Once the pressure in the small chamber had equalized, he stepped out into the vacuum of space. The only appreciable light came from the glow of the distillery and his suit's headlamp, which was far too dim to see anything as far away as the wreck, but he was sure of its relative location to the distillery building, so he walked toward it at the pace that the gravity boots would allow.

It was his first time walking on an asteroid's surface. Other than countless cracks and an occasional impact crater dotting the landscape, it felt like walking on loosely packed dirt. Footprints from exploring workers marked random trails leading in all directions, but the gravity boot tracks diminished as he moved farther from the distillery.

At about the halfway point, his boot caught on a piece of metal that stuck a few centimeters out of the ground. His upper body kept moving, and he landed with his face shield in the layer of space dust that covered the surface. Twisting himself around to sit, he yanked at it, and the chunk pulled free. It was a roughly square access panel of some kind, made of metal so thick he'd hardly have been able to lift it in a standard gravity environment. He turned the unremarkable piece over as it floated in front of him, but it had no markings. Instead of letting it float as a potential hazard to ships, he shoved it back into a surface crevice before continuing away from the cloud of debris that his miniature excavation had caused.

In a few minutes, the wreck site became visible. But as he got closer, what had looked like an entire ship from a distance turned out to be only a few large pieces of hull sticking out of the ground. Desiccated green slime surrounded the base of each fragment where it disappeared into the surface. If more of the ship was here, it was completely buried. One of the large pieces of metal had unfamiliar markings that looked a lot like *DAG*. The letters were obviously just part of some other symbol from the ship, but now he knew how the asteroid had gotten its name.

It was unclear whether the scattered material was from a single shipwreck or was there for some other reason. What *was* clear was that whatever had happened, it hadn't happened recently, since the sections of wreckage that were near the ground had been buried by a thick layer of dust that would have taken a very long time to accumulate. There were no signs of any recent activity, and there weren't any clues that would lead him to the Guardian. It was a dead end.

43

Tom sat on the loading ramp of his ship and scrubbed some charred insulation from a wiring harness with the hope he'd soon have something to connect it to. It was time-consuming work, but it gave him something to focus on while he waited. Flip fluttered in from somewhere else in the hangar. *"Snacking many times good."*

Tom looked up at Flip, who had a bit of green liquid dripping from the corner of his mouth. "Tell me you didn't just eat some of that slime from the wall."

Flip licked the last bit into his mouth. *"Tasty slime. Better even pocket bars."*

"I don't think you're supposed to eat that until it's refined."

Flip hopped over to perch on Tom's tool box and knocked off two large attachment nuts that bounced down the ramp and into a small tunnel dug out of the wall of the hangar.

"Thanks. Now I have to go and find them."

"Jumping rolling pieces."

"Yeah. Try not to touch anything else." Tom put down the harness and had to duck to enter the small opening, which looked like part of an unfinished utility shaft. Someone had dragged in a portable lighting cable that was only partially working, and the flickering glow was barely enough to illuminate the thick trails of green slime oozing from the walls.

"I can hardly see in here. Can you bring me a light?"

"*Heavy too much light lifting.*"

There was no sense in trying to get Flip to make an attempt. He didn't like dirty spaces and Tom would be out before he could convince him to try. "Okay, fine."

Tom felt around on the slanted dirt floor for the nuts, occasionally plopping his hand in a puddle of slime, until he had both wet parts in his hands. "I should have made you come and find them."

Still crouching, he turned around toward the entry hole and took a step, but caught his foot on the lighting cable. His face slammed against the tunnel wall, right into a large blob of green ooze.

"Agh!" He spit out a bit of slime. A second later, he lost his footing completely, and his body twisted as he tipped toward the ground. He was falling but also watching himself fall from a distance, as if from a third-person perspective. His sense of time slowed as his upper body arched over, then his face hit the ground, snapping him back into real time as he was covered in more of the goo.

The tunnel began to change. It wasn't supposed to tilt or spin. It couldn't possibly, but it was. He stared at the *Hefty* through the tunnel opening. It was on the wall now, or was he on the ceiling? Images of small ships flew through space, crashing into asteroids. He flinched as one exploded on impact.

"Flip . . ."

A dull blue planetoid covered in jutting rock formations filled his vision.

"Fall more into feel okay?"

The light at the end of the utility shaft faded to black.

44

The planetoid rolled over and over in his mind. Tom stretched out his hand to touch it, but couldn't reach.

"How is he?" a female voice asked.

Tom's head hurt, and the image faded as he slowly opened one eye to find strangers standing next to him. He was on his back, and the bright light only made his head pound more.

"Coming to, I think. Tom, can you hear me?"

"Not so loud," Tom croaked.

"That's a good sign. We'll let him rest. Try to sleep, Tom."

"Huh?"

"We had to make sure you were okay. Just try to rest."

He wasn't in any condition to argue, or even ask who he was talking to. Tom gladly closed his eye and remained quiet, as his head hurt less that way.

Tom woke to the sound of fluttering as a familiar accompanying breeze hit his face. He forced an eyelid open. The storage room that had been outfitted with a few emergency medical supply cabinets and a bed seemed to have been put together more as an afterthought rather than a dedicated part of the station, but it had been quiet enough for him to get several hours of solid sleep.

"Hey, Flip," he groaned. "It's good to see you."

"*Many happy to waking.*"

Kerra followed Flip into the small room and set a tray of food down on the cart next to his bed. "Congratulations, you're one of the few people to survive accidental ingestion of unrefined dagart."

"What?"

"You got a mouthful of it when you fell in the tunnel. It's highly toxic to humans before it's distilled."

Flip landed on the tray to sample the smells from the hot dishes.

"Want something to eat?" Kerra asked.

"Maybe just a bite."

"So what happened?"

Tom took a sip of synthesized broth from a cup. "I think I tripped over a cable."

"I mean when you passed out. You were mumbling something when they found you."

"I got dizzy, and I saw . . . It was confusing."

"They said you were saying something about rocks and ships."

Tom narrowed his eyes as he worked to recall the experience. "I sort of saw myself in the shaft—from a distance though, but it was more like a *feeling* of seeing myself." He shook his head at the confusing memory. "But then that faded and I saw ships crashing and something Fernius showed me in his collection."

"What collection?"

"Fernius has a sort of odd collection of artifacts." A dull headache made him rub at his forehead. "But mostly I saw a small planet or some kind of large asteroid. I kept seeing that. It had a bluish crust, but I don't remember ever being there."

"Bluish crust . . . like a crystal?"

"Maybe. It was just . . . crusty. I guess it could have been crystal. Do you know what it is?"

"It sounds like one of the planetoids in the Kala field that I pass on my way to get water. It doesn't have a name that I know of, but it's covered with an unusual layer of crystal that looks blue in the dim light."

"I'm just glad the images have stopped," Tom said. "They made the dizziness worse."

"How do you feel now?"

"Rough."

"Well, the good news is that they found a part that'll work for your engine."

Tom finished the cup of broth as Flip tugged at a pastry until a small piece pulled away. "*Tasty bread cake.*"

"That's great," Tom said. "I want to get to my ship and pick up where I left off."

"If you think you're up to it."

He sat up, feeling his body ache from the bruising he took during the fall. "I'll feel better if I'm doing something."

She slid the tray out of his way. "Want some help?"

Tom groaned as he twisted to get out of the bed. "I'd appreciate it. Flip's a great helper, but he doesn't like to get dirty."

She grabbed his arm to help steady him. "It's a good thing

Flip was there with you. Nobody saw you go into that crawl space, and Flip is the one who found help."

Tom looked at Flip. "Thanks, buddy."

"*Awkward flooring is bad bounce.*"

Kerra squinted an eye and cocked her head. "What does that mean?"

Tom shrugged. "He's either saying that the floor was slippery or he's calling me clumsy. Either way, I'm glad he was there."

Tom took an unsteady step, and Kerra caught him. "Are you sure you don't want to rest more?"

"I'm okay. I'll feel better once I get moving."

He was right. By the time they got back to the hangar, Tom was moving on his own. He was ready to get his ship flying again.

45

They both had their hands in the starboard engine compartment of the *Hefty*. Tom strained to reach in as far as he could, feeling for the dropped fastener under the exhaust housing.

"Let me try," Kerra said.

Tom pulled his soot-covered arm out of the space, and Kerra touched her tongue to the corner of her mouth as she reached in, twisting to slide her shoulder into the narrow opening. "I think I've got it."

The small clank of the fastener dropping to the bottom of the engine compartment made them freeze. "I don't got it," she said.

"That's okay. I dropped at least two in there back on Copania. I like knowing that I have a small spare parts supply in there, even if it's just out of reach."

Kerra giggled, and Tom grinned. He wiped his hands on a rag. "I've got more in the parts bin."

As he tromped up the ship's ramp, Kerra looked at Flip,

who perched on a nearby railing. "Couldn't you get the fasteners out of there? You'd probably fit."

Flip looked at the opening, then at Kerra. "*Dirty nongreasy mess is mine.*"

"It's pretty dirty, all right."

Flip pulled a sticky piece of candied fruit from his satchel and licked at it.

"So . . . Flip. I've been wondering why you chewed up the wiring in my ship. Were you trying to stop me from getting to Feth?"

Flip looked at her with the tip of his tongue hanging from the corner of his mouth. "*Tasty insulated spaghetti snacking.*"

Kerra's eyebrows popped up. "That's it? Are you telling me you chewed through my tagalong wires because they tasted good?"

"*Accidental wire breaker covering.*"

"Well, that's good to know, I guess. But couldn't you have gone for a less critical system, like the landing light wiring?"

"*Flavor is tasty blue insulator. Yellow bitter snacking.*"

Her mouth hung open at the unexpected rationale. "I . . . would not have guessed that they tasted different."

"*Mmm, jelly icing.*"

She shook her head. "You're something else, you know that?"

Tom returned with a handful of assorted fasteners and spread them out on the service cart he was using. They picked through them, and he handed one to Kerra. "Try this one."

She reached back into the compartment and leaned against the housing, grinding soot into the side of her jumpsuit. "Got it."

Kerra stood, and Tom attached the housing cover. "Let's find out if that did the trick."

Tom went into the cockpit as Kerra backed away from the ship. "All clear out here!"

The engine roared to life, then quickly shut down again. Tom came back down the ramp, scrubbing his hands with a pasty cleaner, and handed a squeeze bottle of the scrub to Kerra.

"Thanks for your help," Tom said as he wiped the residue from his hands with a rag. "I should be good to go now."

"Tanger has your cargo packed whenever you're ready."

"I'll pick it up after I get everything cleaned up. It should just be a small box." Tom didn't have any leads on the Guardian, so his work at the refinery was done. But there was something about the visions that nagged at him, and he needed to reconcile what he had seen. "When will you be going back to K2?"

"We're planning to get an early start tomorrow."

"Why don't I come along? I'd like a chance to see that planetoid you were telling me about, and it's safer traveling with two ships."

"What about your delivery?"

"Another day or two won't make any difference."

Kerra glanced at her ship. "I have to admit that I'd feel better if you came with us."

Tom tossed the rag onto the service cart. "Just give me a call when you're ready, and I'll join you."

⸻ ◦ ⸻

FROM THE *DAMSEL*'S center level, Firkis glanced at the access ladders to the adjoining decks as he nervously rubbed at the metal trim on his jacket. Most of the miners were having a midday meal in the commissary, and the rest were working temporary jobs at the distillery. He tapped the controls on a small handheld device. It wouldn't be long until someone decided to come back to the ship, so he had to make the call quick.

A moment later, an image of Daihn appeared on a small screen. "I'm pleased that you have survived. Do you have information to share?"

"This is my first chance to contact you, and I don't have much time. They're going back to K2 tomorrow."

"Very well."

"I expect to be paid as soon as you have them."

"Your compensation will be proportionate to your results."

Approaching footsteps echoed off the cargo ramp below. "I have to go, someone's coming."

46

After Kerra had the *Damsel* out of the hangar, Tom lifted off with Flip in his usual position on the copilot seat backrest. There were no signs of other ships nearby, but Tanger had the defense system targeted toward their departure point in case of another attack. The plan was for the ships to hold position within firing range for several minutes in case someone attempted another ambush, then Tom would follow Kerra to K2 once the area looked clear. Most of the miners went along, but a few stayed behind to continue their temporary jobs at the distillery.

Tom's stomach rumbled. "I wish I'd had something to eat at the commissary before we left. Compared to food cubes and ration packs, it was like gourmet cooking."

"*Tasty eating fine doorknob.*"

"It should be a short trip to K2 via the asteroid field, but I'll have to weave a lot, so be prepared for sudden maneuvers."

"*Ready shifting rolling.*"

Flip hopped into the air and fluttered out of the cockpit. A minute later, he returned carrying an entire pastry, flapping his wings as fast as he could in order to keep the heavy load in the air.

"*Snack is fine weather eating.*"

"Where did you get that?"

Flip dropped the pastry into Tom's lap and returned to the backrest. "*Common-scary tasty snack.*"

The pastry left some sticky icing on his jumpsuit, but it still tasted great. "You're a pal, Flip. Thanks."

The *Damsel* was more maneuverable than the *Hefty*, but Tom kept up the best he could through the turns, and he made up time on the straightaways with his ship's more powerful engines.

As the *Hefty* rounded another huge asteroid, a strangely familiar sight came into view—a planetoid with a crusty blue surface. He hadn't passed it before, but the closer he got, the more certain he was that it matched what he'd seen in the dreams. It was strange to have the memory of being there while only now discovering that the place actually existed, and he stared at the fascinating sight. Kerra's transmission brought him back to the moment.

"Tom, we're close. Follow me to the large hangar, but don't land until I contact you. If there are any miners down there, I want to make sure they know you're with us."

Tom tapped the comm panel. "All right. I don't see any other ships, but be careful in case someone else decides to move in."

The *Damsel* moved closer to K2, and Tom stopped the *Hefty* to keep it at a nonthreatening distance.

"*Feeding happy sooner.*"

"If you're saying it's time for lunch, I agree."

Kerra's voice came through the comm sooner than he

expected. "Tom, the large hangar is damaged. Dock in the smaller hangar. I'll meet you there."

"Anyone else down there?" he asked.

"Some of the miners, but they know you're with me."

"We're on our way."

He increased engine power and adjusted course. "Looks like lunch will have to wait a little longer."

Tom entered the secondhand industrial hangar and landed on the worn gravity decking. Scorch marks covered the walls, and several large pieces of mining equipment had been blasted into rubble. Flip hopped into flight and headed for the galley counter as the engines powered down.

"You coming or staying here?"

"*Sooner meal mine now.*"

"All right, save some for me."

As Tom lowered the *Hefty*'s ramp, lingering fumes from vaporized metal burned his eyes. The odor made it preferable to breathe through his mouth, although he could still taste the acrid vapors. Kerra was just entering the hangar, along with two other men. "Tom, I'd like you to meet Shek—"

"Hey!" Shek Windham interrupted. "I know him." He pointed at Tom. "You work for the chekt."

Shek planted his feet and reached for his sidearm. Tom instinctively put his hand on his own. That made the other man pause as Kerra jumped between them. "Stop! Tom is here to help. He didn't have anything to do with the attack."

Shek stared at Tom. "I saw him on a power cell run to Feth, and I know he works for Daihn."

Tom locked eyes with the threat. "I did work for her, but not anymore."

Shek's voice lowered. "You're not welcome here."

Tom held his ground, but a firefight was something he

wasn't sure how to handle. He worked to keep his voice calm, hoping it would make him sound more confident than he felt. "Fine. I'm leaving."

"Tom, wait," Kerra pleaded.

"It's all right," Tom said as he backed up the ramp, his hand still on his sidearm.

Kerra kept herself positioned between the men and followed Tom into the *Hefty*. "I'm sorry, Tom. A lot of miners were killed in the attack, and they're not thinking clearly."

"It's not your fault. I'll wait for you to finish so we can head back to Dag together. In the meantime, I want to get a closer look at that planetoid."

"It shouldn't take us more than a few hours," Kerra said as she backed down the ramp. "Daihn took the last of the good ore that we had to leave behind, and there isn't much left here that isn't damaged beyond repair."

"Call me when you're ready," Tom said, hitting the control to raise the loading ramp.

"*Warm tasty dry watered*," Flip said as he tugged at a dehydrated food pack that was wedged onto a shelf.

"We're taking off." Tom ducked into the cockpit. "It'll have to wait until we get back into space."

47

Tom examined the features of the crystal-covered planetoid as they approached. An endless field of jumbled shards ranging from a few centimeters to several meters long extended over the entire surface, each of them reflecting pale cobalt light from the distant Kala sun.

"I'm sure I've never been here, Flip. But I saw it clearly when I . . . dreamed, or hallucinated, or whatever."

"*Sleeping lucky waking time.*"

"Did anything happen when you ate that slime?"

"*Tasty slime dessert.*"

Obviously it hadn't had the same effect on Flip, but the impression it left on Tom was something he couldn't shake. "I'm going to land to get a closer look."

Landing was easy, since the small body had no atmosphere and just enough gravity to hold the *Hefty* without the need to anchor, but the ship's instruments detected something that Tom didn't expect. "The landing system is reading a high surface temperature. How could a planetoid without an atmosphere be so hot?"

Flip fluttered onto a throttle lever and stared at the landing panel. "*Is warming inside?*"

"It must be."

Flip took flight again and headed into the main cabin. "*Warming snacking time.*"

Tom followed. "I guess this is as good a place as any to wait for Kerra." He pulled a meal pack from a storage cabinet and read the label. "How about a cheese wrap?"

"*Cheezy meal fold.*"

It was the last of the nearly expired meal packs he'd bought the day he'd met Kerra. "What do you think of her, Flip?"

"*Wire snacking ship.*"

"Huh? I'm talking about Kerra, not her ship." Tom sighed. "You know, it would be a lot easier for us to communicate if we got you a better translator."

Flip jumped onto the stove handle and defensively put both hands over the tiny device. "*Favorite this trains-later.*"

Tom leaned against the counter and stared through the stove window at the rehydrating meal. Melted cheese oozed from the ends of the wrap like the slime on the walls of the Dag asteroid, and his mind drifted back to their time there—and working with Kerra. "Communicating with her seems easy, like we have some chemistry or something. Know what I mean?"

Flip hopped onto the counter to get a better look at the warming food. "*Tasty communicating chemistry meal.*"

Flip was probably just referring to his upcoming lunch, but his odd wording made Tom ponder the strange comment. *Communication and chemistry.* The Dag slime was a complex chemical mixture. Was it possible that someone had deliberately encoded information into the slime? He shook his head. That didn't make sense. There was no reason to use such a dangerous method, and also no way for anyone to know that he would eat it to receive the images. But as his eyes wandered across the section of cockpit viewscreen that was visible from where he stood, he couldn't deny that the planetoid was exactly as it had appeared in the visions, and that made something else feel more important. He'd told Kerra that the visions had included something Fernius had shown him, but what he hadn't told her was that it was the Oraca tablet. He'd seen it clearly in the dreamlike experience, and it felt like more than just chance that the planetoid and the tablet stood out so distinctly. It was more like a deliberate message that this place and the Oraca were somehow connected.

"Tom!" Kerra's voice broke his concentration. "We're under attack."

Tom jumped up and ran to the cockpit to answer. "What's happening? Who is it?"

"It's Daihn. She has an attack shuttle headed to the surface, and we don't have any way to fight."

A chill ran through him. "I'm coming."

"No, Tom. You can't get here before they do. Get back to Dag and tell Tanger what happened. Maybe he can—"

Kerra's transmission was cut off. If Daihn still had a debt to collect from the miners and they couldn't pay, she'd kill them to protect her reputation—a pointless slaying to satisfy her alien code of conduct. The troop transport appeared on his port viewscreen, and to starboard were the asteroids that led back to Dag. If he did as Kerra asked, he could save himself. But her life was at stake, as well as the lives of at least a dozen other miners. His hands trembled with cold sweat, and his head swiveled between viewscreens as he processed the dilemma.

"Going friendly asteroid?"

"We can't leave them, Flip, but I don't know how to help, either."

"*Nicely asking release friends.*"

"I wish it were that easy. The only things Daihn cares about are accumulating power and that blasted chekt code."

Chekt code. The connection of the planetoid to the Oraca was only a guess, but Daihn might be willing to bargain for information about his experience. If the visions were a clue to the Oraca's location, it could mean handing it over to an interstellar tyrant, but he wasn't going to let some galactic bully kill his friends if he could help it.

Tom tapped the communication controls to broadcast on an open channel and cleared his throat to speak in his most confident voice. "Exalted Daihn, this is Tom Sparker. I have information to trade." A moment passed with no reply, and Tom amended his proposal. "Information . . . about the Oraca."

Daihn's reply sounded tinny through the *Hefty*'s comm system. "You demonstrate resilience, Tom. What is your proposal?"

"I have information related to the Oraca, and I'll trade it in exchange for fulfillment of the miners' debt and the remainder of my original contract with you."

He might as well go for broke and try to clear his own contract as well. If the Oraca was as valuable as Fernius claimed, even a thin piece of information would be worth more than he was asking.

"What is the nature of the information?"

Nature of the information? He barely had a theory, but he had to come up with something that sounded worthwhile. His desperation pushed out a bold claim.

"A clue to the location of the Oraca." He winced. Even the strong visions didn't support that kind of conclusion. If Daihn went for it, he'd have to do some embellishment to sell the dreams as real.

A moment later, the *Emu Ja'* launched a scanning probe, and it headed for the planetoid. Daihn sounded as confident as ever.

"I wonder, Tom, why have you landed there?"

Tom didn't have a good answer. The planetoid was the clue he had to trade, and if Daihn had figured that out so quickly, he'd already lost his bargaining chip. "I was waiting for the miners to recover their equipment."

The probe anchored itself to the planetoid and began transmitting data to the *Emu Ja'*. "A molten core," Daihn began. "Unusual, but . . ." Her voice trailed off with uncharacteristic curiosity. "There is an object within."

That gave his theory—and his confidence—a sudden boost, and he saw another opportunity. Daihn's slip on the open comm channel meant that anyone could have heard that there was something inside, maybe even the Oraca itself, and it was unlikely she had a way to get to whatever it was before others started arriving, but Tom might.

"Instead of the information I offered, I'll get whatever is in there for you, along with my original terms."

He was answered with silence. Maybe he'd overplayed his hand and now Daihn was angry enough to kill them all. He held the smooth control yoke tightly, ready to make a run for cover if the situation called for it. His eyes darted to his starboard viewscreen as he unconsciously took shallow breaths. If he bolted to the other side of the planetoid, maybe he could get into the field by using the planetoid for cover until he was deep enough that Daihn wouldn't bother to follow. The moment stretched out too long.

"Is your craft capable of retrieving the cargo?"

Good, she was talking. Tom relaxed enough to inhale fully.

"My ship is designed for it, but I'll need a check of my magnetic seals and HF systems before I go in. I'll also need to remove my tagalong, and I might need a grappling device."

"Proceed into the docking bay for the needed maintenance checks and equipment, and we shall proceed as you have proposed."

"I'm on my way."

As he pulled the *Hefty* from the surface, a giant green cloud appeared in distant space. Flip, who had been silently observing, broke the momentary calm. "*Cloudy smoke ship!*"

The diadu that emerged moved straight toward the *Emu Ja'*, and Daihn's voice tensed as it crackled over the comm system. "Circumstances have been altered. You must proceed into the planetoid immediately."

"But I can't without—"

Daihn's voice snapped. "Does your ore-collection system function?"

"Partially, yes."

"The object is merely twenty centimeters in diameter, so additional hardware will not be required to retrieve it. It's approximately two kilometers below your current location."

"I need to make sure the magnetic seals on my ship will hold before I go in."

"There will be no opportunity to check your craft. The object is most certainly a protective container of some type. Bring me this container undamaged and unopened, and I will accept it in accordance with your previous request. Fail, and I will be obliged to exact contractual compensation from the prisoners."

Tom knew what that meant. Either he could risk his life inside the planetoid, or he could run while Daihn dealt with the corporate ship. But if he ran, he'd be abandoning Kerra and the others. If his ship didn't survive the magma excursion, it might mean he'd sacrifice himself in vain, but it was the only choice he could live with.

"How will I get below the surface?"

A more friendly although still tense voice replaced Daihn's. "Stand by, Tom," Mius said from his station on the *Emu Ja'*.

"*Check ship friend.*"

"Yeah, at least there's someone there who isn't trying to kill us."

The *Emu Ja'* stopped its advance toward the planetoid, and a large door on its underside slid open.

Mius's transmission crackled. "Move away from the surface on a course perpendicular to the launch trajectory of the *Emu Ja'*."

Tom quickly put some distance between the *Hefty* and the surface as the *Emu Ja'* launched a hulking object at the planetoid.

"I'm clear."

The device slammed into the rock and anchored itself just before it exploded, focusing a charge into the crust and opening a way into the molten core.

Daihn returned to the channel with final instructions. "I will delay as long as is practical. Return quickly."

The comm switched off. They were on their own.

<h1 style="text-align:center">48</h1>

Daihn kept her focus on the diadu as it drew closer. She pointed at the viewing window. "Hard to port. Get us behind that asteroid group."

The *Emu Ja'* moved with surprising agility for a big ship, and the maneuver shielded them just as the diadu opened fire. Bright flashes of destructive blue and white energy lanced through space and tore chunks from their asteroid shield. But it took only moments for the diadu to maneuver around the barrier and lash out again. Bolts of light splashed off the *Emu Ja'*, and the ship rocked.

"Full ahead." Daihn pointed. "Then get us behind that large one." Her crew worked in concert to put both distance and obstacles between the ships, but it was only a cat-and-mouse game to buy time. More bolts of energy rocked the ship.

Mius steadied himself at his monitoring station. "Shields at ninety-two percent."

Sparks flew from one of the weapon stations, and the human controller dodged them as a saazu dutifully doused the flickering threat with a fire suppressant. She looked back at Daihn. "Should we return fire?"

Daihn held up a hand. "No. Redirect all energy weapon power to the shield system." The diadu was too big for her to do any significant damage, so keeping her shields working was the best way to prolong her distraction of the destroyer—hopefully long enough for Tom to complete his task. But despite the agility and enhanced defenses of the *Emu Ja'*, at some point she would have to leave. "Keep us behind cover as much as possible, but make sure they can see us. I want them to remain engaged. And be certain the interstellar drive is kept online. If anything threatens our ability to leave, inform me immediately."

Daihn's brow furrowed. Her comment on the open channel was a stupid mistake, but it was done. The corporate factions were already pursuing her for her rightful seizure of the corporate yacht according to Kahr, as well as other fair actions she had taken to gain advantages over her competitors. But the open communication had led them straight to her. Now that they also knew of the planetoid and what might be hidden there, they would stop at nothing to get to it first. If the object was a clue to the Oraca's location, she wanted it. And if it was the Oraca itself, it was worth any cost to obtain.

49

Aside from a burning desire to be discharged from service, Tanger's short military career had also left him with cybernetically enhanced reflexes and an array of finely tuned senses. Even if nobody else could feel the vibration, he could. "It's getting stronger. How about excavator number two? And what's the temperature in tunnel three?"

A young conveyor operator did his best to keep up with Tanger's rapid-fire questions. "It's not even online, sir."

"What about the condenser or the wash basin we just installed on the new line?"

"I'll check those next, sir."

His entire fortune was invested in the distillery, and they were already behind on order fulfillment. An equipment breakdown now would mean he'd default on supply contracts. Stellar Dagart was popular, but his competitors had plenty of other options for customers that he couldn't serve, and that could wipe him out financially.

"Sir, something's wrong."

"Don't tell me what I already know."

"Shaft two just went dark."

A muffled explosion made the walls rattle, and both men steadied themselves. The tremor subsided, and Tanger wiped condensation from the control room window. The slowly drifting stars meant that their formerly stationary asteroid was now in motion. "Pull up our orientation."

"To what, sir?"

"To anything. We're moving and I want to know why."

The operator scrolled through data screens and brought up a map of the asteroid field. "We seem to be rotating, but I can't tell if we're moving through the field."

Tanger relaxed his hold on the console panel and exhaled. The minute g-forces created by the slow spin of Dag told him more than the refinery sensors could. He stared into space. "How many delivery shuttles do we have in the bay?"

The operator checked a status screen. "We have two, not including your ship."

Tanger pulled himself from the window and headed out of the control room. "Get our entire stock loaded onto those shuttles, including all of the raw product."

"What's happening, sir? Are we moving through the field?"

"Yes, and we're accelerating."

50

Tom brought the *Hefty* to hover over the hole made by the blast where liquid magma had surged to the surface. The oozing fire was not something he'd ever instinctively go toward, much less into, but his ship was built specifically for this purpose—he swallowed—forty years ago. A quick glance at Flip showed him staring wide-eyed at the viewscreens. "Sorry you got caught in here for this."

"Bubbly orange swimming?"

"We should have plenty of room to get through that opening, but hold on to something. I've never taken a ship into anything like this, and I'm not sure how it's going to react."

Tom positioned the *Hefty* and pushed the nose of the ship beneath the surface of the already cooling access point until the magma drives were covered by molten rock. The attached tagalong drive quickly melted, and its display lit up with alerts.

"So much for tagging out of here." With his ship sticking halfway out of the blasted opening, he closed his engine vents and exhaust ports to protect them from the intense heat they would be exposed to once they were underway.

He'd never even slid open the cover of the subsurface mode power panel that was positioned overhead, but it moved easily, and he flipped the largest of the switches. The interior lights turned red, and the ship's viewscreens changed to display a graphical representation of the dense fluid. Magma viscosity, flow, and density could vary even over short distances, so identifying target ores required the specialized telemetry. It was something Tom had never seen. "Well, that's good . . . I think."

"*Hotter soup riding into redness.*"

"Let's hope the magnetic seals hold . . . and the camera ports . . . and the vent covers." He pushed out a sharp breath. "I never planned to do anything like this."

Formed from a single-piece casting, the hull was designed to maintain its strength and durability at extreme temperatures and pressures. It also had a low friction coefficient, which made movement through viscous liquids easier. But neither feature would help if any of the critical magnetic seals failed. Not only had he made a deal with the most dangerous being he knew, but now he was taking them into the most hostile environment he'd ever been in.

Tom hit the activation sequence to start the magma drives, but instead of powering up, the ship jerked suddenly and began to quickly sink into the thick liquid. He spun to the main engine controls to back the ship out, but it was too late. The *Hefty* was already completely submerged, and exposing any of the conventional engines or thrusters to the intense heat would simply destroy them before they did any good. He returned to the magma drive panel and frantically tapped at the controls.

"*Go inside rocking hot?*"

"I'm trying!" He reset the startup sequence, and his gut went hollow as the panel lights all shut off. They were in the worst possible position—sinking without propulsion and with no way to abandon ship.

"I'm really sorry I did this."

"Making broken working?"

The walls of the ship began to radiate heat into the cabin. "I don't know how. I've never even started the drives." He mentally kicked himself for attempting to use a system that he'd never tested. Magma missions were risky under ideal conditions, and he should have known better than to assume a forty-year-old ship that probably hadn't seen that type of service in a decade would actually work as designed.

"Smelling smoky turnips."

Something did smell like it was burning, but the immediate problem was their uncontrolled descent. The magma drives were the only method of propulsion the *Hefty* had that could function while submerged, and without them, the ship would keep sinking until some other critical system failed. This might have been his worst decision ever, and Tom banged his fist on the controls. The drive panel lit up, and a rumble vibrated the ship for a split second before going silent again. "Wait, what happened?"

"Bumbler rumbler."

Tom's eyes widened. "Yeah, but something must be loose."

Now that he had a possible solution to focus on, he scrambled for a fastener wrench from beneath the copilot seat and pulled the tiny magma drive control assembly from its ceiling mount. The wires that connected it to a cable bundle looked new.

"All the wiring looks fine."

Tom pushed at the components attached to the underside of the small panel, and as he pressed a switch housing, the magma drives jumped again. "Ah! It must be a bad switch."

It was the same type of foil-clad switch that he'd worked on during his gravity decking overhaul, and he knew that pulling open the switch housing would result in the spring-loaded contacts falling out in a mess that would be impossible to reassemble. He flipped the copilot seat up again and dug beneath the spare parts and debris until he found a piece of scrap foil that was left over from the decking job.

"Flip, grab a piece of that bundling wire from the small tool bin."

Flip hopped into his fastest flutter toward the rear of the ship. Tom gently slid the foil strip into a seam on the side of the switch housing and pinched it between the switch body halves. Flip arrived with a piece of stiff wire that Tom used to tightly bind the halves together, then allowed the patched assembly to hang freely.

"Cross your fingers." He flipped the switches in sequence again, and the magma drives roared to life as the *Hefty* lurched forward. "Yes!"

"*Making good ship swimming.*"

"That's right." He clutched the flight yoke with both hands. "Good ship swimming."

The molten rock rubbing along the hull made a sound like a badly tuned bass trumpet, but they were moving forward.

"Let's see if we can find whatever is in here."

The virtual images on the viewscreens began to shift as the sensor data transmitted magma density and flow in remarkable detail. Daihn's acoustic probe had detected the object two kilometers from the surface, and it was a reasonable assumption that the deeper they went, the hotter it would get. Tom followed the temperature increase as he learned how to use the scanning equipment in a hurry. The magma display was mesmerizing, showing streaks and blobs of fluid dynamics as the *Hefty* pushed through.

There was no way to know how long Daihn would be able to wait, and according to his subsurface speed indicator, a four-kilometer round trip would take him fourteen minutes. Hopefully that would be quick enough to retrieve whatever was down there and rendezvous with the *Emu Ja'* before it was forced to flee.

51

"Energy shields are down to forty-one percent," the systems monitor reported.

"Continue to evade. Target the secondary aft weapons at the face of the next asteroid."

The *Emu Ja'* rounded the giant rock, using it as a shield from the diadu's weapons, and Daihn gave the order. "Fire!"

Quick trails of light streamed toward the surface, and as the missiles exploded, a dozen large pieces of rock flew from the face of the asteroid directly into the path of the diadu. Its energy shields glistened as they absorbed the impacts, and it answered with another volley that rocked Daihn's ship.

"Shields at thirty-eight percent."

"Take us up and over, and put more distance between us."

Another blast shook the *Emu Ja'* and Daihn nearly fell out of her chair. The scent of singed electronics drifted through the bridge.

"Our shields have failed in section five," Mius said as his display lit up with alerts.

"Primary shield strength is at twenty-six percent," the systems monitor added.

Daihn clenched her armrests so tightly that her fingertips turned white. "Keep that section directed away from incoming fire, and get us farther away."

The *Emu Ja'* raced to put the next asteroid between them, and the extra distance kept the next few shots from hitting. As the bolts of light streaked past the viewing windows, something launched from the corporate ship toward the planetoid that was too large to be a simple probe. Daihn pointed at the bright flash of propellant. "Move to intercept that craft."

The maneuver made the *Emu Ja'* an easier target, and another volley struck the ship hard. Wisps of white smoke drifted from the rear of the bridge.

"Primary shield strength is at ten percent."

"We're within weapon range," the tactical operator said.

Daihn had a clear view now. It was an automated mining drone, and it was speeding for the new opening she had made in the planetoid's surface. "Fire starboard primary weapons. Destroy that craft!"

Red bolts of light sprayed from the *Emu Ja'*, one of them striking the mining drone with a crippling hit that sent it spinning off into open space.

More fire from the diadu struck the *Emu Ja'*, which corkscrewed to evade the next volley. Then Daihn saw something unexpected in the distance. A large asteroid was quickly moving toward them. Small traces of light sped away from the rock as it adjusted its course to target their position.

"Identify that object," Daihn said. "Is it natural or artificial?"

Mius ran a quick scan of the newcomer. "It's the asteroid used by the Stellar Dagart distillery. Common mineral composition with trace organic compounds laced throughout, but I'm not detecting any source of propulsion that would explain its movement."

As the asteroid got closer, it became obvious that the small dots of light were ships fleeing the surface.

"Maneuver to put the destroyer between us and the incoming asteroid."

The *Emu Ja'* looped into an upward roll, forcing the corporate ship to turn away from the incoming asteroid if it wanted to continue its pursuit. But instead of chasing Daihn, the diadu was already turning to face the new threat. The destroyer pounded the Dag with a barrage of energy weapon fire, but the blasts couldn't penetrate more than a meter, and the Dag's rotation made it difficult for the diadu to concentrate its firepower.

The corporate ship began to back away, but the Dag was moving too fast for it to evade, and it collided with the large ship, sending fragments of rock and scraps of metal into space. The destroyer tried to turn, but the Dag pressed its contact and ground at the hull, forcing the behemoths to move as one. With rock and metal pressed together, the giants wrestled in a winner-take-all death match.

52

The burning odor was getting stronger.

"Flip, see if you can find out where that smell is coming from." His winged companion flew out of the cockpit.

Even if there was no fire, something was overheating. And if it was the magnetic seals that were failing, it would only be a matter of time before there was a breach. The ship's cooling system turned on and rumbled as it worked to maintain a comfortable temperature.

"*Hot not smoking,*" Flip said from the main cabin.

That was good, but they were already over a kilometer deep and the pressure on the seals was increasing. A bright green dot appeared on the forward display next to an analysis marker that indicated a high-density object.

"Aha!"

"*Finding splashy dot container?*"

"I sure hope so, because it's the *only* thing I can find." Tom tweaked their route to make sure it was as direct as possible.

The next minutes passed quickly as he watched the distance to his target narrow.

Without warning, a circuit under the forward console popped, and the port viewscreen blinked off. Tom flinched and waved away the puff of white smoke. "I think we just lost a mag seal on one of the cameras."

The forward display indicated that the object was within a hundred meters, and it was the size Daihn said it would be. Finally, some luck. It should be small enough to fit inside the starboard pod. He opened the ore pod gates and slowed the ship to maneuver more precisely. A tiny display screen near the pod controls showed the exact position of the object relative to the forward collection gate, and Tom carefully moved the *Hefty* to capture it. The green dot on the display that represented the target disappeared.

"I hope that means we got it."

Tom closed the pod gates and engaged the magma drive throttle to full as he swung the *Hefty* as tightly as he could back toward his entry point. He leaned back in his seat, relieved to be on their way out, but the small puff of pungent gray smoke that drifted into the cockpit put him back on high alert.

Flip's translator took on a frenzied tone. *"Orange leaking into fire!"*

One of the upper seals on the main ramp hatch was failing. Magma oozed through and dropped onto the cabin floor.

"Smelling hotter dropping!"

Tom set the autopilot and jumped out of the cockpit to assess the breach. "We're on our way out."

Sparks flickered from the place the magnetic seal was failing. He didn't have an emergency plan for hot magma dripping into his ship, and a frantic search for something to cool the blaze came up with only a single small fire-suppression canister. Using it on hot magma would be like spitting on a campfire. So far, the molten rock was piling onto the gravity deck, and while it was melting through, it would stop once it hit the pecrite hull beneath. He'd save his suppression canister in case something more combustible ignited. Tom pulled the small box of Stellar Dagart from an otherwise empty tool bin and dashed back to the cockpit. If they made it out alive, he'd need to salvage as much as possible, and the delivery was the most valuable thing in the cabin. "There's nothing we can do about the leak. Stay there and let me know if anything else starts burning."

"Making smarter leave soon."

He held his free hand in the air as he looked back at Flip. "What do you think I'm trying to do?"

Tom shoved his cargo behind the copilot seat and checked the subsurface display. Their speed was steady and the temperature of the surrounding magma was decreasing. Hopefully that meant the auto-nav system was correctly backtracking their course toward the cooler surface. He only needed five more minutes.

Flip darted into the cockpit, trailing a wisp of smoke. *"Oranges sparking balls."*

Tom spun toward the main cabin, where several small fires had started. He grabbed the suppression canister and discharged the entire can into the cabin, then slammed the cockpit hatch shut, sealing them inside. "That's it. Let's hope we get out of here before a critical system fails."

Flip sat on the copilot seat and squeezed between the lap belt strap and the backrest. *"No more trips hot rocking."*

"I feel the same way, pal."

A loud bang from somewhere in the ship made Tom jump. The air that blew into the cockpit went still as the ship's cooling system failed. Bright yellow flashes flickered through the small window on the cockpit door as flames licked the ceiling of the main cabin, and the radiant heat from the hull made the walls feel like they were closing in on them.

53

The grinding continued as the diadu fired bolts of energy, but the Dag pressed hard against it, making it too close for any of the destroyer's remaining weapons to score more than glancing blows.

Mius looked between the spectacle and his workstation panels. The scanning capabilities of the *Emu Ja'* were state of the art, and he probed deeper to find some explanation for what they were watching. None of his readings suggested the influence of any technological control over the asteroid or a method of propulsion, but its attack strategy was too focused to be part of any natural phenomenon. "I'm detecting electrical signals running throughout the asteroid, but they're inconsistent with any known system of control."

Scrolling through another screen of readings, he stopped at a graphical representation of an incredibly complex but organized pattern of data that suggested a possible explanation. He looked at Daihn. "The scans show what looks like some kind of neural pattern."

Daihn showed no sign of curiosity about the unusual readings, and instead looked between the planetoid and the battle that was distracting the corporate ship. The entrance they had blasted for Tom had cooled, and was no longer visible.

"What is the status of the surface?"

"No sign yet," Mius said.

He knew that as long as the destroyer was occupied, Daihn would wait. But if her ship was in danger of being captured or destroyed, she would have to leave. Repair crews had begun to restore critical systems and redirect emergency power to the defensive shields, and with some luck, they would have enough time to get the *Emu Ja'* ready for a final round.

A bright light from the battle caught Mius's attention. The destroyer had changed its tactic. Instead of trying to maneuver to use its weapons, its powerful engines flared to maximum. The Dag had a huge size advantage, but the diadu's massive engines countered its push and drove the Dag across space toward the planetoid.

"Move us closer to the surface," Daihn said, "but keep us out of the destroyer's weapon range."

The Dag refused to stop its own relentless press against the giant ship, and the two behemoths remained locked together as the Dag ran out of room. With a crash that splashed great seams of rock and crystal into space, the corporate ship pinned it against the planetoid surface. It was a shrewd move by the captain of the diadu, as the maneuver caused even more damage to the destroyer, but the Dag was now trapped, and the diadu pressed its attack. The destroyer's engines continued to blaze at full power until the Dag began to deform. Its shape flattened slightly under the immense pressure, then visible fractures appeared as the bow of the destroyer pushed beneath its surface. In one sudden jarring movement, the Dag split into two pieces. The giant chunks drifted slowly apart as they spilled streams of green liquid into space, and the unusual electrical activity Mius had read moments earlier disappeared from his readings.

With its attacker neutralized, it didn't take long for the diadu to start moving toward the *Emu Ja'* again, and they were nearly out of options. Even badly damaged, the destroyer was still a serious threat. With the energy shields failing, a single hit could cripple or destroy their ship.

"Get us to the opposite side of the planetoid," Daihn ordered.

The diadu matched its course as the *Emu Ja'* sped to use the planetoid as cover. Several weapon blasts from the destroyer failed to hit their mark, probably due to damage it had sustained during its fight with the Dag.

"Transfer all available power to the energy shields."

An indicator flashed on Mius's holodisplay. "I'm detecting activity at the entry point."

The planetoid's surface appeared calm to their naked eyes, then sparks of light popped up and increased in intensity until breaker gun rounds were shooting out like a fountain.

The *Hefty's* forward momentum carried it out of the molten rock and into space as bits of cooling slag fell away from the slick pecrite. The small ship started its engines and headed for the *Emu Ja'*, which closed in on its position.

"Make sure those bay doors are open," Tom said over the comm. "I'm coming in with some hot cargo."

"Hurry, Tom," Mius responded. "We've got to get out of here."

Slowing the *Emu Ja'* to rendezvous with the *Hefty* gave the diadu a chance to close its distance, and it sent several bolts of fire that lit the space between the three ships as it crested the horizon of the planetoid.

The *Hefty* matched Daihn's course and aimed for the docking bay to make a hasty landing. It splashed through the energy barrier into an automated cargo lift, pushing it along the deck until it crushed it against the hangar bulkhead, cushioning the *Hefty*'s abrupt stop. A tremor ran through the hangar as Daihn activated her interstellar drive, and green haze swallowed the *Emu Ja'*.

54

Tom and Flip were still trapped inside the *Hefty*'s cockpit while the rest of the interior burned, but within seconds, saazu had bypassed the ramp lock and quickly put out the fire in the cabin. Tom opened the cockpit hatch, and Flip flew out ahead of him through the smoke. Choking a bit on the fumes, Tom looked back as he caught his breath. The *Hefty* was in bad shape. Life support had failed as they were exiting the planetoid, and the alerts that had lit up on the panels told him much of the internal circuitry had been damaged or destroyed.

Daihn was first to enter the docking bay, followed closely by Mius and an armed human security force.

"Open the ore pods immediately," Daihn said as she approached the smoking ship.

"It's in the starboard pod," Tom said, pointing.

Saazu workers pried the ore gates open. They extracted the block of glowing rock and slid it onto a hoverdolly as they continued to cool it using a stream of viscous liquid.

All attention was on retrieving the pod. Tom looked around the bay at the armed guards, busy saazu, and Daihn herself, who stood silently with her arms folded, gazing intently at the block of cooling rock. All he could think of was what might happen if he'd missed capturing the object somehow and there was nothing for them to retrieve. But in moments, the recovered object was easy to spot, as it had settled at the side of the block, and saazu chipped away carefully with powered hammers until the dull gray sphere popped free. One of the workers brought the object to Daihn. As she turned it in her hands, the muddy ball smeared the loose sleeves of her otherwise immaculate white robe.

Mius stood next to her. "It looks like a pecrite mine pod."

"No doubt a protective shell for the most valuable treasure in the galaxy," Daihn said.

Mius leaned in to get a better look. "Or something left over from an old mining expedition."

One of the workers scanned the item with test equipment. "I'm getting intermittent readings that correlate to the expected age, but also indications of a more modern source material. It might just be contamination from our extraction process."

Daihn nodded to one of the saazu, who took the pod and carefully inserted it into an elaborate clamping device. A slight scraping accompanied the twisting of the halves, and the saazu handed the weighty unlocked sphere back to Daihn. With the attention of everyone in the bay silently fixed on the pod, she pulled the two halves apart.

There was nothing inside. Another scanner operator examined both halves with a wave of a test probe and shook his head at Daihn. "Solid pecrite."

Daihn glared at Tom. "You have failed."

Tom felt his skin flush. Daihn wasn't casually sending him off to an unknown fate this time; she was accusing him of an unfulfilled bargain. The last time he'd faced her, he'd gone silently to what had amounted to an execution attempt, but not this time. The only tool he'd used with her that had actually worked so far was contractual bargaining, and that gave him a foothold on the moment.

Tom took a step forward. "No." He motioned to the pod. "I retrieved the object undamaged and unopened, just like you said. I did my part."

He was right. That was the deal, as proposed by Daihn herself. She'd broadcast that on an open comm channel, and chekt code would demand that she abide by the terms of their agreement.

Daihn's cold stare mellowed as everyone in the room held their collective breath, and Tom did his best not to blink. She seemed to appreciate his reverence for the details of their agreement, but it was clear that she wasn't happy at being outsmarted. Still looking at him, she dropped the two halves to the floor, cracking the shiny lacquered finish of the decking with a sharp snap, then turned quickly and stormed out without another word, followed by several saazu.

Tom stood and watched as the remaining crew began the cleanup process from the recovery. He needed a moment for the adrenaline to fade and for his legs to stop shaking before he tried to walk.

Mius approached slowly, looking as relaxed as Tom had ever seen him. "It's good to see you stand up for yourself."

"I guess I learned to not let her have the last word."

A saazu walked up and handed Tom a small data chip.

"What's this?" he asked, but the furry being walked away.

"The balance of your contract payment," Mius said.

"She's paying me?"

"The deal was retrieval of the pod as the balance of your contractual obligations. The chekt have eyes everywhere, and they're watching everything she does, especially since she's trying to become their leader. Your payment is part of that contract, and she's honoring the deal, but I suggest you clear out of here as soon as possible."

"Is Kerra and everyone else all right?"

"They're all fine. Daihn has already recalled her people from the K2 installation."

The news helped his stomach settle, and he glanced at the saazu who were already cleaning up the mess from the recovery effort. The empty mine pod halves sat on the bay floor. He still owed Fernius for the hull repairs, and most of the information that he had was already compromised, so it probably wouldn't be of much value. But bringing him a souvenir might be a good way to start a new payment plan negotiation. "Would it be all right if I take those? I know someone who collects stuff like that."

"I don't see why not, but I don't work for Daihn anymore. My contract with her ended when you delivered the pod." Mius cocked his head. "How did you know there was something inside that planetoid?"

Tom didn't want to give away any details, but Mius had saved his life at least twice, and he felt obligated. "I didn't know for sure, but I had an experience at the Dag refinery that made me think it was important."

Mius's eyebrows raised. "On the Dagart asteroid?"

Tom nodded.

"Because after you entered the planetoid, it showed up and attacked the diadu."

"The *asteroid* did?"

"Yes. And a deep scan showed what looked like a neural pattern formed by streams of liquid woven throughout its mineral core. Based on what I saw, I think it was a living creature."

More pieces of the mystery fit together. If the asteroid was a living being, it might have known he'd receive the visions as he fell into the slime. And if the tablets had something to do with the planetoid it had shown him, it might have attacked the diadu to protect what was inside. If he was right, it might even mean that the Dag itself was the Guardian. But the mine pod was empty, so why attack if it wasn't protecting the Oraca? "Where is the Dag now?"

"Unfortunately, it was destroyed by the corporate ship during the fight."

Destroyed. Had an ancient creature been killed because of him? Had his curiosity about the visions somehow prompted the Guardian of the Oraca to act? But why would it show him the planetoid in the first place if it didn't want him to find it— unless the visions weren't deliberate? He worked to process it all. There was no way to answer those questions now, but his role in the events left him feeling at least partly responsible.

Mius's voice softened. "The look on your face tells me there's more to the story."

There was, and with the Dag asteroid gone, it felt safer to share it. "When I was at the refinery, I accidentally ate some of the raw dagart, and I had what I thought were hallucinations. But now I think the creature transferred the image of the planetoid through that liquid."

Mius's brow tensed and his voice hardened. "Did it show you anything else?"

Something in his earnest tone made Tom pause before sharing more. The Dag was already gone and everyone knew about the mine pod. But only he and Flip knew of Fernius's tablet and their covert mission, and despite everything Mius had done for him, it felt important to keep that information confidential.

"Just some spacecraft colliding with the Dag, or maybe being smashed by it. There was some wreckage on the asteroid surface, so maybe that's what I saw. I mostly kept seeing the image of that planetoid."

Mius nodded, and his voice calmed. "Well, from what I know about unrefined dagart, you're lucky to be alive after an experience like that."

"Maybe luck had something to do with it," Tom said as he extended his hand, "but I've also had some help." It was all he could risk saying about Mius's assistance while they were still aboard the *Emu Ja'*—and around the saazu. "There's a lot I don't understand, Mius, but I'm grateful."

Mius returned his grasp. "I've done only what was required, Tom."

An alert sounded in the bay, and Mius looked at the *Celestial Blue*. "Daihn is leaving, and I have to get my ship out of the hangar before she does. The deck crew will hook up a tow module so you can get your ship to the mining asteroid for repairs."

"Where will you go now?" Tom asked.

"I have obligations elsewhere, but my ship will stand sentry until you're secure on K2."

"Thank you, Mius."

"Take care, Tom." He turned and headed for the *Celestial Blue*.

Tom watched as he left, unsure whether Mius was a friend or just a decent guy who'd wanted to give him a break.

One of the tactical shuttles fired its engines, and a saazu approached Tom, gesturing toward the tow ship that had been attached to the *Hefty*. It was time to get a ride to K2 and find out just how bad the damage was.

55

Tom looked over the *Hefty* as the tow module lowered it onto the deck in K2's hangar. All traces of his tagalong drive were gone, and the brightly colored pecrite repair had been turned dark gray by the magma's heat. Aside from the cockpit, the interior sections that weren't melted or charred were covered with a thick layer of black soot. Flip hovered next to him.

"Staying ship cleanup wrenching."

"I hope you like it here, because this is going to take some time to fix."

He owed Marcus a call to let him know what had happened, too. Although the tagalong drive had served him well, it seemed right to let him know that it had been destroyed. And now he even had his own tale of heroism to share, though any feelings of pride about saving the miners were dulled by the *Hefty*'s condition. Being a hero wasn't his thing anyway. That was Marcus's department, and as far as Tom was concerned, he could have it. For him, it was enough to just have good friends and earn a decent living.

Kerra approached from across the hangar with a warm smile. Instead of pausing when she arrived, she threw her arms around him and hugged tightly. "Thank you for saving us."

Tom wrapped an arm around her shoulders. "There wasn't anything else I could do. I couldn't just run and leave you to Daihn."

She took a half step back and looked up at him. "You could have left, and it might have even been the smart thing to do. But it was brave of you to stay and help."

Tom was glad that he'd stayed, too, although it might have been more out of fear than bravery—fear of what might happen to her and also of how he'd feel if he didn't stand up to Daihn when it mattered most. But whatever the reasons, he knew he'd made the right choice.

A pair of miners pushed between them to remove the lifting straps from the *Hefty*, which would have been a scrap-yard haul in most parts of the galaxy. The ramp door was stuck partially open, and the ore pod gates that the saazu had pried at were twisted beyond repair.

Kerra looked at Tom's ship. "How bad is it?"

"My tagalong is gone, and who knows what other systems are damaged, not to mention I have a lot of cleaning to do." The *Hefty* settled onto the deck as the straps were removed. "How is everyone else? Mius told me that the Dag was alive and got destroyed fighting a corporate ship."

Kerra nodded. "That's what everyone is saying. Nobody's heard from Tanger or any of the Dag workers yet."

"I hope they got off the asteroid before the battle."

"My mother said that Tanger is," she mimicked Winnet's tone, "'one of the most capable administrators I've ever known.'" Tom smiled at her impression as she continued. "If that's true, I'm sure they got evacuated in time. And she asked me to thank you, too."

Tom gave a nod. "I guess we all need to get settled again." He looked back at his ship. "But I'm not sure where to start."

"Mius is leaving soon," Kerra said, "so I thought we could take the *Damsel* to Koyla Center. You can complete your delivery, and we can resupply."

The payment from Daihn wouldn't be enough to cover his debt to Fernius, and he'd need that money to get another tagalong drive anyway. But he could at least make payment arrangements and maybe get some parts to begin repairs on his ship. "That's a great idea."

Shek Windham walked into the hangar and glared at Tom from a distance.

"Everything okay with him?" Tom asked.

Kerra gave Shek a glance. "It'll be fine."

Tom made sure not to turn his back toward the man, just in case.

Kerra bit at her lip. "What are you planning to do once your ship is fixed?"

Tom leaned against a storage bin. "Well, I thought about asking if there was work for me with the miners."

Kerra's voice softened. "I'm sure we could use a good pilot. And I'd like that, too."

56

Mius checked the secondary mooring latches on his starboard shuttle and climbed through the docking port back into the *Celestial Blue*. It was good to have his ship back in space and in a safe holding position near K2. While the twins were busy getting the interstellar drive ready, he headed for his private quarters.

The sounds of the ship's systems faded to silence as he stepped into the simply furnished room that provided some refuge from his daily duties. He'd managed to keep his energy high for the past few months, but now that his work with Daihn had ended, the full weight of it settled onto him. The trip back to headquarters would give him a welcome respite, but he still had one more duty to perform before they left. He tapped on a holocom console to initiate a call, and an ethereal image of a man illuminated by auburn light appeared.

"Hello, brother," Mius said.

"How does the search go?" the man asked.

"All we found was an empty mine pod."

"So the Oraca remains lost."

"My contract with Daihn is finished, but she'll probably keep looking."

The man nodded. "Then our mission is also incomplete."

"There's nothing more I can do here, but I have some new information to share when I arrive."

"We look forward to seeing you."

Mius gave a nod and the image disappeared.

He pulled off his tactical vest and entered a small round alcove. A gentle glow of light automatically lit the area as he knelt on a round cushion and closed his eyes. With a deep breath, he began a short but much-needed period of meditation after his long mission—one that left him with an uneasy conscience.

57

While Kerra shopped for food and supplies for the colony, Tom and Flip visited Fernius. His office typically had a box or two filled with surplus parts or some other kind of odd equipment sitting on the floor near his desk, but the dozen new crates that were stacked neatly against one of the shelved walls were a strange addition.

Fernius looked up from his work. "Welcome, my friends!"

They approached his desk, and Flip landed to examine Fernius's computer screens as Tom clunked a handled bag onto the floor. "Hello, Fernius. It's good to see you."

Fernius stood. "Your delivery of Stellar Dagart has been received in good condition." He waddled close and put a hand on Tom's shoulder, looking at him with anticipation. "And now, Tom, what of your primary quest?"

"It seems that the Dag asteroid wasn't an asteroid after all. It was alive, and I think it was the Guardian."

"How remarkable! But you say it *was* alive?"

"It's a long story, but the Dag showed me a planetoid in the Kala asteroid field, and I went into the molten core looking for the Oraca. The Dag was destroyed in a battle with a diadu while I was searching, but all I found was an empty mine pod."

Fernius's shoulders relaxed. "So the quest has failed." He shook his head. "Disappointing."

Tom reached for the bag he'd brought. "I brought you something as a souvenir for your collection." He heaved it onto the desk and pulled out the heavy pecrite halves. A thin film of coolant still covered them, and a hint of the sweet odor drifted into the air.

"Is this what you found?" Fernius smiled broadly. "How thoughtful of you! It will make a fine addition to my collection —a memento from the quest for the Oraca."

"I was hoping you'd like it. I need to make arrangements to pay off my repair debt though. My ship took some damage in the planetoid, and I lost my tagalong, so I'm out of business until I can fix it. It's going to take a while before I can earn enough credits to repay you."

"But you already have!"

Tom cocked his head. "I don't understand."

"The only source of Stellar Dagart has been lost, Tom. That will make the supply you've brought worth a hundred times its previous value."

"So you'll clear my bill?"

"I'll have the lien on your ship removed immediately."

"Thank you, Fernius. I'm grateful."

He still had a broken ship, but at least he wasn't in debt anymore.

"If I gather additional clues," Fernius said, "perhaps we'll work together again to resume the search for the Oraca."

The fringe systems were dangerous, but Tom had found opportunities there. Even though the Oraca search had been a bust, the experience left him with new friends and a fledgling career, and he was ready to do it all again. "Count me in."

Flip jumped into flight from the desk. "*Numbering mine too.*"

"Let's celebrate your safe return with a drink," Fernius said. "We just finished the renovation of the Satellite Pub." He shook Tom's shoulder. "And I want to hear every detail of your quest!"

Risul shoved the door open and tripped into the room carrying a stack of tattered boxes. "I've got more junk here. Where do you want it?"

"Thank you, Risul. On my desk, please."

Risul looked at Tom over the top of the stack. "Hey, Tom. Welcome back."

"Thanks. It's good to be here."

Fernius walked from around his desk and placed his hand on one of the pod halves. "Risul, we're going out. Please find a place for these in the back room."

— ⋅◦⋅ —

As Fernius led the way out of his office, Risul plopped the boxes onto the desk. He lugged the metal pod halves into the large storage area and looked around at the packed room. The only empty space was on a high shelf nearly three meters up.

"You need to get rid of some of this junk, old man," he mumbled.

He climbed a ladder and heaved the two halves into the empty space before returning to the floor and patting the dust from his clothes. One half of the pod sat firmly with its flat side down, and the other rocked gently on its curved side until it came to rest. Risul switched off the room lights and locked the storage room door.

EPILOGUE

The storage room was still. Then a tiny bright pinpoint of white light appeared over the half of the mine pod that balanced on its curved side. It quickly expanded into a three-dimensional matrix of dimmer points that hovered above the pod. A blurry image appeared within the matrix, and overlapping metallic whispers filled the room. In a moment, the sound faded into echoes as the matrix reformed into a single bright point of light, then disappeared.

"Alas, the treasure remains lost. But I am richer for having pursued it."

— FROM THE JOURNAL OF FERNIUS POH

Thank you for reading *Oraca Discovery*!

If you enjoyed this book, join my email list at JPulk.com for new release updates and giveaways. As a special welcome gift, you'll also get a free ebook copy of *Waiting at Eridia*, a light-hearted short story about one of the supporting characters in the Star Reacher universe.

www.ingramcontent.com/pod-product-compliance
Lightning Source LLC
Chambersburg PA
CBHW051215130726
47988CB00001B/100